HIGH WARNING

BOOK TWO:
THE WILDER LEGEND

HIGH WARNING

BOOK TWO:
THE WILDER LEGEND

KIRBY JONAS

Cover design by Clay Jonas

Howling Wolf Publishing
Pocatello, Idaho

Howling Wolf Publishing
1611 City Creek Road
Pocatello ID 83204

For more information about Kirby's books, check out:

www.kirbyfjonas.com
Facebook, at KirbyJonasauthor

Or email Kirby at: **pocatellocowboy@gmail.com**

Manufactured in the United States of America—
One nation, under God

Jonas, Kirby, 1965—
High Warning, Book 2: The Wilder Legend / by Kirby Jonas.

ISBN: 978-1-891423-56-7

To learn more about this book or any other Kirby Jonas book, email Kirby at pocatellocowboy@gmail.com

To the memories of John A. Wagner,
lover of nature and photographer extraordinaire,
and to wild Picasso, who embodied the
spirit of the wilderness and who in my mind became the stallion known as Wilder Heart

And to Sarah, who made John so happy

CHAPTER ONE

South of Oakley, Idaho, 1929
Warning Horse Ranch

HIGH WARNING'S OLDEST BROTHER, Grant, and his wife Cora had bought an acre of ground from their parents, Angel and Lydia, on the west end of the Warning property and built a small home there between the ranch house and the town of Oakley. They had a one-year-old baby boy and another child on the way, and Grant, at twenty-six years of age, now worked full-time at the stone quarry of Jared Wayne, his father-in-law. He still went on mustang roundups, and he came to the ranch headquarters to green break and train horses whenever he had a chance, but the quarry job and his little family kept him pretty busy. Fifteen-year-old High sure missed him.

High was glad, though, to have Cora's skills in the kitchen added to those already well established in the family. Cora's mother had trained her well in the art of fine cuisine before dying of a heart condition only half a year after their wedding.

High's just older brother Seth, now seventeen, had graduated school early. He was working at the bank in Oakley and had his own Ford Model T. He had bought the car on the payment plan, which their father had practically begged him not to do. But Seth had always felt like he knew better than everyone else when it came to numbers, and understanding money, and Seth for years had done as he pleased. He was a good-looking young man, but slight of build, pale-haired, and almost frail looking, whereas High had kept on growing well past the time Seth stopped, around five-ten. High stood six-foot-two now, at the age of fifteen. He was still mostly slender, although broad of shoulder, lean through the hips and stronger than most boys his age.

Twenty-four-year-old Owen was his father's best rider now, for he had yet to marry and he was able to dedicate all his time to the riding of the green stock. But even at fifteen, most of the family recognized one irrefutable fact: When it came to horses, High was the one with the magic touch—to say nothing of also being the only one in the family who seemed to be absolutely lacking in fear, of anything or anyone. This was a trait his mother and father spoke of often, a trait they feared would one day take the life of their little boy who had started out so tiny and frail but promised to be the biggest man in the family by the time he reached his full stature.

Every now and then, in the world of horses, there comes along a person with something unexplainable in his makeup, or hers, that seems to make him one with the animals he trains and rides. Since High was six years old and had first connected with the wild stallion Grant had named Wilder Heart, they knew on the Warning Ranch that he was one of those special, gifted people.

Now that High was fifteen, and by Angel's best guess Wilder must be somewhere between seventeen and twenty years of age, the stallion—still kept intact and used as a stud for many miles around—was a phenomenal animal. Following his childhood dream, High had trained the horse to do many spectacular things on the most subtle command. He would lie down on either side and let High walk across his body, a feat which High always performed in socks because he didn't want to bruise his friend. Wilder would also lie down on his belly to let children climb on him, and even when there were mares in season around, Wilder was a predictable, gentle animal, much different from most studs when it came to mating time.

Wilder could bow, count to ten with either front foot, dance, leap to the left or right, forward, and for a few feet even backward. Angel had balked at High teaching the stallion to rear up on his hind feet and paw the air, but High had never been one for listening too closely to his father's advice about what tricks to teach his horse, and he taught him anyway. Wilder would work fine under a saddle, but High often rode him bareback. Even when jumping three- or four-foot hurdles with his eyes closed and his hands held out to the sides, like wings, he would do it, mostly to show off.

Around Memorial Day, the Fourth of July, July 24th—which locals called Pioneer Day—and Labor Day, as well as whenever there was a county fair going, Angel often let High ride Wilder all the way to whatever the event was, or sometimes Angel would haul Wilder there in a special trailer he had designed, which he would pull behind his Chevrolet. Any parade or fair was in Angel's best interest to take High and Wilder to, since not only did the spectacular team bring in a good amount of cash between spring and fall, but the publicity for the Warning Ranch was immeasurable. Many new buyers from around the state became aware of the Warning Ranch thanks entirely to High and his trick horse.

There was only one regret High still had. Every year he had begged Angel and Lydia to let him strike out on his own with Wilder and ride him at will around the country, collecting tips to show off his wonder horse. Along with his friend Murk Bowen, he had even quit school three years earlier than Seth in hopes of following that dream, but it was the one thing in which neither Angel nor Lydia had any give.

It seemed that High was as grown up as any of their children—except when it came to leaving home.

As for the subject of leaving home, one of High's greatest heartaches had come when his beloved sister Ava had found some asinine rich banker's son, gotten married and moved all the way to the town of Paul, close to thirty miles away. Her name was Ava Strickland now, and the baby they simply hadn't been able to wait to add to their family tree was Rudolph. High found the name to be a simply ridiculous moniker for a baby. But it was the first name of Ava's rich father-in-law, so High guessed she had been pressured into it.

High wouldn't have minded so much having the sister he treasured so deeply get married, but with her husband Sidney Strickland being such a complete, pompous ass, and High being a young man who rode and played hard and often went places dusty, muddy, and sometimes even bloody, depending upon what his day had consisted of, he never felt very welcome in Ava's new abode. There in that prison, Sidney had High's poor sister scrubbing the floors daily and would most likely have had her cleaning their sinks with a toothbrush if she would have stood for it.

Sister Eve was married now as well, a disease which seemed for the past four years to have been spreading all over the Warning ranch, but which High swore to invent a cure for. Luckily for Eve, she had married Luke Barnes, a local redneck who liked to cowboy and worked at the same stone quarry Grant did. Luke had bought for his wife a modest little home of orange brick, only five miles or so from the ranch.

Little Clem, who preferred to be called Clementine, was eleven, and smart as a whip—in fact too smart for her own good when it came to school. She was the one Angel always said someday might be the area's first lady doctor. Fortunately, Clem had started becoming a pretty decent sort to have around, now that it was for all intents and purposes only her and High as the Warning children—although High shuddered to think of anyone calling him a child.

In spite of Clem's high intelligence and a bad ration of freckles across her nose and cheeks that some boys seemed to think were cute but which High thought made her look like she had been splattered with mud, she was a splendid companion to have on a horse ride. She was a daredevil of a girl, and the two of them might be seen on any Saturday—or even, heaven forbid Lydia should catch them, a Sunday—racing horses around the ranch bareback and screaming like Shoshone warriors.

High's friend Tommy Hawk had gotten a job on the Diamond S Ranch way back when High was eleven, ten miles up the canyon toward Utah, so he lived a short ride away from the Warnings. One Saturday, Tommy rode his most prized horse over, a beautiful blue roan, dragging with him Murk Bowen, with whom High also spent a lot of time on the horses. They had been out riding, along with Clem—who insisted especially that particular day on being called Clementine since there were non-family members around. They came riding back home to find Grant in the yard, leaning over the hood of his Dodge, talking with Angel and Owen.

Tying the horses to let them cool off, they went to visit Grant, since even as close as he lived they didn't get to see him often. Clementine ran ahead of them and gave her big brother a huge hug.

After greeting Tommy, Murk and High, Angel and the other boys fell back into a quiet conversation. Grant had been trying to tell Angel there was talk around the rock quarry about the stock market having a bad time. Angel seemed to take it in all seriousness, but High had to laugh.

"Horses and cows ain't sellin' too well, huh?" In all reality, he should have taken *that* much more seriously, since it was their livelihood, but he guessed Grant was talking about something else entirely—probably something to do with money. He had no knowledge about any of that. If it didn't have to do with horses or cows, they might as well have been talking about satin and lace.

"I'm not gonna lie, Son," Angel said, rubbing his chin. "I've heard about the stock market, but I really haven't read up on it. What does it all mean exactly?"

The look on Owen's face was even more baffled than his father's, so High instantly knew he was in good company.

Grant shrugged, looked around at everyone else as if someone might help *him* explain. He might as well have been looking at a bunch of tired blood hounds just returned from a twenty-mile run. If only Seth were here right now.

"Well, I'm not real sure either, Dad. Somethin' to do with some sort of market in New York City, where I guess people take their money and buy up pieces of different companies they like. You know, like General Electric, maybe, or Union Pacific. Or Ford. Or the Chevrolet company. Things like that."

Angel stared at his oldest son and finally blinked, like an aging range bull that has been asked to breed too many times that day. He pursed his lips thoughtfully. "I wish I could say any o' what you just said made sense. So ... if this market you're talkin' about has a bad time, then what?"

"Well, Cora's dad was sayin' people could go into some kind of panic, and try pullin' all their money out of the bank when it really isn't in there in the first place, and ... Well, jeez, Dad. I'm not real sure what-all it means, but Cora's dad said it would be pretty bad for the whole country if it keeps up. Maybe even for the whole world."

Finally, Angel shrugged his broad shoulders. "Well, Son, I doubt it will affect us much all the way out here in Idaho, if it's somethin' happenin' in New York City. That's a long ways from here."

"You think so? Her dad sure seemed worried. And he *did* say the whole world."

Angel knitted his brow, then shrugged again. He turned and looked at High and the others, reaching out to tug one of Clem's pigtails. "Why don't all you woodpeckers go wash? Mom just set out two plates of cookies that are gonna have to get eaten up—no matter what happens to the stock market in New York City."

On Monday, Grant drove over right after work, looking grim. Angel was on a green colt in the round corral, giving it its first good rounds under a saddle. He saw the look on Grant's face and jumped off the colt immediately, tying it to the snubbing post. High, who had been watching his dad from the top rail, came down, and the two of them strode over to Grant, Angel striking the sweat and mud off his face with a handkerchief. High felt suddenly almost sick, because he could read the look on his father's face, and on Grant's. In his gut, he knew the world was about to change.

"Hi, Son. Is everything alright?"

"Dad, maybe you should come to town with me. My father-in-law says to get near a radio if possible, and I was thinkin' we could go in to the general store."

"I don't understand. What's the problem? Son, I've still got time to ride two more colts before dark."

Grant clenched his jaws. "Dad, I think you better come. It's about that stock market again."

Angel searched his son's eyes. "You look like you saw a ghost," he said finally. "Do you think I should bring Mom?"

"No!" Grant said, his eyes grown big.

"What about Roper?" Angel rested a hand on High's shoulder.

Grant looked at his little brother, who was now almost as tall as he was, and tried to smile. "Yeah, that might be a good idea. He should know what's up. Where's Owen?"

"Out with a colt. Can we fetch him?"

"I don't think we have enough time."

They drove into Oakley to the general store. Both sides of the street out front were packed with automobiles, some of them parked in a very sloppy manner, and they had to push inside through a crowd of people already gathered there—other folks without radios, or, like the Warnings, without electricity at all.

Nathanial Silver had his radio on the counter, and the volume was cranked all the way up. A man's grim-sounding voice was coming across in crackling syllables. Silver looked over and saw Angel and his boys, and his usual smile didn't materialize. Not one of the people in the store was smiling, even though almost all of them were people High recognized who were fond of his father and always friendly toward him. Frail Freda Silver, standing next to her husband, came rushing out from behind the counter and hugged Angel, something she almost never did. Tears streaked her cheeks.

Seeing that scared High almost more than anything.

CHAPTER TWO

THEY CAME TO CALL that day "Black Monday", and even it paled in comparison to the following day. That "Black Tuesday" the New York Stock Exchange crashed so hard that rich men became paupers overnight, and people who had gone so insane as to take out loans with banks solely to invest the money on Wall Street lost everything they had. Many took their own lives.

The Warnings had never been wealthy. They had their little horse ranch and their acreage, with a large vegetable garden in the back and a cellar filled with Ball and Mason jars bulging with colorful vegetables and fruit from the garden and the orchards. They had stores of dried apples and fruit, they had jerked meat, and they always had cattle and hogs, sheep, goats and rabbits ready to be butchered whenever the need arose, chickens, dozens of eggs, both for their own consumption and to be sold up and down the road and in town. They had fresh milk from the two Guernseys they always kept. The Warnings might want for new clothing or shoes, but they would not starve.

It was those who had taken to living in town who suffered most, and High's poor sweet angel, Ava, among the worst.

There was no telephone or power line running all the way out to the Warning Ranch. If anyone wanted to talk to them, they had to do it the old-fashioned way, by driving, riding, or walking to their house and yelling, or trying to be civilized and knocking on the door.

High, Murk Bowen and Tommy Hawk were out working—or more aptly playing—with Wilder when the pale green and cream five-passenger 1927 Cadillac Victoria pulled sedately into the yard, a thin cloud of November dust coming up behind it even as tiny, hard pellets of snow had begun to patter out of the gloomy gray sky.

It was an automobile High had seen a few times too many, in his estimation: It belonged to Sidney Strickland, Ava's husband.

Stepping away from the stallion to go do his duty of greeting visitors, High handed Wilder's lead to Murk, who stood nearest to him. As he got closer to the car, he realized there was only one person in it, or at least only one adult. The real surprise was when Ava, dressed in a lilac-colored, multiple-ruffled dress that came to down below her knees, and a cloche hat, got out of the driver's seat. High couldn't stop the huge smile that came to his face.

Ava without Sidney Strickland was a rare treat.

But this wasn't a treat. Ava saw High coming, and she began to walk toward him, her hands clenched in fists down at her sides. High's sister didn't spend a lot of time out in the sun, but she had inherited their father's dark skin tone. Today it wasn't dark. It was almost as pale as if she had been coated in a film of flour. Ava's face was beginning to contort the closer she got, and when she was nearly to him her knees almost gave out.

High ran the last few steps to her and caught her, his big sister who now seemed dainty and frail standing in front of him. He stopped staring at her face, hiding sudden fear in hugging her tight to him as she broke into loud sobs. For a full minute, he couldn't ask what was wrong, but he feared the worst. He could sense Tommy and Murk watching from behind, and the silence was broken only by what sounded like a concerned nicker from Wilder.

Ava finally peeled herself away from High. Her face was drenched in tears, and her eye makeup, something she had taken to wearing only because her husband insisted on it, stained her cheeks.

"Ava! What's wrong?"

"Sidney. High, he took his own life."

Later, the family sat quiet in the living room. Angel was next to Ava on the couch, and with one big, long arm he had drawn her close to him, letting her cry into the side of his chest. Lydia held little Rudolph, who had gone sound asleep, and Seth sat with Florence Starbuck, one of the twins, with whom he seemed to spend most of his time these days, if he wasn't at work. Clementine sat still as a statue between High and Owen.

Tommy and Murk had vacated the property at their first opportunity, but they had headed over to Grant and Cora's place on their horses to tell them they needed to come home at once. Eve would have to wait for the news until Ava had the strength to drive to her house.

The story had come in solemn tones. Ava admitted how Sidney, feeling proud and wealthy, had bought their nice home, and their beautiful, nearly new Cadillac, and done it all on credit, because his job at his father's bank paid him so well he knew the future was bright ahead of them.

Without even asking Ava's permission, because he was the modern man of the house and knew what would bring them vast prosperity, like his father had amassed, he had taken out another loan of twenty thousand dollars and invested every dime of it in the New York Stock Exchange.

By Black Tuesday, they had lost every penny. Sidney just never bothered to let Ava in on the secret.

She didn't know until she found the note explaining everything pinned to her husband's vest where he lay out in the woodshed with a .38 bullet in the center of his chest and the revolver near his hand.

*   *   *

Things continued to look bleaker and blacker as time passed. Grant's wages had been cut back severely at the rock quarry, as had those of Eve's husband Luke, in order to keep all employees working as long as possible. Eve and Luke were forced to abandon their new cute little house and move in with Grant and Cora, and of course Ava and her baby, whom she and the rest of the family called Rudy, and High had named Rascal, had moved back into the girls' old bedroom with Clementine.

Seth kept courting Flo Starbuck, while her prettier twin sister Lilia, with the big blue eyes and fine blond hair, seemed to have her sights set on High. Unfortunately, although Lilia was an appealing girl to look at, at least her face, and she was charming and eager to please, she was slender to the point of looking bony. That wasn't the biggest problem in the way of a relationship between her and High, however. Harder to overcome was the fact that High was in love with Valentina Torreales, whose father and mother still made the best tamales in Idaho and who always opened their home to him when he could break away from the horse ranch long enough to go into town to see her.

One Saturday, he got on Wilder and rode into Oakley, waving at people as he passed, but hardly stopping until he reached the Torreales place. In a very un-ladylike way, Valentina came rushing out to meet him, and as he climbed off Wilder she threw her arms around him.

"I guess you're happy to see me," he said with a grin.

"I guess I am! What do you want to do today?" she asked, her teeth bright white against the deep brown of her skin.

"I have two dollars, and I want to take you and your brothers over to the movie house and watch a cowboy show. There's a film playin' called *The Big Trail.* How would you like that? I have enough for popcorn and soda pop too."

Valentina's smile grew even larger. High didn't know how she managed to do that when it seemed sometimes like her face was already about to break. She hugged him again. "That sounds like fun! Are we going now?"

"I don't see any reason to wait around, do you?"

She laughed, and they went to round up her three younger brothers, turned Wilder loose in the family's pasture, and set out on foot for the movie theater.

High loved to go into the theater, which was attached to a little diner where they had a black and white checkerboard floor, a long counter with red-topped round stools where they served hamburgers and hotdogs, sodas and sundaes, and where a huge popcorn maker sat and filled the place with the scent of unspeakable goodness.

He bought a bag of popcorn for all of them, and they went on into the dim-lit theater room, where the magic happened. The movie was recently released. It was the main actor's first starring role, they said, and as the words left the screen and the film began, he watched the big man in the decorated buckskins and dark hat move across the screen gracefully and hoped he would star in more films. There was something about this young actor that drew High in immediately. His name was John Wayne.

Hunkered down in the plush seats of the theater, in the darkness with the flashing light of the film flickering across the seats, and the swarm of eager, mesmerized faces, with the aroma of popcorn permeating the huge, warm room, High put his arm around the girl he was head over heels for. For that two hours of his life it was easy to pretend all the world was right, and that prosperity had returned to the United States, who would of course save the rest of the world now as well. Young John Wayne, broad-shouldered, grinning and strong, filled the room with his confidence until every person there must believe that nothing could ever go wrong in the world again, and that good would always prevail.

They came out of the theater later, blinking against the bright sunlight. "What do we do now?" asked Valentina.

"Do we always have to be doin' somethin'?" She looked up at him, and of course he was grinning. If anyone should be asking that question it would be her. High was the restless one who always had to be on to the next reckless adventure.

"We don't!" she said. "Let's just walk around town, okay?"

And so they did. They walked around town, the boys tagging along, laughing, playing, sometimes racing each other up and down the street. Then they walked around the country, admiring the pretty orange brick homes with the white trim that were such a telling symbol of the area. It was hard to believe that so many of the people in these homes were struggling to put food on their tables.

After the boys finally got bored of strolling and went off on their own, High and Val ended up on the huge metal swing set in the city park. He pushed her for a while until he got so exuberant about it that she almost fell out of her swing and refused to let him push her anymore. Then they sat side by side on a bench and watched little children play and dogs run around.

"Do you think we'll ever get married?"

Valentina's question was so abrupt it almost made High swallow his lump of Doublemint gum. He looked at her to see if she was smiling playfully. She wasn't. She was maybe the most serious he had ever seen her look.

"What do you mean? When we're older, you mean?"

She studied his eyes for a while, then drew in a deep, quick breath, and let it sigh back out. Reaching over, she took his hand in hers.

"My big sister Linda married when she was sixteen. Did you know?"

High had turned sixteen that April Fool's Day, and it was early June now. Valentina had been sixteen for a month longer than he had. He swallowed hard.

"I didn't know that," he said casually, as a pretty brown, black and white bird caught his eye. "You ever see a bird like that around here before?"

She looked at the bird with about as much interest as she might have looked at the broken stub of a pencil on the sidewalk. "It's pretty."

"I wonder what it is," he said. Long silence followed before finally she quietly spoke his name. "Yeah?"

"What do you want to do? I mean with your life?"

"Pretty much what I'm doin' now. Except I want to take Wilder and ride around the country—or maybe even the world. I want to show everyone his tricks and take up a collection and get rich."

"Then what? Come back here and settle down?"

"Sure, maybe. That'd be alright I guess." He noticed his hand was starting to sweat.

"If we got married, we could get two horses and ride around the country together. Or we could just ride together on Wilder. He's strong enough, isn't he?"

High's heart was pounding harder and harder. He had roped wild horses, gotten on their backs for some hellacious rides, broken bones in a lot of different circumstances and climbed barefoot up almost sheer cliffs. He had even once tried to flush a huge black bear out of a copse of willows he had seen it wander into. But nothing seemed scarier than Valentina Torreales did right now. The scariest part was she actually made what she was talking about sound inviting! But he had so much more he wanted to do with his life before being roped and tied, as Angel referred to marriage, always with a grin.

High was only ever going to be young one time!

Valentina Torreales didn't speak about marriage for a long time after that, much to High's relief. The world seemed to keep spiraling ever deeper into poverty, while disgusting rich people back east boasted of things such as being the "Hostess with the Mostest" and threw lavish parties, sometimes to the tune of millions of dollars. The stories sprawled all over the pages of the local paper, until High began to deplore the rich.

It surprised him, though, that people continued throwing pennies, nickels and sometimes dimes and quarters in his bucket whenever he rode Wilder around, advertised by his full name, Wilder Heart, and showed off all his magnificent tricks. High's accompanying sign, his poster of advertisement which his mother had made for him with great pride, in foot-high letters read: **HIGH WARNING AND WILDER HEART!!! A show no one should miss!** With his big plan of taking all his money and heading out across country the moment his parents gave him the go ahead, High had saved up two hundred and fifty more dollars to go along with another two hundred and ten dollars he still had from Smoky Wanamaker's purchase of Wilder. He guessed it was more money than most kids his age would see in five years, and especially during the hard time.

High would have had a whole lot more, but sometimes he would go on a binge and buy groceries for someone like Murk Bowen and his mother, or Tack Siddoway, or he would go to the Oakley general store and purchase shoes for some kid he might have seen walking to school barefoot. His mother had caught him at the store once, and she had started in preaching to him about how he should save his money for a rainy day, but when she found out he was buying a new dress for a little girl at church whose dress looked like it had gone through four or five older sisters, Lydia was quieted. It was the last time his mother ever tried to talk to him about saving money. That night he had come home to roast beef, mashed potatoes and gravy, his favorite meal, and with a big apple pie, to boot. The best part of all, though, was the huge hug she gave him, and her telling him how proud he made her.

High found himself not going into town as much to see Valentina as he had before. It wasn't because he didn't want to. She had taught him to kiss, and between that and snuggling with her, he wasn't sure if that might not be almost as thrilling as galloping on Wilder. But her talk of marriage had scared him down to his toes, and even though she hadn't mentioned it again much over the past year, the memory still haunted him.

Seth still had his job in town, although it barely paid enough to make his car payment, and he continued living at home and eating off his parents' table. High had a feeling his brother was getting ready to propose to Florence Starbuck, but he didn't know what his older brother thought they were going to do for money to get a place to live. He sure as heck couldn't move them into the bedroom he shared with High.

Still, Seth always found enough to put seventeen cent-per-gallon gas in the tank of his car and go riding in the country with Flo, and more often than not the two of them had taken to inviting High and Lilia along. Lilia was a good year older than High, making Flo a year younger than Seth. But it didn't seem to matter. Folks always thought High was the older brother anyway. He stood six-foot-four now, and outweighed Seth probably by fifty pounds, and he was proud to say it was mostly hard, sinewy muscle. Seth had stayed soft and fragile looking, but that suited him and his lifestyle, and being big and tough as rawhide suited High.

One day while they were driving all the way out past the little farming community of Paul, with High and Lilia in the back seat, she slid her hand over and put it on his leg. Just like that, as if it had been meant to be there all the time.

He froze and tried to swallow a lump in his throat, but he couldn't let a mere girl know he was scared. He looked down at her, and she was smiling demurely. Neither one of them said a thing. What could they say anyway, with Seth and Flo in the front seat?

In a desperate move to get Lilia's hand off his leg, he finally put his hand over hers, and that was her signal to intertwine their fingers and rest their hands on the seat between them. It didn't seem like much of a tradeoff to High, who thought he should have left her hand on his leg. Taking it in his now seemed like he had surrendered, and what would Valentina think if she ever knew that?

When High was out riding a few weeks later with Murk Bowen and Tommy Hawk, they came upon Lilia walking along the roadside by herself, pointed toward the ranch. They slowed down and stopped beside her until High politely told the others to go on to the ranch without him.

"What are you doin' out here all by yourself, Lilia?"

"Just walking. I like to walk on beautiful days like this."

He had to admit it was beautiful. It was April the second, he had just turned seventeen years old the day before, and between that and the incredible warm weather they were having, things could not have been much sweeter. The way he figured it, he was only one year from being old enough that his parents would have to agree to let him start traveling the world!

"You're not goin' anywhere special?" High asked, hooking a leg over Wilder's saddle horn.

"No, nowhere special. Just walking. Well ... I had been thinking about stopping over at your place, though."

"Oh. You wanna ride?"

"Umm ..." By the look on her face, High knew she had been waiting only for him to ask, but of course she couldn't seem anxious—or so he thought. "Why sure!"

He already regretted his offer as they started off with her sitting behind the saddle and she locked her arms tight around his middle. He regretted it, but then again he didn't. She was still skinny little Lilia Starbuck, but darn, she was pretty.

But so was Valentina Torreales, and she was in the ranch yard visiting with Tommy Hawk and Murk Bowen when High rode in with Lilia Starbuck, looking far too much like two mating June bugs.

CHAPTER THREE

THE FIRST THING HIGH'S mind did was flash back, and suddenly he wished he were dragging behind a goat, shooting at a man who had stolen Wilder and getting subsequently knocked unconscious by a panicked horse, or even watching his mother's legs get taken out from under her on her way to the outhouse by a scared, fleeing cow. Most anything would have been preferable to this moment in this heretofore perfectly peaceful yard.

One moment he saw Valentina smiling up at him that beautiful smile, and the next it was raked from her face as if by a giant talon. That was about when her eyes fell to his middle, and after a few moments' quiet reflection she must have realized he hadn't really sprouted two extra arms, dainty ones at that, and that most likely there was someone sitting behind him who owned those arms, and by the look of them that the someone was most likely female.

With Lilia behind him, High couldn't swing a leg back over the cantle of the saddle to get down. Instead, he swung one forward. Then made a jump that was meant to be graceful over the horse's side. Most sensible people would have let go of his middle somewhere in that sequence of motions, but later when he had time to mull it over he realized that, Lilia Starbuck being a girl, she wasn't expected to be sensible. Maybe Lilia had a death-grip on him and was determined that he would never get away. Or perhaps it crossed her mind that sitting on a wild mustang stallion, behind the saddle and far from the reins, wasn't quite as safe as sitting on a sofa, or behind a desk in school. She could even have been daydreaming and didn't know a hellcat with fire in its eyes was staring up at her would-be lover, ready to unleash a hundred-ten pounds of hell's worst fury of flailing arms and gnashing teeth.

Whatever the case, Lilia held on until past the point of no return, then let go. She couldn't sit back upright. Her upper body was heavier than her lower, and was now aimed downward, and since she wasn't a cat, she couldn't simply spin about and land on her feet. She couldn't sit up, couldn't land on her feet, so the only reasonable course for her seemed to be landing on the side of her face.

The hard fall didn't save Lilia from anything, but it might have saved High from serious bodily mutilation and Spanish curse words, which was at least *something*. The sudden appearance of Lilia lying on the ground grazing dirt, and the comical dismount she had performed to get into that position, left everyone in the yard speechless and immobile. High was staring at Valentina, who was staring past him at the ground, but as yet he didn't know at what, since he was yet to be made aware of Lilia's clever mode of dismounting. It wasn't until Lilia's feet completed the entire act, with a wonderful little thumping sound in the dirt, that High sensed something might be amiss besides the fact that the girl he loved had just watched him ride into the yard spooning with the girl who loved him.

He whirled and found Lilia on the ground at his feet, lying there as if worshiping the ground he walked on, except he didn't understand immediately what the crimson spots were falling on the ground by her face. When he did, he gasped and dropped to his knees, trying to help her up but getting the back of her head under his chin instead, as she tried to bolt upward in a rush.

High's head spun, and he pivoted to put out his hands and found Wilder standing there stoically. He looked for all he was worth like some calm horse from a pastoral painting, casually chewing on grass. High rested his hands against Wilder until his head decided it would be okay to move again. By that time, Lilia had already gotten up and had nothing more polite to do than stand there with her hand on the side of her head while a trickle of blood wept out from under her palm. She looked like she had just crushed a handful of ripe strawberries against her temple.

Murk Bowen ran over and grabbed Lilia by the waist, thinking he was keeping her from falling, which maybe he was. With that immediate tragedy on hold, High whisked his attention back to Valentina Torreales. But now it was only her ghost. Thin air. Still feeling a bit dizzy because for all her tiny body, Lilia Starbuck sure packed a man-size wallop with the back of her head, High scanned the yard.

If Valentina Torreales was a fast-moving train, all he could make out of her was her caboose, and a cloud of dust.

Valentina was homeward bound, and even Tommy Hawk was smart enough to grab High's shoulder and jerk him back when he started after her.

"Hey, man! You plumb crazy? There might be a lotta times t' tackle a woman, but this ain't one of 'em."

High looked at him, blinking to clear his vision. "What do I do, just let her walk all the way home?"

"Maybe not, but my father once gave me some advice that might be good for you: If you got a runaway train, at least let it use up most of its steam before you try t' jump on it."

High didn't have any plans of jumping on Valentina, at least no time soon, but deep in the remote recesses of his mind he found some sense in a Shoshone elder's wisdom. Now what about Lilia?

It was sink or swim for High, or possibly both. Lilia was a sweet girl, but she wasn't the one who put his head and heart in a whirl. He didn't want to hurt her emotionally besides physically, but he could only stay with her so long to comfort her right now. He guessed Valentina was walking at a good four-mile-an-hour clip, which meant if he intended to run her down he had less than an hour to do it before she got home. Not that he really thought running after a wounded grizzly was a wonderful idea, but this was one grizzly he was afraid was going to become an entire den of them if he didn't tame it sometime in the next hour of what promised to be hell, with butter on it.

By now, Clementine, sweet beautiful Clementine, had come out to the rescue, having witnessed the carnage of her brother beating girls both in the head and in the heart. She came bearing with her a wet towel, which she placed on innocent Lilia's head, then, making a scared-worried face at High, put her arm around the older girl's waist and walked her toward the house, talking soothingly.

High started for Wilder, and Tommy spun him around again. He pointed down the road. Valentina was only a hundred or so yards away. "You don't listen so good, uh? Look! That train ain't hardly even rollin' yet."

"What if somebody else gives her a ride and she gets home?"

Tommy thought about that until a look of alarm came into his eyes. "And her mother's home, uh? That's a good point, Roper. The last thing you wanna do is let a aggravated woman get all the way to her mother, and with sore feet. Maybe you better go, at that."

High thought while riding out of the yard at a fast walk that he had hit upon a plan that not only would allow him to follow the advice of Tommy Hawk's father, the Shoshone elder, but would avoid letting anyone else stop to help the maiden in ire. He would simply walk Wilder along behind her for a mile or two, keeping far enough back that she wouldn't hear him. Then, when she appeared to be slowing down, and the steam of her engine stopped coming so hot out of her ears, he could ride up and start doing all the apologizing he could invent in the next twenty minutes.

It seemed like a good plan, at least, except for the human need always to be checking its back trail, if only to see if someone actually cared enough to give chase.

When Valentina whipped her head to look back, High was caught there, perhaps not flat-footed, but at least paint-stallioned. The horse must have sensed high danger, for his ears shot forward, and he jerked to a halt. Valentina whirled back forward and started running, her red dress flowing out behind her. It might have made a beautiful painting, but to High right now the dress only represented the flames of his love burning to the ground.

High's first instinct was to look down for his lasso, but then he recalled that Valentina only had two feet and that his mother had once quite effectively cautioned him, with the punctuation of an axe handle on his butt cheeks, to count the number of feet on any animal he went to roping. That was of course just in case one of them might have only two, the way Clem did the day he roped her feet out from under her, then took a good twenty feet to get his excited horse calmed down before he could stop laughing and run to his four-year-old sister's rescue.

As he recalled, there was no one who came to his own rescue that day when his mother caught up to him. That, if memory served him, was the Night of the Hog-Tied Sister, and High had spent five days at hard labor for it, one of them on a forced fast, with no time allowed even to touch a horse's hide until a parole committee of both his parents and all three sisters met and decided he could walk free. No brothers were allowed on that committee, since all three of them had made the mistake of laughing when they heard the story.

After deciding he couldn't rope Valentina, and he most likely shouldn't bulldog her, High decided simply to cut her off like a wayward calf. He galloped up close, which by the look of terror on her face as she wheeled to face him might not have been his best choice, and then Wilder stopped. With this two-legged calf now facing them but not trying to bolt in any direction, the wind was kicked out of both High's and Wilder's sails like a pocket-knife jabbed into a balloon. They stared down at her until at least Wilder had the common sense to avert his direct gaze.

"Stop following me!" The girl's face and voice reminded High of the eerie sound of a bobcat he had listened to out in the brush one dark blue evening. Any need to get closer to the sound had diminished one hundredfold, and the girl's screech had the same effect now.

"Val, wait. I didn't tell Lilia to hold onto me like that. That was her own doin'. She was just goin' to the house to visit Seth, and I offered her a ride!" He guessed she was going to visit him, not Seth, but she had never flat-out said that, so there was no point in inserting inflammatory information he would only be guessing about.

Valentina didn't have a good rebuttal, so showing her backside to him seemed the next best thing. She skirted around him and took off walking again, now the escaping calf Wilder liked to see.

With a flurry of hooves, the stallion ran ahead of the startled girl once more and spun back facing her.

"Let me by!"

"Val! Come on! You're the only girl I care about." He leaped off Wilder, and for the first time almost as far back as he could recall dismounting horses he lost his footing and almost fell. He didn't like that Valentina had to stifle a laugh, but maybe that was a good sign.

"I'm all head over heels for you, Val," he professed. "I want to marry you."

The look of anger disappearing off Valentina Torreales's face was like some invisible hand peeling an orange. She charged him, and he should have turned tail and run for the hills, but he didn't. Instead, he met her rush head-on and squeezed her tighter than he had ever held onto any human being since the early morning he rode back into the city of Caldwell with Bandy Drake, Sheriff Boone, Smoky Wanamaker and the posse to find Ava standing there waiting for him.

It didn't take Valentina Torreales, who fantasized about being called Valentina Torreales-Warning, very long to start getting their wedding all planned out with her mother. High, still trying to figure out how that loop not only had gotten thrown around his feet but had been tightened and tied before he knew it, let Valentina run with the wedding plans. He didn't understand any of that kind of stuff in the first place, and in the second place he had plenty on his mind trying to figure out how in mud buckets he was ever going to support a wife, much less his own damn foolish self. He guessed he and Valentina could take over the abandoned shed he remembered putting the Indian horse hunters up in. If old Tack Siddoway would loan them the same sheepherder's stove, they could shack up there—or at least *shed* up there—and be fine until they ran out of jackrabbits and packrats to shoot, at which point they could quietly starve to death, living on love—until they stopped living.

Sometimes when he thought about how ludicrous it all was he had to hold back a good belly laugh. He guessed that was the reason why folks were supposed to get married young, because that was the age most people still didn't have brains enough to realize there was no way they could survive real life, in a real world.

CHAPTER FOUR

FRIDAY THE THIRTEENTH WAS always considered to be bad luck, but High never knew why. For him, it would always be *Wednesday* the thirteenth. But he actually had a good reason. Wednesday, May 13, 1931, was the day that changed High's life, and the lives of his family, forever.

He was riding back from Oakley by the light of a beautiful sunset when a car came barreling up from behind, blowing its horn. Turning, he recognized his father's Chevrolet, and it slid to a halt, sending dust everywhere. "Hey there, Roper!" his father yelled out the window with a big grin. "Son, that is one calm horse you got there." He looked over at Seth, who was in the passenger seat, and High heard Angel say, "Here, give me that dang thing!"

When Angel turned back around, he was holding a ring up between his thumb and forefinger. "Take a look at that, would ya? Take a look!"

He held it up higher, and High reached down over Wilder's side and took it from his father's hand. It was just a plain iron ring someone had painted to look silver. "What in the—" High stopped himself and looked over at Seth. "You didn't! You and Flo are gettin' married?"

Seth nodded, with a smug smile. "Sure are."

"Well, I'll be danged," said High, and whistled.

Angel chuckled. "Yessiree! How you like that, huh, Roper? It's just gonna be me and Mom and Clem at home if all you kids keep up the nonsense." He mercifully didn't mention the fact that widowed Ava still lived with them as well.

"More likely it'll be all your *married* kids livin' back home with you," High replied with a laugh, reaching down to give back the ring.

Angel laughed gleefully. "Well, Roper, Seth's gettin' married right away. And I mean *right* away—two weeks from now. He didn't want his younger brother beatin' him up to the altar, I reckon. What you think about that?"

High returned his father's laugh and looked over at Seth again, giving him a wink. "That sounds fitting. Seth never did like me beatin' him at anything."

"And you never could!" shot out Seth from the other side of the car. "Get back to the house fast, huh? Mom's gonna make strawberry shortcake, and Flo's comin' over."

"Not Lilia too, I hope."

"Oh hell no! Not after that last fiasco! I'll bet she *never* comes to our house again!" said Seth with a laugh. "See if me an' Flo ever try to set you up again!"

"Well don't do me any favors!" High yelled at the top of his voice at the car as it raced off down the road.

He was walking Wilder along easy, thinking about life and enjoying the remarkable evening. The sunset had been spectacular, and now so shortly afterward the land lay in purple shadow, with a pink alpenglow shining off the snow on the mountaintops. He had spent the last two hours of his day in Oakley, listening to

Valentina go on and on about their wedding, which they planned
to take place on June first.

They both laughed about his original idea of taking up residence in an abandoned shed, because as it turned out that was
exactly what they were going to do. The shed was on the Warning
Ranch, however, not some abandoned outbuilding in the hills,
and it was well-built and would be easy to put a stove in. Any
other time period it probably would have seemed odd to set up
housekeeping in a shed, but right now during this hard time the
country was suffering through, it seemed perfectly normal. High
knew for a fact it wasn't just him and Valentina living in quarters
like their shed, and even worse.

It still made him chuckle when he thought about Seth getting
all worked up and being determined to get married first. But nothing about it surprised him. Seth wasn't competitive in a lot of
things, but that was one where he would be, since he had been
courting his girl serious long before High had accidentally asked
Valentina to marry him.

He moved Wilder into a jog and was going along laughing
about everything when he saw a cloud of dust and smoke suddenly come up ahead of him in the gloaming. It appeared to be
right in the road, and he peered closer. Whatever had happened,
it was so far away he could make nothing out. But the cloud of
smoke was getting higher now. All of a sudden, he got a sick feeling in the pit of his stomach. Bells began to go off in his head.
Something about the scene ahead was not right.

Tickling Wilder's ribs with the rowels of his spurs, he put him
into a high lope. As he rode, and a dark mass in the road far ahead
loomed larger and larger, his guts got tighter still. Was that a ve-
hicle in the road? The smoke had died down now. That was good.
But the very strange-looking black lump in the road of which he
could make out no detail remained there, motionless, in the fail-
ing purple light of the day.

Wilder kept loping along, and he was not relaxed about it. High knew the horse had long since picked up on the tension in him, and unlike their normal runs this one wasn't something that made Wilder feel carefree. The distance closed. It closed fast—but not fast enough.

There were two cars, and one of them was on its side. At six hundred yards, he could finally make it out. There was one tall, slender shape of a human that appeared to be lurching around the cars. Had the driver of the second car gone somewhere for help?

They were very close now. Close enough that High saw the single person drop to his knees. His guts were all tied into knots now. He kept having to blink tears out of his eyes, only partly from the wind hitting them.

The kneeling person must have heard him, and he jumped to his feet and became a scrawny, bare-headed man in black pants and a blue shirt. An unreasoning fear began to clutch High's insides, and something told him to ride no closer—so he kept riding anyway.

The man was staring at him. It was Washington Starbuck, the father of Lilia and Florence. One side of his face was covered in blood. His car was upright, but the whole front of it was smashed and still spouting the steam, in much lesser amounts, that might have been what High had seen from the distance.

He stopped in front of Wash Starbuck to ask him if he was alright. He had just started to open his mouth when he looked at the overturned car. His eyes stopped on the hood. He could only see one piece of it, but it was a smoky blue color.

He started to whirl away from Starbuck, but the man grabbed his shoulder and spun him back. High stared into his eyes. Even in the near dark, it was suddenly obvious the man was drunk.

"Don' go over there, boy."

"Why?"

"Just don't! I'm a-beggin' you!"

High tore away from Starbuck, almost making him fall. He went in long strides and leaped sideways over the smashed hood of the tipped car.

The sight he saw froze him cold. It was his father, lying with his legs still up inside the car, his right arm under the passenger door, and his cheek on the ground, surrounded with blood.

"Son ..."

High could only stare. Had he heard his father speak?

"Get 'im, Son ... Roper. Get 'im. Get your brother."

Running close, High dropped to his knees. His father's arm was pinned under his own body weight on the car door, along with the weight of the car. "Dad! What do you mean? Where is he? Did Seth go for help?"

"Seth was in here with me. Goin' to the blacksmith's to order a weddin' ring."

High took a moment trying to comprehend that before realizing Angel must be delirious, or at least dazed. "Dad! I know. You showed it to me already. Dad, I have to get the car off you."

"You can't. Stop! Go get your brother."

"Dad, I don't know what you're talkin' about. You're not makin' sense. Where'd he go?"

"Find him, Rope. Find that dumb kid."

Angel's head settled down onto his shoulder.

"I'll go for help, Dad. I'll be right back. You stay here." He didn't realize how stupid that sounded, as if his father could get up and leave.

He lurched up, but something made him look back down at his dad, who was still staring up at him. But something wasn't right. "Dad? Dad!"

He fell to his knees again and put one hand under the side of his father's head. Angel's eyes were open, but the sight in them was gone.

High lunged up backward and almost fell over into the grass beside the road. In the growing dark, he searched frantically around the car before whirling toward Washington Starbuck, who stood at his broken car with a blank stare.

"Where's my brother? Mr. Starbuck! Where's my brother Seth? Did he run for help?"

"Son ... I don' know. The car rolled. It ... It uz jus' all sudden," he said, slurring his words. "It uz jus' all sudden there'n front o' me, an' my car hit it, an' it rolled, an' ... people ... Somebody flew." The look in Starbuck's staring eyes was vacant.

"Somebody *flew?*" repeated High, almost screaming. "What are you talkin' about, somebody flew? Where?"

The man raised an arm to point down the road, toward the ranch. High started along the road, sweeping everywhere with his eyes. He found Seth in the shadows only because one severely broken leg lay at the edge of the road. The rest of his body lay crushed in the grass, surrounded by so much blood no one could have survived the loss of it. Seth's right hand lay only partly open. Looking down at it, High was shocked to see the ring there at the joint of his palm and fingers. It lay there, a cheaply made but perfect little circle that was supposed to signify how life, and marriage, went on and on into forever.

High never even thought about crying. His eyes were dry as he picked the ring out of Seth's hand, slowly pushed to his feet and went again to kneel by his father. His eyes were still open, like Seth's, as High stared down at him until it got too dark to see. High turned and slipped the ring Seth had been so proud of into his pocket.

Night was closing around them now. Only the stars would remain here to see the carnage as High left Washington Starbuck standing alone in the road and galloped the last half mile toward home to bring back help. Now more than ever he wished at least someone out here had a phone, so they could call for help from town.

At the funeral held in the cemetery that Friday morning, as the sun shone bright but gentle on the masses gathered there, Florence Starbuck was inconsolable. She spent most of it on her knees beside the fresh grave of her fiancé, with Lilia crouched beside her, holding her without talking. Their mother, Tamar, and their three brothers clustered together behind the girls, like frozen bodies in wax. The one man who was the reason for the funeral wasn't here, and probably for the best. It wasn't likely that anyone here would want to exchange pleasantries with Washington Starbuck.

High remained stoic, still too shocked and angry for tears to come. His mother was doing surprisingly well here in public, and staying strong for all the family, but he had heard her crying alone in her room until deep in the night.

He helped lower his father's plain wood coffin by ropes down into its lonely hole in the ground. The earth now was being fertilized by the best man he had ever known. He thought ahead and prayed someday he would be able to come here alone and see if the tears would finally come out of him. For now, they merely felt like blocks of ice behind his eyes.

He next helped lower his brother Seth into his grave at the foot of Angel's, feeling the ring in his pocket and wondering if he should go give it to Florence, or if that would only make her grief all the worse. Someone started playing taps, not with a bugle, but on a violin. He looked over to see Freda Silver, from the general store, plying the bow across the strings of her instrument as her hands shook like leaves in a high wind, and tears poured down her cheeks. Her husband Nathanial was crying as well, and that made High silently glance around the hundreds of people who had come to see Angel and Seth off on their long eternal journey.

He had never noticed so many people crying at one funeral. He had never stopped to think about how beloved his father was in this valley. It struck him then that his father, Angel, truly was an angel now.

High gave it only until the next morning, when everyone else was asleep, and he got up in the dark and got dressed in a black shirt, Levi's jeans, and his Justin boots and pale gray hat. Last of all, he strapped his Frontier six-shooter on his hip.

He took a lantern out but didn't light it until he was in the barn. He had kept Wilder in a stall that night, and now he gave him some molasses feed in a nosebag. While he ate it, High threw his saddle on and cinched it down. The second the stallion stopped chewing, he stripped off the nosebag and threw it over on a pile of straw, then flung himself into the saddle, easing the Colt back and forth in the holster.

He leaned over and blew out the lantern where it still hung from its rusty spike in one of the barn poles, and then he rode Wilder out of the barn so quietly that no one could have heard. As he left the yard and turned on the main road toward the Starbuck place, he couldn't help thinking of the morning all those years ago when he rode away from Ava this same way, to go after Wanamaker.

The only difference was back then he was only going to retrieve a stolen horse. Even though it had turned out much different than he planned, he had had no real intention whatsoever of using the pistol on his hip.

Today his intentions were entirely different.

CHAPTER FIVE

HIGH RODE DIRECTLY TO the Starbuck place, and before he reached it it was growing light. The sun wasn't up yet, or even touching the hilltops, but the early gray light was plenty to see by. He sat Wilder out at the main road, watching shadows now and then move in front of a dim light that glowed through one of the windows. The window he was watching he guessed looked into the living room, whereas the light was glowing from farther inside, probably from a kitchen on the back side of the house.

Wilder blew patiently, and High patted his neck, then in the same motion of his hand reached back and touched the butt of the Colt. He had worked long and hard over the past two days convincing himself to do this, and how. But now that he was here, his resolve was crumbling. First, it was this place. He had no reason to think the entire family wouldn't be in the house. How did a seventeen-year-old walk in and shoot a family's bread winner, husband and father, then just walk out?

Then there would be the question of his own guilt, not only in his mind, but with the law. That meant no marrying Valentina Torreales, who likely would be married to someone else before he ever got out of prison for what he intended on doing today.

Well, he would at least go scare the man. He had to have *some* punishment, since the local sheriff had decided to mark the whole incident down as only an accident, and he hadn't even charged Wash Starbuck in the deaths of Angel and Seth.

High rode into the yard and on to the barn, watching the house to see if anyone might look out. As far as he could tell, they didn't. At the barn, he looked around carefully for any light or other sign of activity. There was none.

He tied Wilder far at the back of the barn and waited.

When the back door of the house finally opened, as he stood inside the big barn doors, his heart leaped. This was it. His big chance. He wondered what Wash Starbuck would feel like having the bore of a cocked .44 shoved in his face. He wondered what it would feel like to be on his knees in front of High, begging for his life. If nothing else, he hoped it scared Starbuck into giving up alcohol.

But it wasn't Wash Starbuck on his way out. It was rotund Tamar, his wife, headed out to the chicken coop with an egg basket.

Was her husband even here?

Tamar must have sensed High in the barn. She must have seen him out in front when he arrived. She was gone to the chicken coop for five or ten minutes, and on her way back she didn't head for the house. She stopped some ways out from the barn door.

"High? High Warning?"

He froze, feeling suddenly ill. One thing he was not was a skulker. He couldn't simply pretend not to be here. "Ma'am."

It took only his acknowledgment of her presence for her to continue on, and she stopped at the door. Her eyes glanced across the holstered Colt, then back to his face. "You came to see Wash."

"Yes, ma'am."

"He isn't here, High."

He let that digest for a moment, wondering if it was true. "Where is he this time of day?"

"I'm not sure, but the cemetery, I'm guessin'. Would you like to go find him there?"

"If that's where he is, I guess I would."

"I think you'll have to. He doesn't come back very soon when he goes," she said, her eyes glittering with moisture. She paused for quite a long time, staring at him as if trying to decide what to say. "High, would you go for a walk with me?"

"I guess you're gettin' ready to cook breakfast."

She tried so smile. "I am. You're welcome to stay, if you'd like."

"I don't guess I better."

"Why did you come, High? To kill Wash? I think you're too late."

He stared at her. "Too late?"

"Not truly too late. My husband's body is still here, physically. But that's all. Can we walk?" she asked again.

"I guess." He didn't know where they were going to walk, but he wondered if he should bring Wilder, in case he didn't want to come back when they were done—in case he wanted to ride from here straight to the cemetery.

She took off walking to the house, so he left Wilder and went with her. She set the basket of eggs down on the cement stoop outside the door, then turned. She started around the front yard, in which Washington Starbuck had planted nice green grass, which was at its most lush this time of year.

"This is where Wash grew up," she said after they had made the rounds of the yard once. "Used to be dirt here, but he put the grass in when the girls were born. Wanted them to be clean and have a nice place to play."

She stopped by the gnarled trunk of a massive willow tree and put her hand on it. "Wash's father planted this tree when he was a little boy. Look at the size of that, would you? See that limb? We always had a swing on it. Do you remember?"

High was surprised that he was able to smile. "I do. I used to come over a lot before the goat thing." It was funny in all that time he had never thought to follow the girls into the house.

Tamar laughed, a sound he had never thought she would make at mention of the "Wild Ride of the Starbuck Twins". She laughed again, then repeated the name, startling him. He thought that was a private thing only among his family.

"You didn't think I knew that, huh? Seth told Florence how your daddy used to come up with names for all the shenanigans you pulled when you were young."

He blushed. "I reckon I'm still doin' them, ma'am. I'm sorry I never came over to apologize for when Lilia fell off my horse. I sure am sorry that had to happen."

"Oh, she was fine, honey. You know, those head wounds just bleed like there's no tomorrow. Three days after it happened you could hardly tell she ever got hurt."

High took a big breath. He wondered what Wash Starbuck was feeling this morning. Why he had gone to the cemetery. Suddenly, he just wanted to go fetch Wilder and leave.

"Wash lost his job a couple of months ago," said Tamar after a deep inhalation. "Then he did the very thing he scorned other men for when they got in trouble. He went and found a man who sells moonshine, and ... He feels lost, High. He can't feed us, other than what we grow ourselves. Can't buy the simplest things anymore. Do you know what it's like for a man when all his pride is stripped away? And now ..." Her voice faded off, and he looked at her to see her chin trembling. Trying to be kind, he looked away.

"Now he killed your father and Seth, and he is the most broken man I've ever known. He once told me your daddy was the closest thing to a perfect person he ever met."

Shocked, High stared at Tamar Starbuck, trying to digest her words. When they finally sank in, he felt sicker than before. It suddenly hit him how gut wrenching it had to feel to look up to someone so much and then know you caused their death. The only thing he could compare it to was if he had caused the death of one of his own family members.

"I guess I should go," he said.

"I'd like it if you stayed and ate with us. Please. It would mean a lot—to all of us. I'll go in and talk to Lil first—tell her you're coming."

High wanted to be anywhere but here right now. He at least had to get the gun off his hip. "I'll stay, ma'am. If you're sure it'll be alright with Lilia. I'll just go back and tend to my horse for a minute."

They parted, and he walked as fast as he could to the back of the barn, took off his gun belt, then buckled it back together and hung it from the saddle horn.

He waited in the shadows until he saw Tamar five minutes later come to the back door and motion to him.

Feeling nervous as a beetle in a hen coop, he walked to the back door, and Tamar came and let him in. He walked up the back stairs into the kitchen, where they had a small oval table that called for some serious family closeness to sit at. The Starbuck boys greeted him cordially, but it was plain that no one knew how to talk under the circumstances. Everyone knew that High had lost his father and a brother and that their father, their husband, was solely responsible for the loss. High couldn't blame them. He didn't know what he would have said in their place either.

Florence came in from down the hall and did a little curtsey to High. He smiled at her. "Good morning, High Warning." He wondered if he was the only person who realized she had made a miniature poem, but then the youngest boy giggled. So High was not alone.

"I'd like to come later and pay my respects, Florence," he said, awkwardly knowing he had to say something but not really sure what that meant.

"Alright, High," Florence said. He noticed that she looked prettier than she ever had before. Her dishwater blond hair, hanging down long and straight, framed her face perfectly.

Lilia came in next. He could tell she had tried to put her hair up, and she wore a dress that seemed too nice for a family breakfast table.

"Hi, Lilia. I hope your head's okay." He wondered if he would have been better off to bring his gun in so he could shove *that* in his mouth. At least it was smaller than his boot.

"It's fine, High. I was clumsy. It wasn't your fault." Snippets of everything they had both been wanting to say to each other, but neither had found the right time or place. It was all a conversation he might have liked to carry through to satisfaction later, but not here in front of everyone.

They ate quietly for most of the meal. Tamar tried to keep a conversation going, but it was about like a herd of cows. They bawl and bawl when they're hungry, but once the hay is on the ground, time for talking is over. Of course, a cow herd's silence at mealtime probably has very little to do with feeling awkward. It is only that cows with hay before them have better things to do than engage in idle chitchat.

High ate faster than was probably polite, but it didn't seem like there was a whole lot else to do in a room so quiet. He had never seen the twins so reticent, nor the boys so lacking in the skills of obnoxiousness. He wondered if this spell of silence was something that ran farther back than the accident. If he were betting, he would have put money on it. He would bet that the silence was born when their father began his drunken downward spiral.

"Well, I reckon I prob'ly should get movin'," he said finally, eternally glad his plate was clean and there was nothing more to offer him.

"A cup of coffee before you go?" asked Tamar.

Now he knew she was trying to stall him. "No, ma'am. I prob'ly should move along, but thank you."

He left with little word and got to Wilder as fast as he could, but not fast enough. He was leading the horse out of the barn when Washington Starbuck came walking his own horse into the yard.

High was glad he had postponed putting his gun belt back on, but still it hung from the saddle horn like a pimple in the middle of a schoolgirl's nose. Starbuck glanced over at it, and his eyes froze. He stepped off his horse and looked casually at High, avoiding looking again at the gun.

"Mornin', son. I'm pleased to see you."

You might not be if you knew why I came, thought High.

"I heard about your job," High blurted out, then felt foolish.

Starbuck didn't seem to know whether he wanted to shake his head or nod, so he did a combination of the two, ending up sort of making circles. "I worked there for twenty years, High. Twenty good years. Shoot. They didn't have a choice, ya know. Closed 'em down. Right down like they never even existed, after all those years."

Starbuck twirled the ends of his reins around in his hand. "Don't know if I can find enough work to keep the family here. My old family place, too."

High nodded. He could only imagine how Starbuck must feel. He felt guilty for ever wanting to shoot him.

"See that tree over there?" Starbuck said, and he pointed to the same willow tree his wife had talked about. High waited for the same stories.

"Yes, sir."

"I always wanted to build the kids a tree house up in there. Boy, that tree seemed so big and strong. Look at that trunk! What a tree. Nothin' could hurt that thing, ya know? And then one year branches just started to fallin' out of it. I'm not talkin' about those little branches that always get knocked outta trees like that when the wind comes howlin'. I'm talkin' about some *big* branches. Then all a sudden one mornin' I come to realize that just when you're thinkin' somethin' is invincible-strong, that nothin' could ever make it weak, that just kinda seems like the time it starts provin' you wrong.

"If I woulda built that treehouse, and my kids were up there in a big windstorm, the one thing I thought was strongest coulda turned into the one thing that was weakest. I coulda killed my own children."

This story Wash Starbuck was telling wasn't about a willow tree. He might have thought it was, but this story was about Starbuck himself, a man so tough and capable, who was always there for his family, strong and able. And then suddenly his branches started to fall, and everyone who had seen him so strong knew how weak he was.

"Can I tell you somethin', High?"

High nodded. "Of course, Mr. Starbuck."

Now the man couldn't look in his eyes. He sniffed and looked off at the mountains. He tried to talk a couple of times and each time stopped and waited, biting the insides of his cheeks. "Ha. Guess you never know where your strengths are, son. Never. I just wanted t' tell you ... 'bout your daddy ..."

To High's horror, Wash Starbuck suddenly broke into tears. He started crying so hard his entire body shook, and he couldn't speak. He came toward High as if he were going to embrace him, and High would have let him. Even though this was the man who had killed his father, at the moment Starbuck felt ironically like the man who was emotionally closest to him. At the last second, Starbuck stopped himself, probably embarrassed, and put up a hand, patting High soundly on the shoulder several times.

He scrubbed hard at his eyes and stopped his tears that way. Then he stood staring at the ground, holding his reins, and trying to get himself gathered up. At last, his chin shaking, he raised his head again. "High, your daddy ... I wish ..." Suddenly, it was all more than the man could take, and he gave High a little wave of apology and a nod, then turned and stalked to the barn, leading his horse.

High leaped on Wilder as fast as he could and put him into a lope.

The next morning, Washington Starbuck didn't go out to the cemetery to see Angel Warning. He went two days later because they carried him.

The Methodist pastor was driving in his old Ford to church early Sunday morning when he passed the Starbuck home on his way. It was he who found Washington Starbuck hanging from the limb of the old willow tree.

That gnarled old, untrustworthy limb had reserved just enough strength to take care of one last job.

CHAPTER SIX

THE TEARS HIGH WARNING had been missing at his own father and brother's funeral found him the gloomy, windy morning
they laid Washington Starbuck in the ground. It didn't make sense
to him. He had felt gutted over the deaths of Seth and his father,
but he couldn't get tears to come even when he was all alone.
Now the man responsible for their deaths was being eulogized to
his eternal sleep, and High had to fight tears with everything he
had.

The same pastor who had found Starbuck hanging from the
willow tree in his yard spoke over his grave, and High was certain
it was a nice service, but the wind batted most of it out of the
pastor's mouth even as he was speaking the words. He hoped at
least Tamar and the children could hear it, and perhaps they were
close enough to. They were even downwind of the pastor. But
then High started wondering what kind of words you would speak
about a husband and father who had cowardly taken his own life
anyway, leaving his wife and children to try and struggle through
their lives alone.

Not only Florence, but this time the entire Starbuck family,
stood with tear-washed faces. For them, and for him, he wished
the rainclouds that were threatening would get their dirty work
over with. It is much easier to cry when the heavens seem to be
crying with you, and when the rain covers tears.

High thought of the supreme irony of how badly he had
wanted Wash Starbuck dead two days before, and how sad he felt

about it now that he was. He watched the twins and ached for them, remembering his own recent torment over his family, and knowing that at least his father and brother had died by an accident.

Six men lowered the forlorn coffin into the ground, all within sight of Angel and Seth's graves. High sucked in a deep breath and gritted his teeth hard as the girls and their mother stepped close and let go of the flowers they had been holding, watching them flutter down onto the top of the coffin.

When everyone began to disperse except his own family and the Starbucks, after everyone else had paid their respects, High looked at his mother. She made the wrong move reaching out to squeeze his arm, because for some reason it was the catalyst that almost made his tears come down. "We'll be going over to visit the family later," Lydia said. "But you can stay now if you'd like." As he had known his whole unfortunate childhood, she was reading his mind.

"Yeah, Mom. I think I'll stay with them. For a while."

"Okay, Son. We'll see you at the house."

Ava walked over with Owen, who was holding her baby, and gave High a squeeze. "You alright, Bub?"

He could only nod. She reached up and patted his cheek, then walked off. Grant came to join Owen, and they both stood by High in silent solidarity. Neither of them spoke. They only looked quietly down at the top of the coffin, and the cast-off flowers.

High finally went over to the family, where they were huddled on the other side of the grave like lost souls. Tamar stepped away from the boy whose shoulders she had been squeezing and gave High a hug, holding on for a long time. Finally, she patted his back and let go. "I'm glad you came to see him, High. I know it might not seem like it right now, but that meant an awful lot to him."

"Thank you, ma'am. I wanted to tell you something."

"Yes, dear?"

"I just wanted to say if you need anything, you let me know. And I mean anything at all. I'll do everything I can so your family doesn't starve."

He sure didn't mean his words to make Tamar Starbuck start crying again, but she did, and she wrapped him in her arms again and held him for an even longer time. It seemed like five minutes.

When Tamar finally let go of High, he stepped back to see that Florence was on the ground by the grave, much like the other day, and Lilia was trying to comfort her again. Feeling breathless and lost, and really having nothing in his mind to say, he walked to them. The moment Florence saw him, the girl who for so long had seemed to hate him for tying her to a runaway goat, she jumped to her feet and hugged him so fiercely it almost scared him. She started crying so loud he thought her whole family would look over to see what the matter was, but instead they all averted their eyes. The whole while, Lilia stood there patting her sister's back and avoiding the eyes of the boy she loved, the boy who was engaged to marry another girl.

"Your family will be alright," High said, after searching his mind to find something that might help. "I'll do anything I can to help you." And he meant it. That woman alone, with three young boys, was going to need help. Her daughters were eighteen, maybe nineteen by now. They might find someone soon who could care for them. But what on earth was their mother going to do with those three growing boys?

High mounted Wilder twenty minutes later, when the Starbuck finally headed home, with a local farmer friend who had stayed with his sedan to give them a ride. He watched the long black Chrysler make a loop around the cemetery, pass through the gate, and rattle down the road bearing with it a million tears yet un-wept.

He sat the stallion for a while, feeling the wind whip against his coat, nearly pulling the hat off his head. At last, the tears of the angels began to patter against the brim of his hat, and he turned Wilder slowly toward the ranch.

The rain drifted down all day, never fierce, but never relenting. The wind ceased, but the rain came and came, pooling in the dark yard, making Wilder and the other horses look miserable as they stood hipshot under the overhang of the barn with heads hung low.

The family was eating together today, with all the siblings gathered at the ranch. High couldn't shake his thoughts about the Starbuck family. Part of him felt responsible for them, and he couldn't make himself understand why. Had something about his visit to their home caused Wash to hang himself? Was he feeling obligated to Florence because she had thought Seth was going to care for her, and now he wasn't, and High was the closest thing she had to his brother now? Many thoughts came to him. Many questions. He couldn't sort through them and come to any better understanding than what he had had at the gravesite.

He was sitting alone out on the porch after supper, a bead-decorated elk hide coat buttoned tightly around him that his friend Tommy Hawk had asked his grandmother to make for him. Nobody, not even Ava, sat out here with him because everyone in the family finally understood he needed to be alone. He didn't know why no one's company was helping him, or why he needed this quiet time. He didn't know until he realized God had made him come out here, so he would be here when the horse came into the yard.

He had watched the horse and rider coming down the sloppy, drenched road for some time, jogging along in the drizzling rain. He knitted his brow and pondered the senselessness of someone traveling in this weather. Yet on they came, regardless.

High's sharp young eyes finally made out the female form that was shrouded in what appeared to be a giant coat and maybe even a blanket on top of it. She was wearing a broad-brimmed western hat, but she was female, plain enough, even though she rode astride her horse, as most women did these days.

He wasn't surprised when the mysterious horsewoman rode into the yard. He didn't know why, but he had suspected she might. A second later, he recognized the horse as a sorrel the Starbucks owned. He hadn't known it sooner only because it was dark with the rain.

The horse clopped up to the porch a few seconds after High stood up to watch. The rider raised her head enough for the late evening light to strike her face. It was Florence Starbuck!

He started down off the porch into the gentle-falling rain and gave her a hand as she came off the tall horse. It still seemed shocking to High, who had for so long known the spiteful glare of this girl, when for the second time in their lives she threw her arms around him. He wrapped her bulkily clad body up tight and waited for her to speak. At the moment, to his consternation, she was weeping again, but this time out loud, mournfully.

She finally looked up at him, but only after they had stood there in the rain with her disgruntled horse nearby for a full five minutes. This girl looked as distraught as High had ever seen anyone. Could she still be grieving this hard over Seth and her father? Alarm bells rang in High's head, and he grabbed Florence by the shoulders and searched her eyes.

"Flo! Did somethin' else happen? Are you alright?"

"No. No, High. No!" She burst into tears again, and he grabbed her just as he realized she was about to fall to her knees in the mud. He turned to look toward the house, hoping no one had seen them.

Ava was standing at the window with the curtain pushed to one side, watching them. Politely, she backed away, and the curtain swayed closed.

"Florence. Talk to me," High pleaded. "What's happened since I saw you at the cemetery?" Try as he might, and he had a good imagination, he couldn't fathom what could be breaking the girl's heart this way.

She looked up at him, and he wasn't sure he had ever seen such pathetic pleading in the eyes of another human. "I have to talk to you, High. I have to tell you something. I can't tell anyone else."

"Okay. Tell me. Please! What's wrong, Flo?"

"I—" She stopped again and stared at him, then lost her nerve. "Oh, High!"

Turning, she took off at a run across the yard toward the barn, leaving him standing there with her father's horse. Feeling sick with worry, he grabbed the reins of the horse and trotted after the girl, catching her lying in a pile of bedding straw on one side of the barn aisle. She was crying so loud it was more of a wail.

Dropping the horse's reins, he fell to his knees beside her and took her arm, turning her face up to him and pulling her toward him. "Florence. You have to tell me. Come on. Just don't look at me. Maybe it will be easier."

Wracked with her torment, she pulled herself up and buried her face against his coat. She moaned words of which he didn't understand a single one, and he told her so.

She pulled her face away from his coat, but she stared down at the straw between them, avoiding his eyes. "High! Oh, please help me. I don't know how I'm going to tell Mama. I'm going to have Seth's baby."

All night long after spending an hour in the barn holding Florence Starbuck, trying somehow to bring her comfort that never would come, High lay in his room alone, six inches away from where Seth had lain near him all the years of his life.

Aw, Seth, how could you let that happen? he kept thinking. *What did you go and do? You should be here now. This mess is your doing.*

His stomach ached, along with his jaw muscles and teeth, from gritting them so hard through the long hours of emotional torture. Poor Florence. How would she tell her mother? How would she even tell Lilia? And what would the people of the valley think of her? Besides that, what would everyone think of Seth? This wasn't the memory High would have hoped for for his brother. If only their planned marriage had gone through, then they could have kept their secret safe forever!

It struck him hard the real reason Seth had been so bent on marrying Flo so quickly. It wasn't to beat High to the altar at all. He was only trying to fix his mistake the only way he could see how, and trying to get Florence married as fast as possible in hopes that no one would notice how fast the baby came.

It must have been two in the morning, High still fighting the ache in his heart, when he pushed the covers off and swung his feet to the floor. Reaching down, he picked his Levi's up off the floor and fumbled in his front pocket. His trembling fingers came out holding the painted iron ring Seth had ordered for his soon-to-be bride.

He rolled the ring over in the palm of his hand, staring at it. He thought of Valentina Torreales, who at this very minute might be lying there in bed, thinking of their June wedding if she was awake, or dreaming of it if she was sleeping. He thought of Lilia Starbuck, Flo's sister, who had openly adored him for so many years, in spite of the goat incident and the scar she still carried on top of her head, and now the second one from falling off Wilder.

Then he thought of broken, lonely Florence, and of Seth, his big, citified brother, who might have tried to save High's honor too, if ever he had seen a way.

There was only one way to fix what Seth had done. Squeezing the ring in his hand, High slid down to the floor with his back to the bed, hung his head and wept.

CHAPTER SEVEN

AVA STILL WORE HER nightgown as she sat on the couch, her sleeping Rudy cuddled close to her. She looked at her younger brother, who had grown to be so much bigger than she. All the love of seventeen years was collected in her eyes.

"I'll never forget when Mama and Daddy brought you home," she said with a smile. "You were so tiny you didn't even seem real. No doctor thought you could live. But Daddy did. And he made Mama believe it too. He kept on milking that old sow and bringing it in, telling Mama it was from the cow—what was that old pig's name?"

"High-awatha," said High, grinning.

Ava giggled. "That's right! I don't think she had a name at all before you, but you're right—Daddy named her after you." Her eyes turned wistful. "I sure miss Daddy."

"Me too."

Holding her baby, she studied him for a long time in the gentle light of the one lantern they had glowing. It was so early in the morning the eastern sky was still a steel gray color, and Venus was glowing in it. Yesterday's storm clouds were gone.

"Babies sure do change everything about your life," she said. "I was only six when you came, and you sure changed mine forever. Are you sure this is what you want to do, Bub? I don't think you can ever go back."

He smiled at her, hoping to look strong. But there are certain kinds of strength hard for seventeen-year-old boys to come by.

"It's what I have to do," he said. "For Seth and Flo."

High spent the day with Owen and Grant, who had been laid off from the quarry, training horses in hopes that they could still interest someone in buying them, even if it was only for half of what they were worth, or less. A lot of the day, he sat on the top rail of the round corral, watching first one brother, then the other, soaking in everything about them.

His older brothers must have thought he was coming down with something, since he usually wanted to be right in the middle of everything, but when he wasn't watching them he took frequent breaks and went in the house to spend time with his mother, Ava and Clementine. Grant's wife, Cora, who was about ready to burst with her second baby, had also come to spend the day.

High sat on the couch listening to their chatter in the kitchen. He watched his mother and hoped she really was doing as well as she seemed. Maybe it was only those times alone in her room at night when her world seemed to be falling apart, those times he could hear her crying when he listened at her bedroom door. In the day, she seemed like a real soldier. He wished he could tell her goodbye, but he knew she wouldn't understand.

Only Ava knew his plan. Only Ava was stuck with knowing his secret, until he had a big enough head start away from the ranch on Wilder for her finally to come clean and let everyone else know what he had done.

When it was night, and Grant and Cora had gone home to put their baby to bed, High sat listening to Ava play the flute. Of course he couldn't remember it, but she and his parents had told him many times how when he was a tiny baby she used to sit by the shoebox they started him out in and play her flute, then sing for him. Even when Lydia had fallen asleep beside her from exhaustion, six-year-old Ava would sit there playing him soft music, and when the Mason jars they used to warm his blankets cooled off, she would change them out with others full of newly heated water. He wondered if deep in his memories that flute sound remained, and if that was why he had always loved it so much—and why he had always loved Ava like the earth-bound angel she was.

After everyone else had gone to bed, and Ava had put Rudy down, she came out to sit by her brother and put her hand on his leg. They sat in silence for a long time before she said, "Bub, I think you should go tell Valentina. I think you owe her that."

"I don't know how."

"There is no 'knowing how', really. I think you just go do it. Say a lot of prayers on the way over there, then hope God will help you."

He knew she was right. She was always right, and he had been thinking about Valentina all day himself. But how did a young woman's fiancé break news like this to her? Especially when that young woman had all of his heart, and had for as far back as he could remember?

After Ava had gone to bed, High went out and saddled Wilder, then rode him mostly at a lope to Oakley, with a stretch of galloping here and there. He made town within fifteen minutes after leaving the house.

Riding through town at a jog, he got out to the Torreales place to find it completely dark. Had he simply ridden too slow? It seemed like the pounding of Wilder's hooves had jolted all conscious thought from his head. He had tried to pray, but nothing had come. And no words came to him now either.

Did he knock on the front door and wake the house? Did he knock on Valentina's window and scare her to death, then bring her out here in the dark of night to destroy her dreams? While begging God to help him, he rode around and around the house in the shadows, walking Wilder slow.

Finally, he stopped by Valentina's window and stared at the moon reflecting in it. For so many years he had dreamed of spending the rest of his life with this beautiful girl. Now fate was pulling her from him, and he could never return.

With an aching heart, he turned around and rode home at a plodding walk. He didn't get home until after midnight.

Sleep must have come to High sometime in the night, but it had to be fitful, for in the morning he felt like he hadn't slept in a week. He lay there staring at the ceiling, aching just the way he had all the night before. He had to go to Florence today. He had to tell her. Maybe she would talk him out of it all. It was something that in the back of his mind he had been praying for—a release from his own foolish sense of honor.

But she wouldn't. He knew it down deep. And so he couldn't change his mind either. And he wondered how long into his future he would suffer for what he planned to do.

High and Clem milked the cows together, side by side. She sprayed him playfully with milk, and they laughed. They laughed even harder when he recounted the story of Gulliver the rooster. She had heard it many times before, but childhood stories like that never grow old. Afterward, she asked to hear again about the Night of the Goat, and Gutter, who had been put down five years ago, some six years after the roping incident had made him an infamous part of the Warning Ranch.

It had been a while since he thought about Gulliver the rooster, and of Gutter the goat, and old Gertrude the Jersey cow. Those had been rough incidents, but the laughter they had brought over the years was priceless. He was going to miss this ranch. He was going to miss Clementine, who had grown to be such a beautiful fifteen-year-old young woman.

He wished he could tell his little sister goodbye. In his own way, he was—it was just that she didn't know it.

Clem and High collected the eggs together and fed the stock. Then he saddled Wilder, took a deep breath before swinging into the saddle, and pointed the stallion for the Starbuck home.

It was on a Thursday, May the twenty-first. Five-thirty in the morning, and High was well on his way along the highway beyond Oakley—final destination, the great big West beyond the Warning horse ranch. Behind him trailed a packhorse he had trained, from the wild herd. It was weighted down with packs full of supplies—bedrolls, pots and pans, cups, plates, bowls and utensils. Enough food to keep him going for a long while, and money to make sure there was always more.

Beside him, and still with the sadness in her eyes from her farewell to the only homes either of them had ever known, rode Florence Starbuck.

Deep inside her she carried the baby High Warning had promised himself to be the best father for that God could help him be.

On Florence's left hand rode Seth's iron ring.

CHAPTER EIGHT

HIGH WARNING HAD BEEN to the city of Burley several times, but never when he was the one person responsible for getting around, and for keeping anyone else who was with him safe. In fact, it had always been pretty much the opposite, with either his father or mother to look out for him and make sure he was safe.

Other than the same sick, nagging feeling he had been suffering from, deep in his guts, the feeling that he was basically running away from home with one of the last girls he would ever have considered being with permanently, this trip had seemed like a big adventure. He was finally getting his chance to go off alone—or at least almost alone—to roam the country and show off Wilder Heart.

One thing High had thought a lot about over the years while lying in bed at night, when everything was quiet, was how to go about the business of advertising. He had seen different salesmen, in Oakley, Burley and Paul, either in town or at different fairs, trying to hawk their wares or get the attention of a crowd so they could demonstrate something. This wasn't something that came natural to him, so he had had to do a lot of self-convincing, but he was pretty sure he was mentally to the point that he could do it. The easy part was the fact that his stallion's beautiful, muscular and wild appearance drew people to want to see more of him. He had found that many times he really didn't have to say a word to convince people to begin gathering around. They simply gathered.

This was the case in Burley. He found an empty lot that wasn't far from the town center, and here, while Florence Starbuck shyly went to watch from a shady bench, High began asking Wilder to perform some of his tricks. The attention of a few individuals and families had already been drawn to Wilder, and as High began getting him to do simple things like shaking hands, pawing the earth, shaking and nodding his head, those people drew nearer. Others stopped while walking past and began to watch as well.

After twenty minutes or less, High had noticed automobiles were even stopping as they drove past. Others would circle the block abruptly and come back around, finding a place to pull in and park.

One tall, lanky man in overalls and a fedora put his hand on a skinny, pig-tailed blond girl of ten or so and guided her within thirty feet. The girl's eyes had a large appearance already, due to the emaciated look of an apparently hunger-stricken face, but now, watching Wilder as he nodded and spun both directions in a circle, his long, thick, black tail furling and unfurling like a flag and his mane flapping over his deep chocolate eyes, her eyes looked like the bottoms of Coca-Cola bottles. When High glanced at the man, evidently her father, he didn't seem much less wide-eyed.

"How long you been at teachin' that stallion, son?" the man finally asked, his battered, long-fingered, bony hand still resting on the girl's shoulder under a pigtail with fraying ends.

High looked over at him. He loved knowing how much attention was being directed at him and Wilder from all around. "I started to train him when I was six." High went on to tell the man a severely abridged version of the story of Wilder Heart, feeling the other people standing around, seeming spellbound.

An immaculately dressed man in his fifties stepped out of the midst of the crowd wearing a big white cowboy hat that looked brand new—and expensive. Besides the hat and wool suit and tie, the man had a smug, all-knowing little smile on his face as he walked close to High. He kept only twenty feet between him and the now suspicious-looking stallion.

Taking off his hat to reveal a thinly-creased forehead and deep brown hair streaked perfectly with silver at the temples, as if by design, the man laid the expensive hat, crown down, on the ground in front of his feet.

The man's voice rose out of the mumble of sound from the crowd, a sound both clear and startlingly deep and important. "Friends, you've seen only a little of what this young man and his horse can do. Only a tiny sample of the feats of which the two of them are capable! Step up, step up! Walk this way and show the young fellow and his horse how much you appreciate them. This show was worth the price of at least a dime! Of course you agree! Don't be shy, friends. Don't be shy! This young man and his lovely bride are traveling the West, showing off this beautiful mustang stallion to the world. Let's help them have the means to travel on, to let the rest of our struggling world see such a fine sight as this.

"Step right up! Step right up, my friends."

High felt almost hypnotized. Mesmerized, at least. And he guessed most of the crowd felt it too, for much to his dismay, the sea of onlookers began, slowly at first, then picking up momentum, to surge forward. One by one, then sometimes in twos and threes, they would bend over and place something in the overturned hat. Some of the bolder young men even tossed coins from six or seven feet away, grinning and nodding at High and at the well-dressed stranger as their money tinkled brightly into the pile already down inside the crown of the hat.

Not actually making eye contact with High, the stranger threw his hands up in the air, yelling exuberantly, "Well, take a bow for the crowd, young man. Take a bow!"

High had seen people bow at the end of one kind of performance or another, but he had never had cause to do so himself. Now he did, and it felt strange, but exhilarating, to hear the burst of applause from his audience.

"Now for one last moment of triumph, my friends. One last moment of triumph. Son, show them your big trick—the one you've been holding back."

Stunned, High stared at the man, whose eyes still seemed to rove everywhere except to meet High's gaze. A big trick? A trick he had been holding back? Who was this man? Did he know about High and Wilder? How did he seem to be reading High's mind?

A big trick? There was only one trick that High felt was worth being called a "big trick he had been holding back." He didn't know if either he or Wilder were ready to perform it in public, yet the stranger's will seemed too powerful to resist.

Using the signal only he knew, High got Wilder to lie down on his belly, and he threw a leg over him and took a seat on the broad, beautiful back. Nudging the stallion to rise, High took a looped rope rein that was attached to Wilder's plaited hackamore. Then, not daring to look at anyone, he clucked his tongue as he had done so many times before and told Wilder in a loud and commanding voice, "Rise, Wilder. Rise and walk!"

He was squeezing his legs tight as the great horse reared upward, to the sound of gasping from the crowd. Then, with a grunt, Wilder began walking forward on his hind feet. One step. Two. Three. Four! The crowd had gone utterly silent. High could no longer even hear the sound of a single bird.

"Down, boy. Bow!" High felt the thrill of goosebumps running up and down his skin as Wilder dropped to all fours again, then lowered himself into a generous bow, before standing back up to his full height and nodding his head vigorously, as if trying to dislodge a cricket from his ear.

The crowd erupted with applause and cheering again as High pranced Wilder around in a wide, proud circle, then once again back the other way. People who hadn't already been near to contribute anything to the stranger's hat changed that now, and some who had already given came to give more. High looked long enough to see that there was plenty of copper in the hat, but there was silver and paper as well, and a surge of happiness rose in his chest. How had this happened? And who was this strange, benevolent man? He had hoped to make money showing off Wilder, but already this had far surpassed even his biggest dreams for his first day away from home.

A fair number of people came over to congratulate High and to get a closer look at his magnificent horse. The pigtailed girl stared at both him and the horse with awe, making him a little more than uncomfortable. When all but a few of the onlookers had finally drifted on, after half an hour or so, and the few who remained watched from a distance, the wealthy-looking stranger sauntered over to High. The way he walked gave High his first moment of warning bells. This man's walk reminded him more than a little of Smoky Wanamaker, stealer of young boys' dreams.

Reaching down, the man retrieved his hat, and it suddenly hit High that he had been used. With a sinking feeling, looking into the man's eyes, he knew that none of that money was going to go to him. The stranger had put his own hat on the ground and asked for donations, in a time when times were hard, and people were desperate, even starving. And now he was keeping the take all for himself!

High felt anger rage up in him as the man came over to stand close to him and Wilder. He steeled himself for whatever the man was going to say.

"You must have a leather sack somewhere, don't you, son?" The man gave High a thin-lipped smile, before looking down at all the coins, and the crumpled bills that seemed nearly to fill the hat. He looked back up at High.

"What's that?" High managed to reply.

"Well, I sure don't mind letting my hat be used, for a good cause. But I'd like to have it back on my head sometime soon if you can find someplace to stow all this loot."

High, taken aback, felt his eyes flicker. "Sir? I don't understand."

The stranger gave a little shake of his head. "What's to understand? You just made yourself a pile of money. But you made it in my hat—that is unless you want to buy my hat," said the man with a grin.

The stranger had a sly look in his eyes, which High studied blankly for a few seconds, trying to figure out the man's angle.

"James Martin," said the man, thrusting out his right hand like a knife blade between them. "But most of my friends call me Jim."

Only a little hesitant, High shook Jim Martin's hand. "You mean you're really going to give me all that money?"

It was Martin's turn to stare. "I'm not sure I understand why you would think otherwise. I'm not *giving* you anything—just handing over what you already earned yourself. That was an impressive performance, and I simply think you deserve to be well compensated for it."

"Thank you, sir. Mr. Martin." All of High's polite upbringing came suddenly rushing back in, and he gave several hard pumps to the hand that was still holding onto his.

"You're welcome. So ... to whom do I owe the pleasure?"

High felt his face flush. "Oh, I'm sorry! High. High Warning." He blushed harder, feeling self-conscious of his unique name for the first time in years. Something about this man, Jim

Martin, seemed really important, made High feel like he was in the presence of some kind of royalty.

"High Warning ... High Warning! Well, that is one cracker-jack of a name! And the horse?"

"My brother named him Wilder Heart, but I just call him Wilder."

Martin gave a little shake of his head, looking at Wilder, who gave a snort. "He isn't too fond of strangers, I'm sensing."

Thinking suddenly back to Martin's introduction of him to the crowd, of all the things he had said that hit so close to the mark, High was reminded that maybe he shouldn't be all that certain of strangers himself. "He's never liked grown men too much."

"Except you, of course."

Again, High blushed. "Well, yes, sir. But I was six when my dad brought him home."

"I see. Say!" Martin indicated Florence. "Was I correct in my introduction of you? Is that your little bride over there waiting so patiently in the wings? She sure looks proud of you."

"No, that's just—" High stopped himself short. What was he doing? *His little bride?* Of course she was, or as good as! Whether High was happy about the circumstance or not, he and Florence were pretty much one, even if they hadn't made it official by going to any preacher or judge.

"Well, yes, sir. That's my wife, Flo."

"I'd very much like to meet her," said Martin. "Do the two of you have any plans for supper? Do you have a place to stay?"

"No, sir. Nothing yet," admitted High, remembering that Martin was still holding his hat full of High's money.

"Well, I would be obliged if you would let me take the two of you for some steak. We could put your horse in the hotel stable where I'm staying, if you'd like, and there are empty rooms there as well."

"Umm ... Sure. Sure, Mr. Martin, I think we'd like that. But I'll buy the food, since you were so kind to me."

"Oh, no! Nonsense," said Martin. "Nonsense. It was my offer, and I'd be offended if you tried to take the honor from me."

High grinned, feeling silly. "Then yes, sir. Thank you."

They walked over to Flo, who stood awkwardly with her hands folded behind her back as they approached. Her eyes flitted back and forth between them as they came to stop before her.

"Flo, this is Mr. Martin," introduced High. "Jim Martin. This is Flo, Mr. Martin. My wife." Saying the words the second time out loud didn't get any easier. It felt sort of like thinking you were biting into an orange and finding out it was a lemon instead. He didn't look at Flo to catch her reaction, mostly because he simply didn't think of it.

"I'm very pleased to meet you," said Martin with a graceful bow. "You are a beautiful young lady, and the two of you make a striking couple. Say! Did you see the way all those people re-sponded to your husband? I think you made quite a haul over there."

Flo looked shyly at High. "Why yes, I did see that. And thank you for stepping in. That was very kind of you." She looked at High again as if to judge if he approved of what she said, and he smiled a kindly smile at her, unfortunately not the kind of smile a young groom gives to a bride with whom he is in love. Flo's face showed that she knew where things stood between them, and her eyes dropped.

After High had fetched a cloth sack from his warbag and put all his new-found wealth in it, probably some twenty or thirty dollars, and Martin was wearing his hat again, he marched them down on Overland Avenue to the Palace Hotel. He offered to put Wilder up for them, but High politely deferred and paid the two dollars himself, the extra being for corn and grain, besides the regular hay. High already felt guilty enough for giving in to let Martin pay for their supper, but he had been very adamant.

They went into the hotel dining room, a fairly elegant setting, but dark because of tobacco smoke and the dark-toned woods used for the tables and chairs and the long counter. On the floor was a wine-colored carpet, decorated with a floral design.

When the bowtie-wearing waiter came by, Jim Martin greeted him amiably, and after making sure both High and Flo were amenable to beef steak, he ordered their plates for them, along with burgundy wine of a deep maroon color much like that of the carpet.

High had never tasted wine before. He watched Jim Martin and simply copied whatever he did, the way he held the glass, and how he sipped the drink almost cautiously, then smacked his lips.

When Flo put the glass to her lips, High had to hold back a laugh at the sour face she pulled. It didn't take much guesswork to know she hadn't had wine before either.

"Not to your liking?" asked Jim Martin, his observation making Flo blush. "I'm sorry! Would you like me to order you something else?"

"No, thank you. You're very kind," said Flo, and High found himself feeling sorry for her. Even more than he, she was really out of her element of comfort.

"It's an acquired taste, I suppose," conceded Martin. "But really some of the best pinot noir I've had in these parts, or even over in Boise."

When the steaks arrived, cooked to medium rare perfection, they were much more to High's and Flo's liking than the wine that was taking them time to get accustomed to. All the while, High kept wondering exactly why they were here. Suspicions brought on and then made strong by his acquaintance with Smoky Wanamaker had High's mind whirling. He kept trying to think of reasons why this seemingly kind and gracious stranger would take the two of them under his wing, then buy them a steak dinner, especially when times were so hard and so many were going hungry.

It was as if Martin, like High's mother, could read his mind.

"I'll bet you young folks are sort of wondering what interest I have in you," said Martin out of the blue, as he finished lighting a long, black, highly noxious cigar.

High felt his face grow hot. It was a sensation he should have been getting used to by now with Martin, but he wasn't. Still, he had to play the part of an adult. He couldn't allow himself to look like a rube.

"Yes, sir, I was sort of wondering, to be honest with you."

"Well, that's fair. I would wonder too." The man looked back and forth between the two of them for a few moments longer, studying them as their curiosity built; they now knew that Martin was not merely being sociable.

Martin settled against the back of his chair. He took a deep mouthful of smoke, savoring it for a while, then blowing it toward the ceiling as he squinted his eyes to let it pass. His eyes lowered to bore into High's.

"High, I'm a businessman. I find and make successful people. Show people. What do you think about the idea of being famous?"

CHAPTER NINE

JIM MARTIN DID NOT like being told no. When High turned down his idea of making him famous by arranging shows throughout the West, and even possibly across the country, Martin had a hard time masking his disappointment. It was the first truly uncomfortable moment between the three of them, and for a time there had been cold silence at the table.

They parted ways amiably, however, with High and Flo carrying their bags to a room on the upper story of the hotel and telling Martin good night as he wandered down to his room facing Overland Avenue.

In High's pocket, he carried the one thing Jim Martin insisted he not turn down, in case he ever changed his mind—it was Martin's calling card, with the address he called home in Boise, and a phone number.

As the door clicked softly shut behind High, he turned into the room. Flo was already sitting on the bed, which had a crisp new bedspread across it, and two plump pillows at its head. She was staring up at High, and in her eyes he could see there was something big on her mind, but she looked away from him after only a couple of seconds.

"You alright?" High asked.

She nodded, looking at her small, soft hands, which were folded in her lap. She nodded, but she said nothing.

High walked over and set his bags down against the wall by the bed, looking around the room without much real interest. It was a pretty fancy place compared to anything he was used to. A lot like the hotel in Caldwell, in fact. But fancy furniture, rich carpets and expensive beds didn't mean much to High Warning. He preferred the humble surroundings out on the ranch.

On a whim, he walked over in front of Flo, picking her bags up off the floor. "Where do you want me to put these?"

Her eyes darted upward. "It's alright. You don't have to do that for me."

"But ..." He looked helplessly down at her middle, then felt his face go hot.

She let a sad, brief smile cross her lips, but it was a smile without even showing her teeth. "I know I'm in a family way, High. But I'm not far along—and certainly not helpless."

He shrugged with both bags still hanging from his fingers. "Well, I already have 'em. So where do you want 'em?"

She smiled again and indicated a place by the wall, on the opposite side of the bed from where he had put his own bags. When he had deposited them, he turned to her again. This time she held his gaze.

"Why did you turn him down, High? You and Wilder Heart, traveling all around the country? Making all that money? You saw how eager all those people were to pay you. You saw how much Mr. Martin made for you, in such a short time. High, isn't that your dream?"

For a moment, it stunned High that this girl understood so much about that part of him. They had never talked about it before, and precious little had been said on their ride from Oakley to Burley.

"Sure. Sure, it's my dream, but ..."

"But what?"

"Well, you heard him. He'd be making all the arrangements. I'm sure he'd make me sign a contract with him. I'd have to go wherever he told me to."

"So? Would that be so bad?"

He stared down at her helplessly. Finally, he blurted out, "Flo! Don't you understand? When the baby comes, he'd try to tell me you couldn't come with me anymore. He'd try to send you home."

Flo went silent, and after a moment she dropped her gaze to the floor. It took High only a moment longer to tell there were tears in her eyes, and suddenly one of them ran down her cheek.

High Warning had fought a boy almost twice his size, almost more a man than a boy. He had braved a wild stallion no one else would try to ride. He had done things that would make great men pale. But nothing could abate the fear he felt seeing a girl cry, and especially alone in this room. And a girl he had committed to marry, to boot. What did he do? He didn't know, so he quietly left the room.

All the way along the hall to the communal bathroom, High was cursing himself. He felt no need to relieve himself, but since he was in the bathroom he did it anyway. He washed his hands, then on an afterthought washed his face, which usually only got washed if it happened to rain. Who needed to waste good water, after all? He stuffed his hands in his pockets and sat back against the sink, feeling sick. Flo Starbuck, the girl who had been engaged to marry his brother, was in a room crying, now by herself. He wasn't sure why, so what could he do about it? Of course, the fact of the matter was even if he did know what to do he might not have done it. He had never been particularly scared of girls, that he could remember. But he had never been put in charge of one, and especially one that was crying.

When he stepped out of the bathroom, the first thing he saw was elegant-looking James Martin, walking down the hall toward him. Martin hesitated in his stride, caught off guard as much as High was. Martin recovered quicker.

"Hello, young man. Nature's call, right?"

It took a moment for the comment to register on High, and then he gave a silly grin. "Yeah, I reckon."

Martin pulled another of his strong cigars from his pocket, and a match from a different one. He bit off the end of the cigar and spat it right out on the floor. That surprised High, since Martin had seemed too upstanding to do something that felt so crass. The man put the cigar between his lips. He struck the match on the rough floral wallpaper next to him and puffed the smoke maker into life. High didn't move that whole time. It was as if Martin was holding him in place with an invisible rope.

"Son, have you had time to think my offer over any more?"

"No, sir, Mr. Martin. I haven't. Flo's a little upset about somethin', an' my mind's on her."

"I see. Well, after all, it's only been a few minutes, right? But I do hope you keep thinking about it. You and that horse have a lot of potential to amaze and entertain people, and both of you deserve to be seen. Besides, the money it could make you, especially during this hard time when a lot of folks aren't making much at all ... Well, just mull it over before you rule it out. You give me a call on my telephone or send me a letter if you change your mind. As long as you haven't gotten too far away, I'll gladly bring a truck and come to find you."

High gave Martin a shy nod. "I'll keep thinkin', Mr. Martin. I promise." And of course he would keep thinking about the offer. How could he not? But the faster he and Flo could get out of this town and move to the next one, the better. Jim Martin was an altogether too persuasive man, and High was afraid he might change his mind.

High wanted to go down to the stable and see Wilder, if nothing more than as an excuse not to go back in the room with a crying girl. But if Flo had to be his wife, he guessed he had better get used to emotional outbursts, even if he never knew how to deal with them.

When he opened the door and peeked in, Flo was lying curled up in the fetal position on top of the bedspread, facing the opposite wall. He was almost overjoyed to see she was still fully dressed.

High didn't have any idea what time it was, but other than to go walking around town he didn't know how to spend the evening except to sleep. He sat down in a leather-covered chair against the wall and pulled off his Justins, all the while keeping an eye of trepidation on Flo; he was afraid she might turn to look at him, or want to talk, or other things even far more frightening. He looked down at his feet and frowned at the filthy socks he was wearing. They had been newly washed that morning, but there was a lot of grime built up inside those boots. After contemplating whether to go back down the hall to the bathroom, wash his feet, and put on new socks, he decided not to. Who did he have to impress anyway? The would-have-been bride of his brother? A girl who had never had much use for him from the start?

With a deep breath, he settled back into the chair and closed his eyes. He had a feeling it was going to be a long, long night.

After ten minutes or so, High heard Flo stirring on the bed. He feigned sleep.

"High, you can't sleep in that chair all night."

He opened his eyes to see her sitting cross-legged on the bed, her hands folded in her lap. She was watching him with an expression almost devastatingly sad.

Well, of course he could sleep in this chair! Where else was a seventeen-year-old boy in a room with his brother's fiancé going to sleep, when there was only one bed? "I'll be fine," he said, realizing that his voice sounded brusque, but only realizing it after he had already spoken.

Flo gave him a sad frown. "Please don't. It's alright if you sleep in the bed."

"But you—"

She stared at him until she realized his tongue was caught good and he wasn't going to finish his thought.

"I'm what? I'm in the bed? I promise I won't touch you. Would that make you feel better?"

Of course it would! But even a kid as dumb as High wasn't dumb enough to say that out loud.

"It's not that. It's just ... Well ..."

"Please just come lie on the bed. You can keep all your clothes on. High, you won't be able to go around showing off Wilder if you don't ever get any decent sleep."

It still took him a long time, but finally, when the silence grew too heavy to bear, and the bottoms of his feet began to hurt, he got up and went to the bed. He was still wearing everything but his boots, everything including his tightly drawn belt. He lay down on the bed, so far over on his own side that he was in danger of tumbling off if he fell too deeply asleep. But that was a chance he would have to take.

Flo was well on her own side of the bed, her back to him. As he lay staring up at the black ceiling, he heard a quiet sniffle. He knew Flo wasn't sick. That left only one other possibility, so he froze, trying hard to decide whether to feign sleep or simply fake his own death.

Exhausted youth has its benefits, and one of those is an ability to fall asleep in situations where no conscientious adult possibly could. High awakened deep in the night to the sound of Flo softly breathing. In time, he decided she was really asleep, which was almost as surprising to him as learning that he had been. On a nervous whim, he slowly rolled up off the bed, went over and put his boots back on. Then he slipped out of the room, down the hall to the stairs, and finally out into the soft glow of the moonlight.

The town was a tomb, noise-wise, and almost as deeply dark. To be fair, he guessed it wasn't exactly like a tomb, for he could hear the chirp of crickets from off in the night, and as he shadowed along, making his way toward the stable, he heard a big, coarse-voiced dog barking in the distance.

Wilder nickered in his stall when he smelled High making his way down the dusty aisle toward him. His sharp-whiskered lip found High's cheek when he got close, tickling him and making him giggle. He spoke softly to the horse, the one being in this town he wasn't afraid to kiss. For a while, he even contemplated crawling into the straw in the stall and spending the night here. Wilder Heart the stallion was his protector, his confidant and his closest friend. But High had responsibilities now too, and one of them would not allow him to stay here.

After caressing the big horse's face and neck for a while and assuring himself that he was contented and would be safe here for the night, High returned to the hotel room, trying to enter as soundlessly as he had left.

No amount of sneaking would have mattered, as it turned out. Flo had a lamp lit, and she was sitting up on the bed when he came in. Her eyes were puffy red, and her face was wet with tears. Did this girl *ever* stop crying?

High froze, wishing Flo were a crouched mountain lion, a raging grizzly, a giant tornado or even a fiercely rotten tomato.

Instead, she was a crying young woman, the most frightening creature in the known world.

CHAPTER TEN

MORNING CAME, AND HIGH was the first to wake up. Or at least the first to show outward signs of being awake. In all honesty, he expected Flo probably really was asleep, for after he had awkwardly gone to lie down on the bed with his back to her, pretending he hadn't noticed her crying, he had heard her sniffling until long into the night. She would have to be exhausted now, because emotional struggles always seem to be more draining than physical ones.

High pulled his boots on. They, and the belt he had gotten up in the wee hours to take off because the buckle kept wanting to twist and dig into his belly, were the only things he had removed for bed. He sat staring at the floor, feeling his hair stick out in all directions but too tired to do anything about it.

He couldn't help thinking about Flo. Why was it that not very long ago, the afternoon she had come to him with the news that she was pregnant with Seth's baby, he had been able to hold her, but now he couldn't? He could do nothing to comfort her. Every time he thought of even touching her, his blood ran cold.

It was because now everything had changed. He had taken on full responsibility of this girl and the baby she and Seth had made. He had done it only out of pity for her, and in honor of his brother's memory. He was in love with Valentina Torreales, the only girl he had ever wanted to marry. He wasn't in love with Florence Starbuck. Not only was he not in love with her, but he didn't even love her. He felt hardly anything for her at all, and he never would.

So comforting her in her sorrow was the last thing he wanted to do.

Oh, how High had messed up! He had ruined his entire future. Everything he had ever wanted was lost. Even the glory of showing Wilder off around the country was tainted because Florence would be with him every step of the way, always reminding him that no matter what happened in his life, he would never have the right to put a ring on the finger of beautiful Valentina Torreales.

If anyone had a right to cry, it was High.

High's stomach growled loudly—more of a snarl. He wasn't hungry, though, which was the ironic part. All he could think about was Flo Starbuck, a girl whose reputation he had obligated himself to protect, a girl who within eight or nine months would have a baby that wasn't even his, a baby he would have to give a name to and raise as his own. Lowering his head into his open-palmed hands, he scrubbed his scalp vigorously, trying to rub all the desperate thoughts right out of his mind. He stood up and tried to smooth his hair back down, then went over and got his Stetson, pressing it onto his head as he wondered if he shouldn't go to the bathroom in the hall and clean up, the way his mother always told him civilized people did, especially when they came to town.

But High didn't feel like a civilized person. He smelled like a horse and probably even looked a little like one, long legs and all. In truth, he had always thought he was more horse than human.

"We gotta go, Florence," he said, his voice more brusque than he had intended. "Flo!"

The girl stirred. For now, that was enough. High picked up a sack with some things he had brought, then left the room and went down the hall to use the bathroom, staring at his face in the mirror as he rubbed it with water, more to wake himself up than to get clean.

He used a bar of soap from his sack to work up a lather on his face, then pulled out an ivory-handled razor and took off two days' growth of fine, dark beard. High had never thought too much about it growing up, but Valentina had always told him how handsome and rugged he looked. As he stared in the mirror, it struck him that maybe she wasn't just saying that. Maybe he really was. And maybe his looks would help him on the road to becoming famous, both him and Wilder.

But what was he ever going to do about Flo Starbuck? What was he going to do but take her around with him, protect her, give her whatever comforts of life he could, whatever comforts she deserved as the intended fiancée of his brother, and pretend to the world that he loved her?

In the hall, High looked toward Jim Martin's room and thought again of the man's offer. He thought about all the money he and Wilder had taken in the day before, money they might never have made if it hadn't been for Martin's help. Was he making a huge mistake not taking Martin up on his kindness? Or was there more to it? Surely Martin wasn't only trying to help out of the goodness of his heart. Surely he would want a huge take of whatever money came in. Was his ability to draw attention, to work a crowd, enough to pay for whatever he would take out of High's pocket?

High thought again how much Martin reminded him of Smoky Wanamaker, and that thought was enough to drive him back to his room. If not partnering up with Jim Martin was a mistake, at least he would never know. And at least he would remain a free man, not indebted to some greedy, unscrupulous stranger.

When he stepped back in the room, Flo was sitting fully dressed on the bed, her arms folded as if she were cold. She glanced up at him, but her gaze wasn't strong, and it fell away. "Are we ready to go?" she asked quietly.

"Not yet," he said, although he wanted to say yes. "You prob'ly should get some food in you, huh?"

"I'm not so hungry," Flo replied.

High fidgeted a little, thinking about all the pregnant mares he had ever been around, and all the other animals on the farm that had given birth to young. His father had always pressed it home to High and the other boys how important it was that especially the expecting mothers had a good, nutritious diet, even if the other animals had to get by on a little less. He had spent as little time as he could manage around pregnant women since he was old enough to remember, but women couldn't be that different from animals.

"Reckon you oughtta eat anyhow," he replied. "On account o'—" He stopped, gesturing helplessly in the direction of Flo's belly, the last place he wanted to think about.

Flo drew her arms together tighter. After a while she nodded. "Yeah. I guess you're right. Do we have enough to eat?"

The honest query struck him hard. After a pause, he stepped toward her, stopping only a couple of feet away. "Hey. This isn't gonna be like how it was in your house, Flo. I won't let you go hungry. I promise."

High was looking at Flo long enough to see her eyes moisten again with tears before she looked quickly down to hide her face. He wished he knew why. He wished he understood women better—or at least this one.

Leaving their meager things in the room, they went downstairs to the hotel restaurant, High leading the way. He wondered if he should at least take Flo's elbow the way his dad had always done with his mother. But he couldn't bring himself to make that move, although he wasn't sure why.

After Flo was seated at a dark corner table, and a somber waiter with hair parted in the middle and greased down to either side had taken their breakfast orders, High excused himself to go check on Wilder. The stallion was eating a breakfast of his own, but he greeted High eagerly and gave him a hearty shake of his head, making the mass of black hair fall over his eyes. High couldn't help thinking how by all rights he should be here eating with his horse instead of dining in a fancy restaurant the likes of which he had never seen before his trip to Caldwell.

After begging a cube of sugar off the hostler, an old man with a gimp and a patch on one eye, High gave it to Wilder. He was rewarded with a big snort and a face full of spit. Laughing, he wiped his sleeve over his face and returned to the other world, the one he had no way to comprehend or deal with—the world populated by a pregnant girl he realized he barely knew.

Sitting in cold silence, High and Flo ate their eggs, pancakes, and bacon, a meal many people these days, especially people living in town, without animals and land, could ill afford. Before they were finished, Jim Martin made his appearance. High saw him as he came through the door, looking around with an almost anxious expression before seeing High and Flo and coming over to them to give a tip of his hat.

"Good morning to you two young folks. You off on another adventure today?"

"Yes, sir," said High.

"Bound to where? May I ask?"

"I'm not sure. Just the next town, I guess."

Martin nodded. "I can't help but wish I was traveling with you. It's a fine day for it, and I'm excited to ..." He stopped, looking back and forth between them. He smiled at Flo, but her return smile was pathetic and forced, and High knew Martin was savvy enough to see it. "Say, you haven't perhaps changed your mind about my offer, have you?"

"No, sir," said High firmly, impolitely taking in another mouthful of scrambled eggs. "We have to do it alone, but I do thank you for your kind offer."

Martin nodded and tried once more but failed to hide the dis-appointment in his eyes. "Well, remember if you change your mind, you have my number. And if you lose it, most people in Boise know how to find me. The offer will always stand."

After Martin went off to be seated at a table of his own, High felt Flo's eyes on him for quite a while as he tried to shovel the rest of his food into his face. He finally looked up at her, and she somehow uncustomarily held his gaze. "What?"

"Nothing."

"What, Flo? What are you thinkin' about?"

She searched his eyes for a moment. "Maybe I should go home, High. I don't belong here."

He stared her down, his heart starting to race. What was she saying? Was she really giving him an out? They had yet to find a preacher to make their arrangement legal. He was still technically a free man. Well, why not? Why not let her go home? After all, she was in her situation by her own doing, and Seth's. It wasn't his fault they hadn't been careful, or his fault they hadn't been able to wait.

But then the thought came into his mind of the little commu-nity of Oakley, how everyone there liked to talk, about everything that was or wasn't their business. He had seen how intolerant and judgmental many of those people were. He had heard them whis-pering behind other people's backs, often right after pretending to their faces that they were their friends. It also came into his mind that Flo Starbuck knew all this. And she was trying to sac-rifice herself—for him.

"You were gonna get married to my brother, Flo. Now you're gonna get married to me. I'm not lettin' you go back to Oakley an' have the whole valley talkin' bad about you an' Seth."

The tears welled in her eyes again, the tears he was long sick and tired of but knew nothing about how to stop. She quickly rubbed her eyes and looked at him, a wondering look in her face. "High ... are you sure? Really sure?"

"Of course." Which he wasn't. Well, he was sure he was destroying all the plans he had carefully laid for his life, but that was the only thing he was really sure of. "Of course I'm sure. And you know, even if you took off and tried to desert me, I'm not gonna sign any contract with Jim Martin."

Her lip trembled. "Really? You promise you wouldn't?"

"I promise. So you can just forget that idea. If you were to sneak off, I'd just be all by myself." He couldn't believe the words he was hearing from his own mouth. He couldn't believe that his own freedom, his one chance to live his dreams, had just reared up before him, and he was cutting it down, like a lumberjack might carelessly cut down a beautiful oak tree.

"I'll stay with you then, High. If you want me, I'll stay with you. You just ..."

Whatever the last of that statement was supposed to be, her eyes fell to her plate, and she didn't finish her thought. High was too scared to ask her to say more, so again they fell quiet, and Flo finished her meal, treating the food much more gently than High had. She was looking down at her plate, and her fork, but when High looked at her he caught a little smile on her lips. For the first time in a long time, Flo Starbuck actually looked happy.

And High felt as miserable as a rooster locked out in the rain. But seeing the happy look on Flo's face, he knew his own unhappiness was something he would forever have to lock inside, and until the day he died no one would ever know the truth, especially not Flo.

CHAPTER ELEVEN

AT A TEXACO SERVICE station on the far edge of town, a sign showed a high-bucking bay pinto with a rider in a white ten-gallon hat sticking like he was glued to the saddle. The caption read, "Wet gas makes your car buck. Use dry—Texaco-Ethyl."

Even though he knew he was drawn in for no other reason than the painting of the bronc and the buster, High reined Wilder in here and tied him off to an iron ring attached to the side of the station. He helped Flo off her horse, and they went in the store and got two bottles of Hires root beer out of a cooler. There was a Gulf Oil Company "Info Map" of the western states on the counter, and High took it and slid it with the two icy cold soda pop bottles across the counter, smiling at the nice-looking older gentleman behind the counter.

"That's a right nice-looking stallion you have out there, son." High thanked him. "I don't suppose that's the horse I've been hearing about. The one that knows all the tricks."

Surprised, High said, "Why, yes, sir. Yes, sir, it is."

"Well, I'll be darned. I was sure hoping for a chance to see him. My luck you stopped in today!"

When High tried to pay the thirty cents for the bottles and the map, the man waved him off. "Oh, no, you don't. On the house, son. I'll just take me a closer eyeball of that horse in trade, if you don't mind."

The man followed them outside and stood with his hands on his hips, admiring Wilder from a ways off after High told him the horse didn't usually take well to strangers—especially adult males. Before they left, the man told them about a cousin of his who owned a café in Paul, which was only a ride of less than eight miles. He offered to call ahead and let him know there was a sensation coming that way, and he knew his cousin would treat them like royalty.

That friendly word and the kind offer were the deciding factors that sent the little troupe off on the road due north toward Paul, rather than heading off toward the larger settlement of Rupert, to the northeast, or Hobson or Greenwood, both communities much farther along on two different roads toward the west. High wouldn't have wanted anyone to know it, but most of all he just didn't want Flo Starbuck to have to travel any farther in a day than she had to. He might not be in love with her, but that wasn't going to stop him from taking care of her in a way that would make his mother proud of him.

The Roadside Café, on the outskirts of Paul, looked from a distance like some giant child had dropped a square white block in the middle of a country of green fields and then forgotten it when called home to supper.

The town itself, if such it could be called, boasted not quite four hundred residents, about five hundred less even than Oakley. From half a mile away, High admired the sprinkling of little homes and businesses as he and Flo approached on their horses. He thought he was going to like Paul, which he had been to before but never paid any undue attention to.

Drawing in at the Roadside Café, he climbed down and helped Flo off her horse again. Even as much as he didn't want anyone to think he was in love with her, he was glad she was lady enough to let him help her down, like he had always seen Seth do. His dad would have skinned him if he ever saw him traveling with a girl and not helping her down.

There were only three cars, a black Model A, a dusty brown Chevrolet pickup, and a dark green mid-twenties Dodge Model B sedan whose lower door panels were stained with what appeared to be splattered cow manure. This was going to be High's kind of place.

Out the front door of the café came a man and woman, both of them in stained, once-white aprons, the man dirty blond, the woman with black-hair pinned in tight curls close to her head.

"I declare!" said the woman, smiling as exuberantly as her husband. "Why, you must be the two kids Charlie telephoned us about."

"I'm Willie Hart, and this is my wife, Catherine," the man cut in, grinning. "You two must be tuckered out—and famished!"

"I bet Fl— I bet my wife is," said High, reaching over to squeeze Flo's elbow. "I'm High Warning, and this is Florence. Pleased to meet you."

"Same here, son, same here," said Willie Hart. "Now listen—why don't you two go on in with Catherine, and I'll put your horses in the shed out back with some grain."

High looked nervously at Wilder. "I think I might better go with you. Least till I see how my horse is gonna treat you."

Hart grinned. "That sounds fine. Catherine, you take Florence with you now, will you?"

It didn't take High long to see that Charlie from Burley hadn't been lying—his cousin and his wife treated them much like royalty. They fed them until they were ready to burst, for which they wouldn't let them pay, and then offered to let them spend the night in a back bedroom at their house. It was an easy walk, between the café and the town itself.

After the meal, Willie and Catherine sat with High and Flo and told them about the little town of Paul, introducing them to the other diners in the room and letting them know they had informed people in town they would be coming. They said excitement in the little community was already building, with people anxious to see this fabulous paint stallion and the young man who could make it perform fantastic and marvelous feats that would dazzle the mind.

High found it hard to contain his excitement. He had always dreamed about this time of his life. The reality of it was starting out as more than even he had dared to dream of.

That early evening, High and Wilder enjoyed a fantastic crowd not only of citizens of Paul, but many spectators who came in from the surrounding farmlands specifically to see the show. They made even more money in Paul than they had with the im-promptu help of Jim Martin in Burley, then were treated to ice cream cones by Willie and Catherine Hart after the café closed for the night.

When the excitement of the day ended, the horses were fed and put up for the night, High and Flo sat on opposite sides of a double bed in a tiny room at the back of the Hart home. Flo was silent, and High was trying to decide what to do. Did he attempt again to sleep on the uncomfortable-looking chair the Harts kept nearby for people to sit in while dressing? Or did he crowd his big frame onto that tiny bed with the girl who was supposed to be his wife, and his lover, but who in reality was neither?

In the end, when Flo turned the lamp on her nightstand off, High lay down quietly beside her, the dust and sweat newly washed from him with a wet washcloth. He stared up at the dark ceiling until he heard Flo's soft snoring. Sometime deep in the night, she rolled over and threw an arm across his chest. He froze and prayed she was still sleeping and wasn't aware of what she had done.

In the morning, things turned out much the same as they had the day before. Willie and Catherine Hart had friends in the nearby town of Rupert, and they offered to send High and his "bride" that direction with a telephone call of introduction. It was an offer High could hardly refuse, especially because he had heard Rupert, which lay in the verdant Magic Valley, was a good-sized city, a city which boasted the distinction of being one of the first in the world to have its streets lit by electricity, after the Minidoka Dam was built in 1906. Over 2,200 people lived in Rupert, most of them typical country folk, and generous. Willie Hart promised he wasn't gambling when he assured High he would make a lot of money there.

It was Saturday, and the Harts had employees who had gone in to open the café, so they stayed over at the house to keep High and Flo company and to cook them another large, filling breakfast. Their five children clamored around the guests, firing questions at them, mostly about Wilder, and about High's escapades hunting wild mustangs.

High was seated next to Flo at the breakfast table, but as was his habit, he kept as much distance between them as he could. When Flo went after breakfast to use the outhouse, Catherine told High she wanted him to come with her to see all her flowers in the yard, and a vegetable garden she was very proud of that provided the café with much of its fresh produce. Of course High couldn't easily refuse, considering all the generosity the family had shown him and Flo.

As they strolled through the garden, Catherine Hart went straight to her true reason for asking High out there. Her question caught him off-guard as much as any question ever.

"Have you not been able to afford a ring for your sweetheart, High?"

For a moment, High couldn't speak. He didn't even know what to say. So as with all good smart boys, he played stupid. "What's that, ma'am?"

"A ring. You plan to give her one, don't you? Because our friends in Rupert own a beautiful jewelry store, and I just know they would work with you if you don't think you can afford anything too fancy."

A ring? What was Catherine talking about? Flo was wearing the ring Seth had ordered made for her.

"I'm not sure what you mean," he said innocently, and with a little embarrassment. "Oh, I know her ring isn't the most expensive, but it was made special."

Catherine stared at him. Finally, she clamped her mouth shut, looking very confused. "Oh. I'm sorry. I didn't ... Well, you just tell me to mind my own business, High. Us ladies, we get carried away with things like that. Never you mind. None of it is any of my affair. Love is what counts anyway, right? Just love."

Love, thought High. *Right. Just love.* A pipe dream for him and Flo.

"Yes, ma'am. I guess that's right."

It wasn't until he was saddling up Wilder and Flo's horse later, getting ready to get on the road toward Rupert, that High saw it—the nakedness of Flo's finger. It was no wonder Catherine Hart had acted so confused at his response to her queries about the ring! Flo wasn't even wearing the ring Seth had bought her.

CHAPTER TWELVE

HIGH DIDN'T CARE TO learn the significance of Florence Starbuck not wearing Seth's ring. He was a little miffed to think with embarrassment back on Catherine Hart's bold questioning about a ring, and his ignorant response to her. He was further miffed to know that even if no one else ever asked about it, there were going to be plenty of people, women in particular, who would wonder. But most of all, he felt slighted by Flo, both him, Seth and their entire family. Wasn't the cheap ring Seth had worked for good enough for this girl?

Eventually, he was going to have to confront her about it. But for now he decided simply to hold his peace and not get into a conversation that was out of his realm of expertise anyway.

The Harts stood waving at High and Flo as they rode away from the house. Even long after they had gone, when High turned to look back, the kindly couple was still standing there, watching them go. He wondered how often he and Flo would find such generous people on the roads they would travel. And he wondered how often they would find vultures and conscience-less thieves like Smoky Wanamaker. He was afraid that man, and Simeon Bristol, Lilia Starbuck's would-be suitor, had tainted his view of a large part of the human race, pretty much forever.

It was around six and a half miles to Rupert, and High and Flo made the entire ride in silence. High's mind was running wild like a mustang between all his dreams of what he and Wilder would do, dreams of all the places they would go, and then back far too often to whatever dark reasons were making Flo choose not to wear her ring. She had to know the rumors it would stir up, or at the least, the boldly curious questions. He also thought a lot about Valentina Torreales and wondered what she must think of him right now. Was she lying on her bed with an unhealable broken heart, or so angry with him that she was already growing to hate him, as she surely would in time if she didn't already? He thought about Flo's mother, who must think him the lowest snake in Idaho, if not in the whole world, for running off with her daughter without so much as a goodbye. Everyone but his own family, if Ava had already broken his news, must think the worst of him, as well as Flo. If they could only know the truth. But it was a truth High would never reveal, not to his dying day. They could all hate him if they wanted to. If anyone ever found out why he had taken Flo away, it would have to come from her.

There wasn't much to stop and look at along the road to Rupert. There was hardly even a tree to rest under and get any relief from the sunshine, which had turned out particularly hot on this late May afternoon. Beautiful farm fields lined the highway, sporadically broken by acres of sagebrush yet to be cleared. Little ranch houses, and some not so little, peeked or stared blatantly at the two riders and their three horses over hills of young grain and potatoes. The people who lived in those houses, and the travelers in automobiles, wagons, and the occasional horseman or woman they passed did the same. Most of the people seemed friendly, but all of them looked mighty curious. The sight of a young couple moving around the country by horseback was not a common one in 1931.

Rupert was a nice little city. The charming town square was just the way Willie and Catherine Hart had described it, like a painting from some quaint town in the Deep South. Rupert Gems, the jewelry store Catherine had told High about, was easy to locate on the square after asking a pedestrian for directions. What the Harts had neglected to mention, and which High and Flo learned in short order, was that the owner, Gino Brambilla, was also the city's mayor.

High couldn't explain why suddenly learning that the man they would be staying with was the mayor of the city made meeting him seem so daunting, but for some reason it did. Now the dust of the road and the sweat stains in his clothes seemed much more noticeable, and more offensive. He looked over at Flo, who walked beside him leading her own sorrel as he led Wilder and Honcho the packhorse, who was a deep dun in color.

Flo didn't always seem able to read High's mind. In fact, she usually didn't seem to get him right. But she did now.

"It'll be alright, High. He'll understand we've been traveling."

Taken aback, he stared at her. He stopped so suddenly that Wilder almost ran into him. "What?"

Flo swept his dirty clothes with her eyes. "I mean all the dust and everything. He won't think any less of you."

"Oh! Well, I'm not worried about that," High lied. "He'll have to take us how we are, or we'll just head on down the road, right?"

"Right." She actually smiled, this time a genuine smile that showed her nice, straight white teeth and made her look almost pretty, although not as pleasant to look at as her sister Lilia, and nowhere close to the beauty that was Valentina Torreales.

"What do you think we should do with the horses?" he asked, suddenly wondering why he cared for her opinion, but only after it was too late to take his question back.

To judge by Flo's expression, it seemed to please her that he would ask what she thought about such a matter. "I don't know. Maybe I could stay and hold them?"

"No!" he replied quickly. "No way I'm leaving you out here in the sun with three horses, especially with one of them being

Wilder—and all these strange men around? You could easy get hurt."

After a pause, Flo smiled again. It was as if she had been trying to decide if he had insulted her or she was pleased to feel he was trying to keep her safe. "I'd be alright. But I bet there's someplace we can tie them. Don't you think?"

"Looking for a place to tie up?" asked a gangly man in wide-legged pants tightly cuffed at the bottom, who had been passing by. "There's an empty lot right over there. It has metal rings set in the foundation—from the old days. Just for travelers like you."

"Thank you, sir," High said, wondering if the man was trying to call him a throwback to another time—which was fine, because he guessed he was. Or maybe he should be pleased at the thought that other people might still travel by horse, and sometimes still ride into town and need a place to keep their stock. Maybe he wasn't such an oddity after all.

They tied up their horses at the place the man had pointed out, and High turned back toward the jewelry store. Flo stopped him. "Maybe I could dust you off a little."

High shrugged. "Sure, if you want to." He stood patiently, trying to hide his embarrassment, both from Flo and from passersby, as she alternately patted and swatted parts of his body, sending out spurts of dust that sometimes seemed like they erupted by the handful.

"There. That looks better." She hesitated and gave him an expectant look. It took a moment for its meaning to register, and he swallowed.

"Do you, uh ... Do you ..." He couldn't quite make himself say the words.

"Do I want you to dust me off a little?" she finished his thought. "It would be nice if you would. Just a bit."

Feeling foolish touching her body, even through her clothing, High went about the basic business of ridding Flo's vestments of the only part of Idaho real estate they could afford. Much of it was probably dust that had just come off him and settled onto her.

"That good?" he asked, his voice more brusque than he had intended. He was trying to cover his deep embarrassment. He wasn't used to touching a girl, and especially not one older than he was. More especially, not this one, a girl he had been at odds with for almost as far back as he could recall.

"Thank you, High." She reached out with a delicate hand and touched his elbow. It was only his imagination, but her touch seemed to feel almost like fire burning through his sleeve.

High turned almost blindly and started across the square, nearly being run down by a passing car that honked an irritatingly loud, obnoxious horn at him. It took him a moment to realize that Flo was clutching his arm, where she had grabbed him as if to pull him out of harm's way. Should he thank her? He didn't feel like she had actually saved him, any more than his own reflexes had, so he said nothing. He didn't want her to feel like he owed her.

Again feeling a strange hesitancy as they reached the tall glass door of the jewelry store, High steeled himself and pushed inside. In his entire life, he had never had any occasion to go inside a jewelry store, and he had had no idea what to expect. There were three people in the big, dimly lit room. Besides a man with perfectly groomed hair who stood behind the counter, there was a couple in their thirties, the woman wearing a ridiculous-looking skullcap of a hat known as a Garbo slouch hat, because actress Greta Garbo liked to wear them and apparently she was someone of influence. The man wore baggy tan trousers and a huge overcoat affair much too warm-looking for a day that must be into the low eighties. All three of them turned to look at High and Flo as they stood there in silence, taking in the people and the glittering jewelry behind the lamp-lit glass cases, the strangely clean but sweetly perfumy smell, and the sound of a dozen different types of clocks ticking.

The man behind the counter kept looking at High and Flo a few seconds after the shopping couple before him looked back down at whatever was interesting them on the countertop.

"Say! You wouldn't happen to be the young folks my friend Willie called about, would you?" the man asked.

"Yes, sir, I reckon," High replied, put suddenly at ease by the wide, genuine smile full of teeth beneath the sharp pencil mustache. Those teeth seemed almost as sparkling as the silver necklaces and strings of pearls. The man's deep, chocolatey eyes smiled too, from behind a pair of glittering spectacles. He wore a tailored gray suit and a cheerful red tie.

"I will be right with you," the man said. "Just a few more minutes."

"That's fine," High managed, looking at the couple, who were watching him again, as if he had purposely intruded upon their shopping experience. Their cold demeanor seemed like a stark winter storm in comparison to the sunrise breaking over the mountains that the man behind the counter conveyed.

After the couple purchased whatever they had come for, they walked past High and Flo. It almost seemed like they both actually sniffed at them with disdain, like a big tomcat walking past a couple of kittens too young and scrawny to be worth his time. The door chimes jingled as they had when High and Flo came in, and the couple passed out onto the sidewalk.

The jeweler, who was almost as tall as High, hurried from behind the counter, saw Flo looking after the retreating couple, and waved them off with a grunt. "Aw, people! Don't you mind them, young lady. Some are too snooty for their own good. They think the world is all beneath them, and it is attitudes like that that make *them* the lower life form. Welcome. Welcome! It is so good to have you. My friends in Paul, they speak so very highly of you.

And the word is getting around town already—about you, and your magnificent horse." He looked suddenly past them, his eyes scanning the street. "Where is he? Where is this grand painted horse?"

High told him, and the man's grin widened. "Well. I shall see him soon enough, I'm certain. Oh! I'm sorry! I forgot even to introduce myself. I am Gino. Gino Brambilla, but please call me Gino. Everyone does."

High introduced Flo, then himself. Gino Brambilla took Flo's hand gently in both of his. "Aw, the young, beautiful lady. You do glow, just the way Catherine described you. Oh, she was so excited. Beside herself. She told me you were the sweetest, most beautiful young angel."

High saw Flo's cheeks turn red. He didn't know if he had ever seen her blush this way with embarrassment, although he had seen her often enough turning red with anger.

Brambilla then turned his onslaught onto High. "And you. High Warning! So it is true? That is your real name? How truly delightful. High Warning! It is like a name from a storybook, no? Robert Louis Stevenson. Charles Dickens! The characters that people their novels, they have nothing at all over such a tall, handsome mountain of a young man—a man with such wide shoulders, no less! And with such a name as High Warning! Oh, my boy, you are going to go far. I am absolutely certain of it."

High was starting to feel like if Gino Brambilla didn't come across as so completely genuine, he would have to mistrust him, just on principle. It usually seemed only people who were trying to get something from someone went on like this man did.

"Well, thank you, sir," High said, smiling and feeling embarrassed by all the attention. "I never thought my name was all that special. Sure not anything to make me famous, I reckon."

Gino Brambilla laughed with delight, sharing the laugh, and the twinkle in his eyes, between both of them. "Oh, you will see, my son. You will surely see. Time will tell you that I am right. I can hardly contain myself, you know. I can't wait for you to meet my wife, Savoia."

Inside, High almost cringed. He wasn't sure if he could take another reception like Brambilla's, if he and his wife were anything alike. But he thought that in only the best way. He had been made to feel welcome in his life before, of course, but never so much by some complete stranger—and a man as important as a city mayor, to top it off!

"So I imagine you two are hungry?" Brambilla looked back and forth between them again. "You've been riding a lot today."

High had to hold back a smile. The ride had been less than six and a half miles, all at a walk. Did Gino Brambilla actually think that was a lot of riding? In High's lifestyle, fifteen miles in a day was only beginning to warm his backside up. But he had to think of Flo now, not himself. He looked down at her, which with him standing six-four, and her about a foot shorter, was quite a look down.

"Are you hungry?" It crossed his mind that to make them seem like a couple he should probably call her something like "honey" or "dear", like his dad used to call his mother. But those were terms he could never use for Flo, and now for obvious reasons would never have any occasion to call someone else.

"I'm fine," said the girl. The flicker of her eyes gave away her obvious lie.

"I think she's hungry," countered High, smiling and making Gino laugh. "Is there a good restaurant close?"

"Oh, is there a good restaurant!" said Gino with his usual exuberance. "There certainly is, and *very* close by, too. I will take you down there and introduce you, because it is owned by my brother Luca and his wife, and they are also awaiting your arrival. But the real dining you will do today will be at my house this evening—and I insist. My wife, oh, she is the finest chef in the entire Magic Valley, and if you have never tasted Old Country Italiano food, you will never be the same—mark my words!"

Gino Brambilla rushed the two of them to the door, where he flipped a sign over to read "CLOSED", and he escorted them four doors down to the Rupert Café, which read on a smaller sign below, "RISTORANTE", a place that assaulted them with a wall of aromatic ecstasy upon walking in. High hadn't thought he was hungry, but he wasn't two seconds inside the restaurant before he decided he must be famished.

With great fanfare, Gino introduced the two of them not only to a cook and two waiters, a boy and a girl, but to every diner in the place. When a man and woman, the man obviously younger than Gino but closely resembling him, made a grand entrance into the room, Gino introduced them as Luca and Angelina Brambilla. High was so stunned by the beauty of the woman, who wonderfully filled out a wine-red dress, even when part of it was hidden by her white apron, that for a moment he could hardly greet them.

"I must return to work," Gino said, a twinkle in his eye after watching High try to unwind his tongue after the introductions, "but you are in marvelous hands here. You must try the roast beef, or the lamb, then tell me all about it when you come back to my shop. Oh—" He stopped, almost mid-thought, it seemed. "And also, I meant to tell you, if you make as much off of your show as I have no doubt you are going to, I will take you down to my cousin Tony's barbershop, where you can get a wonderful haircut, and then to Sally's—that is my brother-in-law, Salvatore— and he will fit you with a new pair of custom-made boots, if you would like." He stopped and reached out boldly, with a gracious smile, to take Flo by the fingers of her left hand, holding them gently. "Then, most important of all, I will show you in my shop some beautiful, beautiful rings. You *must* put a ring on this young bride's finger, for fear some gay young blade may steal her away!"

CHAPTER THIRTEEN

AFTER GINO BRAMBILLA LEFT, High tried to be gracious to Luca and Angelina Brambilla, who took it upon themselves to be not only his and Flo's personal chefs, but also their waiters. But after the embarrassment of once again having the lack of a ring on Flo's finger brought up, he was having a hard time keeping the smile on his face, and a harder time even speaking to Flo, or looking at her.

"Did I do something wrong, High?"

He was almost shocked by the sound of Flo's voice, the first time she had spoken to him since entering the jewelry store. He forced himself to meet her gaze, although he wanted more than anything to ignore her and not have this conversation here, with three other couples not far away from them. After a few seconds, a sense of resolve came over him. Maybe it was time to have this out. After all, she was the one who had brought it up.

"Why aren't you wearin' Seth's ring?"

Flo looked quickly down at her hand, reddening. His challenge had obviously taken her off guard. Her eyes came back up to him. "I don't ... Well, I ..." She was badly stumbling for words.

He simply waited and stared her down. He had no desire to lessen her discomfort. If she had decided she wanted nothing to do with Seth's ring because it was too cheap and ugly, not shiny and perfect like the rings in Brambilla's store, maybe that was her business. But he chose to take it as a slap in the face to his whole family, who were anything but wealthy. And having people constantly bring up her lack of a ring made High look like a cheapskate who didn't care anything about his wife. That was something he didn't think he should have to tolerate. She could at least wear the ring when people were around.

"I'm sorry," she finally said in a soft voice. "I'll try to put it back on."

"Try? Why try?"

"It's really very tight," she said. "I was afraid I might not be able to get it back off when I ... When the baby ..." She blinked as tears tried to fill her eyes. "High, sometimes women gain weight when they're going to have a baby, and sometimes it never goes away." She once more dropped her eyes to her plate, no longer able to look at him.

What was he supposed to say now? In all his life education, nothing had prepared him for a conversation like this. He quickly learned the bitter lesson about what *not* to say when he finally thought of *something* to say. "Well, if you're worried about gettin' fat, don't. It's not like I'd care."

Her eyes flashed up at him, and she jumped up and almost ran from the room, leaving the door ajar in her hasty departure.

To High's monumental consternation, he realized that all three nearby couples were either watching him, or very uncomfortably avoiding any glance his way. Worse, beautiful Angelina Brambilla had just walked in with a pitcher of some wondrous-looking maroon-colored liquid in a clear pitcher, shining luminescent in the sparkle of the room's lights.

In a rush, Angelina was at High's table and setting down the pitcher. "Is everything alright? Your wife, she ..." The woman stopped herself, probably realizing all of a sudden that there wasn't a thing she could say without seeming like she was minding everyone's business but her own.

High almost knocked over his chair trying to stand up, and the napkin he had put on his lap to mimic the other diners fell on the floor. Angelina Brambilla must have read his intention to go after Flo. She put a hand out and clutched his forearm firmly.

"No. No, High, this you should not do. I do not know what passed between you and your wife, but I say the look in her eyes when she went out. This is not the time for you. I will go find her. Okay?"

He nodded dumbly, aware that if she left alone, he was stuck in this now very uncomfortable room with three couples who probably thought he had said something very cruel to his wife. In point of fact, had he? Was what he said rude? At the moment, he wasn't even positive what it was, other than something about being fat. Inside, he swore as Angelina turned and rushed from the dining room, untying her apron as she went.

The door swung shut behind her, and the room went deathly still. That was when Luca Brambilla made another entrance, his expression of concern telling High that he at least had an idea already that something must have gone awry.

Luca, like his wife, was a remarkably attractive person, and under any circumstances it would have been hard not to notice it. Even in spite of the fact that he must spend most of his time indoors running this restaurant, he was somber of skin, and his eyes were nothing short of the deepest chocolate, paling only in comparison to his perfectly groomed, curly black hair.

"Everything is alright?" asked Luca. "Your wife ... you quarreled a little bit, maybe?"

High was starting to feel mortified, knowing every eye was on him and there seemed absolutely no escape from this situation. Luca showed a great tact when he quickly glanced about at the others, then reached out and took High by the elbow. "Come, young friend. Come with me for a few minutes. It will be alright. My darling wife, you know, she is very smart about these matters of the heart. You will see."

Like a dumb beast, High followed Luca through the door into the kitchen, where all the magic happened. Even though High's mind had been very preoccupied throughout the meal, the delicious taste of the food had not been lost on him in any way.

"Here," said Luca, as he put a hand on High's shoulder and guided him past the other cook to a place on the far end of the room. "You should try this. It is ice cream. What we call *gelato*, over in the Old Country."

Still feeling dazed, High looked down at a bowl that was heaped with a pale green, brown and pink concoction in which were embedded what appeared to be bright red cherries, and nuts.

"Try it," said Luca, regaining his earlier exuberance, a trait he and his brother Gino shared. He handed High a small spoon, and with a shaking hand High dug into the mound of ice cream, filled the spoon, and put it in his mouth. He in no way could have stopped the look of delight that must have come to his face.

Luca broke out in a huge smile, lightly brushing the backs of his fingers across High's chest. "Aw, you see? Yes? It is delicious? We call it spumoni, but some people in America call it Neapolitan, except really this is different. Very different. It is like what you might call the nectar of the gods—only frozen."

High certainly had to concur. He didn't believe he had ever tried any nectar of any gods, but if there was such a thing it couldn't be much different from spumoni ice cream. Up until this moment, he had only ever tasted vanilla, and one time chocolate that his father had ordered mixed with strawberry at the drugstore one day when he had sold an expensive stallion and was feeling flush.

"It tastes real good," High mumbled, feeling even as he spoke that he sounded like a country bumpkin of the highest order. Which he actually was, but till today he had never felt too embarrassed about it. Fact was, he normally kind of enjoyed the image.

The two waiters and the cook were busying themselves tidying up and washing dishes, all things it didn't look like needed doing at the moment, at least to High. Luca looked over at them. "You can wait to do this later," he said in a kindly voice. "Go and mingle with our other guests. I think they are almost finished eating, but it will make them happy to engage with us."

It was almost as if the room sighed with relief when the three workers departed into the dining room. Luca watched them go, then turned to High and gave him a close-mouthed smile. "Everything is alright, Mr. Warning? With your wife?"

High nodded. "I think so. I must have said something stupid, but I'm not sure what." This was a lie, because his exact words had finally made their way back into his thick skull. However, he still was not sure why the words would have upset Flo so much that she would jump up and run out. It wasn't like she should care what he thought of her, so long as she didn't have to stay in Oakley and face all the people who would talk about her, and as long as he took good care of her wherever they might go.

"Well, these things, they sometimes happen. You know? I mean, it might look to your young eyes as if my Angie and I are an ideal marriage, but believe me, that woman can be full of fire." He got a sheepish look. "And truthfully, I suppose I can too, sometimes—when it seems worth it."

High tried to smile at Luca Brambilla. He knew he was "full of fire" as well, but he sure didn't think he had ever showed that side to Flo, or at least not *toward* her. The worst fire she would likely ever see from him was the day he beat the big bully, Simeon Bristol, to a pulp. The plain fact was he was never going to understand a woman—any woman. Other than perhaps his sister Ava, who had only baffled him in her extreme poor taste in a husband.

When Luca Brambilla came to understand that High wasn't yet inclined to talk, especially about women, a firm resolve settled over his face. High didn't know why, but it was almost startling, in a way, that a man as handsome as Luca would have such a kindness about him. It wasn't anything High would have expected.

"You know, young friend," said Luca, having to look up at High, who had him by a good six inches, "I imagine you would feel more comfortable out back, away from other people—yes, even such kind ones as me," he said with a teasing grin.

This time High had to grin back. Luca's disarming smile drew it out of him as sure as heat drawing a boil. "Yes, sir. I think I would. But what about the g—" In a panic, he stopped himself just shy of uttering "the girl". She was supposed to be his *wife,* for pity's sake! "What about my wife?"

"Don't you worry. You step out back, make yourself comfortable in the shade. We have chairs—handmade by my other brother, Stefani. He is the ugly one of the family, but a fine carpenter." He winked at High to show he was only joking. "I will come for you when Angie brings your bride back, and I promise you that my wife will set yours completely at ease. She will be—how do Americans say it? Good as new. Better yet, I won't come for you. I will send your wife."

"Thank you," High said, feeling overly bashful. He wondered if this torture would ever end, or if one day he would simply realize that he and Flo had fallen into a routine, a routine where they understood how to live with each other, how to be friends, at least, and how to say the right things to each other. For High's part, he had a hard time imagining anything Flo could say that would upset him, as his flippant words had done to her. But he guessed maybe if she said something along the lines of how he sat a horse like a chimpanzee, or how he couldn't even rope a rocking horse, it might arouse his ire. He grinned at that silly thought as he was walking away from where Luca had opened the kitchen's back door for him. If Flo ever said anything like that, it would be obvious she was spoiling for a fight, and he would figure that was his ticket away from her. He had promised to take care of her, but he had made no promise to share blankets with a shrew—a word he had once heard his father call the woman who owned the local theater in Oakley, with her poor husband.

High sat in the shade behind the restaurant, in a little alcove, a miniature version of a town square, where there were dining tables, chairs, and in the center of the yard, a beautiful, ornate bird bath. Sparrows kept coming in to light at the water's edge to drink, then eventually to bathe, and one time a yellow warbler pair made their appearance. He could have stayed out here in peace for hours. In fact, he would have preferred to, except he knew soon he had to go get Wilder and the other horses and care for them.

He sat there idly thinking about what he had said to Flo about not caring if she got fat. He was slowly beginning to realize why such words might have hurt her feelings. He guessed no normal young woman would be alright with being thought of as fat, and of course even if they weren't a true "married" couple, in the romantic sense of the word, Flo certainly had her pride. He was trying to decide if he should make some kind of clumsy apology—for clumsy it would most certainly be—or if he was better off to pretend the words, like some dying carp, had never flopped out of his stupid mouth.

He heard the back door open as he was watching a new arrival to the bird bath, this time a rufous-sided towhee, which he had never seen in a town. He took a deep breath, and turned to face the woman who was supposed to be his wife. It was only at that moment when he realized he had thought of her twice as a woman, when in reality they were still both just a boy, and a girl.

Florence Starbuck wasn't the person standing there looking at him with her hands clasped in front of her. It was Angelina

Brambilla. He didn't know which of them was the more sparkling, the woman, or her wine-red dress.

"High?" the woman spoke his name even though he was already looking at her.

"Yes, ma'am."

"Luca said he thought it would be alright if I came out to talk to you. Would that make you uncomfortable?"

Oh, hell, he thought. Uncomfortable? She was a woman perhaps ten years his elder, more beautiful than any two-legged creature he had ever seen, and she was going to want to talk about a subject that mortified him—his supposed wife. Of course it would make him uncomfortable!

"Of course not," he said. The lie was so big and so bitter he could nearly taste it.

The woman stepped closer, and now the breeze told him she was wearing a mild yet alluring perfume. He hated it because he liked it so much.

"Florence is such a beautiful young lady, isn't she?" Angelina asked, and this question was going to force an even bigger lie out of High, because never in his craziest dreams would he have thought of Flo as pretty, much less beautiful. Every time someone else talked about her beauty, their words jarred him.

"Yes, ma'am." Was it the lie itself, or rising bile High could taste?

"You hurt her feelings, of course. But I know she will be alright now. The two of us had a very pleasant conversation, mostly about you. Do you want to know something, young man? This is from a very old lady who has seen a lot of married people in her life."

High would have laughed under any other circumstances. *Old!* No person with eyes would have called Angelina Brambilla old. He thought this, but of course he didn't say it. In fact, he was too tongue-tied to speak at all. The part where she had said she and Flo had mostly talked about him would have been enough all by itself to glue his tongue to the back of his throat, even if Angelina Brambilla wasn't so utterly rude as to look like she did.

He could only stare, feeling helpless, until Angelina gave him a smile every bit as gracious and endearing as those of her husband and her brother-in-law. Her teeth were as white as clouds on a summer morning.

"In all of my life, young man, I don't know if I have ever known a young lady who loved her husband more deeply than your wife does you."

High stared at her dully until all of a sudden his tongue vomited up the word, "What?" At least "vomited" seemed to be the appropriate choice of words. *Loved him? Florence Starbuck loved High Warning?* Until this moment, he had felt like Angelina Brambilla seemed every bit as sane as Ava. Now he knew she was as crazy as all the rest of them, and perhaps a fool to boot.

"She loves you dearly, young man." Her next words were as blunt as any he had ever heard a stranger say to him. "But is it fair to ask you this? Tell me why she would say she knows you are not in love with her."

CHAPTER FOURTEEN

THROUGHOUT HIGH WARNING'S LIFE, since at the very least the age of six, he had put a lot of effort into proving to the world that there were very few things that frightened him. To his credit, he could even honestly claim that he wasn't *trying* to prove anything to anyone. It just seemed to happen that way, because the truth was, High really seemed to have been born fearless. In almost everything.

People who knew High would call him courageous, but most of them would also call him foolish. His prideful side enjoyed the first word; his honest side could not deny the second. Ironically, sometimes he got very smart, smart enough to keep everything he was thinking inside, and sometimes he got very cowardly, far too scared to want to know any more detail about something than someone might already have volunteered. This was one of those moments—High was too smart to continue this conversation with a woman who could probably talk circles around him and could tongue-tie him, at best. He was too frightened to ask any details of the recent conversation Angelina and Flo had shared.

High did what any self-respecting foolish coward would do. "Aw, she just hasn't been feeling good lately. I'll sure talk to her. But I'd better go take care of the horses real fast."

He threw that last part in because by some good fortune, at just the right moment, he had found the strength to glance up at Angelina, and in her eyes he saw her gearing up to take this conversation up another notch. Little did she know, this conversation was over, and so was High's stay in this town. He might still do a show here, because Gino Brambilla had advertised it around so much, but when it was over, he was leaving, even if it was dark. He was taking Wilder, and he was taking his packhorse, and if Flo knew what was good for her she had better be ready to travel too. High knew a rat trap when he saw one, and to Angelina Brambilla he must look like the biggest rat around. Her whole family was surely soon to know that as well.

In High's earlier ennui, he had noticed a gate in the patio wall across from him. Because he feared what might await him if he went back through the restaurant—and Angelina was standing between him and the door anyway—he turned on his heel and made tracks for the gate. It didn't sound like the woman was following.

He got to the gate, grabbed the latch, and made a fool of himself trying to pull it toward him. When he started to jerk on it in frustration, he heard the woman close behind him.

"High? Sometimes when we are frustrated, we pull on things that would be better pushed—or push things that should not be pushed."

Confused, he turned to look at her. He was pretty sure his face was already red, but it certainly was when he realized the hidden meaning in her cryptic comment. Without thanking her, he pushed angrily on the gate. It opened as meek as a lamb and allowed him to pass.

Marching with his eyes straight forward, High got out on the street. The warmth of the day had coupled with his discomfort to make runnels of sweat trickle down from under his hat, and down the small of his back. High didn't mind sweating, but he despised it when it was a sign of his having been put in an embarrassing spot.

He scanned up and down the plaza, saw the building they had left the horses tied at the side of, and made his way there at the fastest walk he could muster without looking like he was running from something.

A car blared its horn as he walked right in front of it, and he waved distractedly and hopped out of the way, stepping up onto the sidewalk. He saw it now—Wilder's rump! A much-welcome sight. Rounding the corner, it took but a moment for a much less welcome sight to register on him. Flo Starbuck was standing on the far side of Wilder, brushing the back of her unsaddled horse almost furiously.

As far as High could tell, Flo didn't seem to have any idea of his arrival. For a second he thought about stopping and backpedaling out of there. But even worse than facing Flo right now was the possibility that Angelina or one of the other Brambillas was behind him watching to see what he would do. If he backed away, they would think him a coward! One of the few things in life High actually was afraid of was having someone think him afraid.

Taking a lung-filling breath, he slowed his stride but kept walking forward, finding the sense somehow to clear his throat. He saw Flo stiffen. He steeled himself and used one of the life skills his mother and his teacher had forced upon him from all the conflicts being a kid with a personality like his had gotten him into throughout life.

"I'm sorry about what I said, Flo. I wasn't meanin' to make you feel bad." He hoped he sounded sincere, the way his mother told him he had to sound. Otherwise, he had just depleted his entire supply of diplomacy.

He couldn't make himself go around to the girl, so he hoped none of the Brambillas were eyeballing him from across the street. He went instead to Wilder. That was the natural place for a man who loved his horse, especially for a man in the awkward position of having assumed the care of his brother's ex-fiancée.

Wilder nuzzled High's cheek and neck with his bristly lips and pinched his nose for a second like he thought he was getting a carrot. High grinned and stroked the horse's neck. Even all these years later, he was still so thankful for this horse, and often still amazed that he had won his heart.

It took twenty or thirty seconds of silence before Flo replied. "I'm sorry I ran out, High. I didn't mean to embarrass you."

"It's alright. I gotta be more careful how I say stuff."

"No, you're fine." They were talking to each other with the painted mountain of horse between them, which seemed to make this conversation much easier. "I was just being silly. I know you don't really think of me as anything but the girl that was going to marry Seth. You've never tried to make me believe anything else. I never should have taken offense to what you said. I think maybe it's just carrying a baby that's making me feel emotional. I heard Mama once say it changes a woman."

The word "woman", in association with Florence Starbuck, would never cease to be a jolt to High, for to him she was still only a girl. It seemed funny that at seventeen he thought of himself as a man, but he couldn't think of this nineteen-year-old as a woman. Was Flo indeed even nineteen? He knew she would be nineteen before he turned eighteen, but it hit him suddenly that he didn't know the twins' birthday. He wasn't sure what possessed him all of a sudden to ask.

Flo turned from her horse and bent a little to look under Wilder's neck at High. She let out a sudden, sad little laugh.

"What?" he asked, dumbfounded.

"Oh, it's nothing, really. I guess it just hit me that we really don't know anything much about each other, do we? Not anything very important." High and Flo had gone to the same school for most of their lives, and their families had been friends, so he started to argue with her. He stopped before he got even one word out. She was right. There wasn't much of importance that they knew about each other. The only usable tidbit High had on Flo was that she didn't like riding upside down on a goat. And she could hold a grudge tighter than a bench vise could detain a grass-hopper—something he should have been ashamed to admit he knew all about.

Sometimes the strangest emotions can hit at the most awkward times. High had no sooner thought of the so-called Wild Ride of the Starbuck Twins, and of Flo and Lilia Starbuck's hair all clumped with mud when a giggle escaped him. When Flo came around the front of Wilder and straightened up, looking perplexed, it made him laugh more.

"What's so funny?"

He stopped, but only for a moment. She advanced on him, acting indignant. "What? What are you laughing about?"

This time, he was able to contain himself long enough to try to apologize. Finally he blurted out, "I was just thinkin' about you and Lilia ridin' old Gutter." With the explanation out, the incident hit him full force again.

Flo put her hands on her hips. "Oh, you still think that's funny?"

High wanted to stop laughing. He was afraid that all the ground they had made toward being civil to each other was being lost. But it was like a tension had been building up in him so long he had no control over his laughter. It kept on coming, in tortuous waves.

Through High's tears, he had seen Flo march away toward the back of the horses and out of sight. He was sure she was going to leave him again and they were going to be back in apology mode, or she would be too angry to talk. He was just trying to decide he needed to get his laughter under control when she appeared before him again. Without warning, she jerked the hat off his head, and it felt like she swatted him right on top of his skull, then gave his hair a vigorous rub before smashing his hat back on.

If High needed a way to stop laughing, Flo had found it. "What'd you do?" he said, baffled. Then the smell hit him, and with it a horrible realization.

Reaching up, he jerked his hat off, and something tumbled down past his eyes, hit his shirt, then fell to the ground. His eyes followed it, stared at it a moment, and then he looked back up at Flo. Last, his glance fell to her hand.

"You— Flo, you grabbed a pile o' horse dung with your bare hand?"

A feisty-looking grin suddenly started to take over her face.

"You smashed horse manure in my *hair?*"

It was Flo's turn to start giggling. He stared at her, furious and insulted, until suddenly he again remembered the mud his goat had dragged her head through, and then all the other times he had had animal urine, blood, and excrement, and the blood or vomit of some human or another on various parts of him and his clothing.

Even as High was bending over to scrub the top of his hair and shake his head violently, he started laughing again. They were both laughing like a couple of lunatics, and they kept laughing together even after he reached out and dabbed the remains of horse manure on one of his fingers onto the tip of her nose.

"Oh, you're awful!" Flo exclaimed, then went back to laughing, until both of them, exhausted, found themselves sitting on the ground, with their backs up against the building. The horses towered over them, looking justifiably concerned.

Flo reached over without warning and put her hand over High's, squeezing it. "I'm sorry, but that sure felt good."

"The horse dung?"

She let out a last giggle. "No, silly. Laughing. Plus I've owed you for years."

Flo was right. He had had her revenge coming for an awful long time. But he would never have dreamed it was coming like this, and he would never have dreamed he would be laughing about it. What lady would pick up fresh horse dung in her bare hand, much less smear it in someone's hair?

Maybe Florence Starbuck wasn't too much of a lady at that. But all of a sudden High realized something else—she was no longer that angry little girl he used to think he knew.

CHAPTER FIFTEEN

GOING TO GINO AND Savoia Brambilla's home for supper that evening after a tremendously successful show High and Wilder put on in the town square was nowhere near as uncomfortable as High had been anticipating. In fact, it was quite pleasant. Flo made it that way.

That evening, Flo seemed to be almost sparkling. Her warm blue eyes were alive, dancing about from their hosts, the wonderful Gino and Savoia, to their children, Gino's charming mother, who spoke no word of English beyond hello, thank you, and goodbye, and to the extended clan, which was the other Brambillas and any shirttail relatives who had come over to America to find their fortunes, once all of them had learned how well Gino and Savoia had done for themselves.

Luca and Angelina were still high points for High, because they were such beautiful people, and so friendly. Of course, Gino was only a slightly older version of his brother, perhaps not quite so "beautiful", but every bit as elegant and charming—words High could never have fathomed using to describe men. But he had never seen people before who fit the words, at least not in the males of his species.

Gino's wife Savoia, however, was in another class altogether. High would not have said she was a classical beauty, the type of beauty one might choose to put in paintings, or in film. Her beauty was more tangible, more earthly, and her well-kept hair, a deep auburn in color, framed a face that kept offering this smile to High, Flo and anyone else who looked at her, such as no one but an angel could possibly put on her face. Savoia's most remarkable characteristic, however, was her eyes. There was a gold mine in-side them, a gold mine of kindness, caring, inquisitiveness and unfeigned love. In this woman's clutches, High would have been spell-bound, perhaps even more than he was with Ava. He wasn't sure there was a thing in the universe he could hold back from her if she gazed through him with those wonderful, liquid chocolate eyes and thought simply to ask him.

The meal of which they all partook that evening was on a par with nothing High had ever tasted. Gino described it as being *real* Italian food, the kind Luca and Angelina had decided the Magic Valley wasn't quite ready to embrace enough to serve it exclu-sively in their restaurant, but he predicted would someday be-come all the rage throughout America. Gino went through a whole list of exotic-sounding names, for the two appetizers (he had never even heard of an appetizer before), the main course, the two desserts he was offered and the wine. They also drank coffee, of an indescribably dark, almost bitter, yet exquisite taste that made him wonder if he would ever be able to enjoy American coffee again.

Tomorrow would come early, for owners of a restaurant, so High wasn't surprised when Luca and Angelina had to excuse themselves while the night was young. Luca came over and kissed Flo on the forehead, telling her how wonderful it had been to meet her, and he shook High's hand with a warm grip. "You are a good man, High Warning," Luca said, "and to watch you and that great horse perform, that I will remember as one of the purest, most complete joys of my life. I am glad you came to Rupert and touched our lives."

Angelina had taken Flo quickly aside and whispered something to her to which neither High nor anyone else was privy. Flo blushed and cast her eyes aside at High before turning even redder and losing a battle with keeping a huge smile from her face.

Before High had time to contemplate what might have passed between them, Angelina stepped to him, reaching out unabashedly to take his hand. Hypnotized, High let her lead him a ways across the room, until they were out of earshot for others to hear her whispers.

Angelina took his other hand, holding them both lightly at arms' length, and her dark eyes settled into his, looking almost black in the dim electric lights, yet sparkling like Flo's had been throughout the meal.

A mysterious smile finally overcame the woman's full lips. "You're not even afraid of me, are you, High Warning?"

High laughed, wondering if he *should* be afraid. "No, ma'am. You don't seem too scary."

"Then you haven't talked to my husband enough." She returned his laugh. "I have been reading you tonight, High. Quite a bit, in fact. I wonder if you know what an important man you will be, in the lives of so many. I wonder if you have any idea of the impact you will have before you leave this Earth."

The words puzzled High to the point that he didn't even know how to respond.

"Just remember one thing for me, young man," she said. "One thing."

"Yes, ma'am."

"Remember that almost nothing is ever as it seems, and sometimes it is the things that seem most trivial to us that will alter the course of our lives forever. Never put something aside as unimportant until you have looked at it from every side, and then gone to God in prayer about it. My father said this, and I will pass it on to you: Upon pedestals of the most unimposing stones may rise the world's most important edifices. Never judge a person, a thing, or a situation until you have judged it in the way that Jesus Christ would judge."

The Brambillas put High and Flo in a tiny bedroom that belonged to two of their children. The floor was of spruce, which to lie upon it without padding would feel like lying upon stone. The bed also was tiny, made to fit two children, and hardly big enough for anyone of an older age—unless they happened to be newlyweds, or at least had made themselves out to be such.

High lay fully dressed on top of the covers. He stared at the dark ceiling, lying on his back because the bed was too small for him to lie on his side unless his body was meshed with Flo's. He planned on a really long, uncomfortable night.

"High? Are you awake?"

The question from the dark seemed pretty silly. They had only been in bed ten or fifteen minutes, and he was lying next to a young woman whose presence in the same bed scared him near to death. "No," he replied. "I'm asleep. Fast asleep."

"I'm cold."

After High understood that the girl was going to blatantly ignore his sarcastic reply, it took a while for his mind to shift gears and for the words to register on him. Cold? How could she be cold? The room was so warm he was sweating. And now that her words had sunk in, he was sweating more. He couldn't even think of a way to reply.

"High?" Her voice came out of the dark again, jabbing him in the ears like a sharp stick.

"Yeah?"

"Can you just put your arm around me? Just till I go to sleep?"

Flashes of memory ran inexplicably through High's mind, memories of long, achingly cold winter nights when he and Seth, sharing the same bed, had been forced to snuggle up close to each other, fighting, it seemed, for simple survival. Now here was the woman Seth would have married, asking him to do the same. Maybe it would be alright. Maybe it wouldn't be as terrible as High imagined—and he had imagined the inevitability of it a lot.

Without saying anything, he rolled over, still on top of the bedspread. He gently draped his big arm across the woman everyone believed to be his wife. In a moment, she brought up a hand that felt as cold as creek water and laid it over his. It was a long time before he heard breathing that told him she was asleep. It could have been an hour, but he bet it was more. Half his body had gone to sleep by then, but he himself was frozen wide awake.

Deep in the night, something woke High, and he sat up. It was too dark to see anything, yet he looked around disconcertedly until he heard Flo's voice. It registered after a moment how frail it sounded.

"High? Are you awake?" Where had he heard those words before?

"Yeah. You?"

"I'm really sick. I feel like I'm going to throw up."

Inside, High swore. He tried to remember where the light switch was. He couldn't even remember where the door was! And being in a sudden panic didn't help.

"Hold on, Flo! Let me find the light."

It was too late. Seconds later, as he was scrambling out of bed, he heard that terrible sound, the sound no one ever wants to hear in the dead of night, especially in unfamiliar surroundings. Flo was throwing up, and from the sounds of it there would be little left inside her.

High froze. He was wide awake now, and in one of those situations where no one but a fool would dare move, not until he ascertains his positioning in the room compared to whatever projectiles may have been launched, and where. His memory of the room's layout came back in a rush. As if walking through a field of sleeping alligators, he got to the doorway and flipped the light switch on. Flo was leaning over the side of the bed with her tousled blond hair the only thing showing to him. Cringing, he turned the light back off. All the damage seemed to be already done. Flo sure didn't need him gawking at her—as if he wanted to right now.

Flo started retching again, and he thought suddenly of his own digestive system. How was *he* feeling? Had they gotten some bad food at supper? A brief self-analysis told him that other than a little nausea over what he had just witnessed, he felt fine.

When Flo finally stopped dry heaving, he said, "Do you want the light back on?"

"Yes, please." The sound of her voice, and a huge sob that escaped after she spoke, were his first signs that Flo was crying.

He turned the light on again in time to see Flo wiping the sleeve of her nightgown across her mouth. In near panic, he ran to his bags and jerked out his only other pair of long johns, running over to where she had thrown up on the floor by the bed. He started to bend down, and she clutched his wrist. "No, High. No, you don't have to do that. I can clean it up. I'm so sorry."

"Hey. Flo." He looked at her sternly. "Stop. Okay? Let me do it. You're sick." He stared her down until finally she sank back against her pillow and tears started running down the sides of her face as she tried to look up at him.

Leaning down, he brushed the hair out of her face and tried to give her a smile. Her chin and lips were still wet, so he dabbed them dry. "Hey, don't cry. It'll be okay. I'm sure you just got something bad at supper. We're not used to that kind of food."

"Sure," she replied with a quick nod. "I'm sure that's what it was."

He crouched back down and started wiping up the mess on the floor as carefully as he could. It didn't take long to realize it was going to take more than just his long johns, so he pushed them all over into a pile away from the bed, still trying to breathe out of his mouth so he wouldn't get sick too.

He sat down on the edge of the bed and turned to look down at Flo again. He was trying to make sure his head cast a shadow across her face from the bright light bulb overhead. "Are you feeling better?"

She only nodded. By the moistness in her eyes, he guessed she was on the verge of tears again. "I am, High. I am." He smiled. "High?"

"Yeah?"

"Thank you. I'm so sorry you had to see me like that."

He gave her a lopsided grin. "Well, I guess we'll probably see each other at a lot worse times than that, huh?"

"Yeah. I guess." She let out a shaky giggle. "Maybe God's paying me back for putting horse dung in your hair."

He laughed. "Prob'ly. Hey, Flo?"

"Uh-huh?"

"We don't want to have to smell this the rest of the night, do we?"

Flo stared at him for a moment with a look of hurt mixed with horror. Then after a few seconds' thought, she started giggling and made a horrible face. "I'm so sorry! It stinks, huh? No, I don't want to smell it!"

He grinned. "Alright. Well, I'm gonna have to go get some towels and water and stuff. Maybe some soap. I don't know if the Brambillas will come in, so make sure you're covered."

With that, High got up and left the room.

In the morning, High woke to the smells of breakfast cooking, especially that of coffee, fresh bread, and some kind of meat. It all added up to a much better smell than what he could remember from deep in the night.

Somehow, he had found himself under the covers in the night, and Flo was snuggled up tightly to his right side, much more tightly than he felt comfortable with. Luckily, he still had on everything but his boots.

"You waking up, High?" Her voice was soft as the down of a chick.

"Yeah. You?"

"Uh-huh. I've been awake a while."

He wanted to move away from her, but to do so would mean rolling off his side of the bed onto the floor. This bed was made for two people who really liked each other. "Are you still feeling alright?"

"Better. But really queasy. That food smell is getting to me."

High held his tongue. It had been getting to him as well, but apparently not in the way it was her. "Yeah. Sometimes I feel like that after I throw up."

They both jumped at a sudden knock on the door. From the other side came the soft voice of Savoia Brambilla. "High? Flo? It's Savoia."

"Just a minute," High said, scrambling out of bed. He hesitated before answering the door. If he opened it now, she would know he had slept in his clothes.

"I'll come back in a few minutes," said Savoia, and he heard her go on down the hall.

When High turned around, Flo was watching him, and she had one hand held out to him. Cautiously, he took it. "I just wanted to thank you again. For last night."

"For what?"

"For *what?* You *stayed* with me, High! Seth would have run like a scared rabbit if he thought he had to wipe up somebody's throw up—even mine."

High laughed. "Yeah, he prob'ly would." A vision of his brother's face crossed before him, making him feel sad at the same time that it brought a smile to his face. He wondered how everything would be today if Seth and his father had never taken that ride into town to pick up Flo's ring.

"You stay in bed, alright?" he told Flo, standing up. "I'll just go see what Mrs. Brambilla wanted. Will you be alright?"

She nodded up at him, smiling. It was funny how more and more her smile reminded him of the sweet smile Lilia used to give him. He wondered why it took so long finally to realize that someone was much more pleasant to look at than you ever would have believed. Florence Starbuck was actually a very pretty girl, now that he had started to find out she could be a nice person. He couldn't blame Seth for falling in love with her if Seth saw her the way High did Valentina Torreales.

High walked down to the kitchen, where he could hear soft clattering about of pans and utensils. Gino Brambilla was sitting there drinking coffee, and Savoia was stirring something on the stove. Gino jumped up.

"Good morning, High! I'm sorry you had a rough night, my friend. That is no good. I hope there wasn't something bad in the food."

Savoia turned and looked at her husband, giving him a little frown and a stern shake of the head. "Gino. No." She added a shake of her finger to the other signs, then turned to look at High.

"I'm making Florence a cup of ginger tea. It will settle her stomach, and she will be as good as new. Promise."

"Thanks," said High, feeling miles outside his comfort zone. "She's feeling a lot better already."

"Oh, so soon? That is very good. Then that is no sickness from bad food."

Gino and Savoia made small talk for a while, forcing High to converse with them even if he didn't want to. The manner of both of them was so kind and reassuring that High could hardly stand to disappoint them.

When the tea was finished, Savoia insisted on going down the hall with High to deliver it. She brought two more pillows from another room, and they set Flo up against the headboard in comfort, where she carefully sipped on the hot tea.

Savoia made a strange request of High by asking him to come outside and help her gather eggs, a chore any normal mother would have sent her children to do. But of course there was no way High would say no, especially not when she had been so kind and understanding and helped him and Flo out so much during the long night of sickness and stress.

They went outside and had barely made it to the chicken coop before Savoia turned to look up at him. "High, I would not ask you to help me gather eggs, okay? But I wanted to talk to you away from your sweetheart."

High swallowed. "Alright." He didn't want to learn what she had to say. Were all Italian women into everyone else's business?

"You were planning on taking Florence away today, correct? To the next town? The next place you will perform?"

"Yes, ma'am. I'm tryin' to make enough money to send home to both our families."

"Well, I don't think you should go. That girl needs rest. She badly needs time to recover—and get better."

"We've only been traveling a few days," he said, already feeling helpless against whatever she was going to say. There was a calm, kind strength about Savoia Brambilla that was going to win, no matter what he said or did.

"Oh, High." Savoia's face softened, and the mix of emotions that came over it made him think of Ava, or even his mother, in her more patient moments. "Talk to me. Okay, High? You can trust me. I promise."

A faint feeling of fear began to rise up inside High. It felt like Savoia Brambilla was reading his mind. It felt like there was nothing about him and Flo she didn't already guess. He couldn't even bring himself to reply, so he didn't.

Savoia gave out a long sigh. "Let's just walk. Okay? I want to tell you a story."

So they walked around the little two-acre property, and Savoia opened her soul, to a young man she hardly knew and may never see again.

Like most people in Italy, Savoia's and Gino's families were devout Catholics. As far back as any of them remembered, they had gone to all their church meetings, they had prayed, they had paid their tithes and done communion. In short, they were model Catholic families.

Then came that dark night, caught far away from home, in that tiny village where they never had any business going, knowing it would see them home far too late. Gino and Savoia were too madly in love. They had kissed far too many times, and felt each other's embrace, sometimes for far too long than was prudent for two Catholic teenagers.

Attraction and love led to lust, and Savoia ended up with child. In light of what they both knew about their church, and what they believed they knew about their families, there seemed no choice for them but to flee, as far from home as possible. So they took the endless-seeming two-week sea voyage to Ellis Island, in New York, and the start of a new life that eventually would see many of their family members following them.

"You know why I am telling you this story, I hope," Savoia finally said. "You can trust me, High. This I will always promise.

And also, I promise you this—that no mistake you have made in the past is so bad that it cannot be made right."

CHAPTER SIXTEEN

HIGH KNEW THAT SAVOIA Brambilla wanted him to make a confession. He was certain that she, like some evangelist, believed he was guilty of great sin and that if only he were to break his silence and get it off his chest he would feel better. But he had done nothing wrong. He wasn't going to say he did just so she could feel good. He had been wrong about Savoia Brambilla as far as one thing, and for that he was glad—she, in fact, could *not* read his story, and she in fact had *no* idea why he and Flo were together. She thought she did, and now he understood where her mind had gone, but she was wrong. He would have loved for her to know she was wrong about him, but there was no way on earth he would give away Flo's shameful secret. He would die first.

He thanked Savoia for her kindly advice, and for confiding her story in him. He thanked her once again for helping him clean up after Flo when she was sick in the night. He also thanked her for washing his long johns, a thought which mortified him. But he had planned simply to throw them out, so she had done him a huge favor. Now, like a dark pink flag, they hung out on the clothesline in the May morning breeze, a reminder of all his shame.

They returned to the kitchen, where Savoia left High with Gino to fry eggs, and she went down the hall to invite Flo to eat.

Savoia came back alone.

"I'm sorry, High. I guess that your little bride will not be join-ing us. She said the ginger tea made her feel better, but she still is not strong enough for food to sound good."

High nodded. What could have happened to Flo? Why would she suddenly get so sick?

"So tell me, High," asked Gino sometime later, 'where will you go next? Do you have any plan where to take your beautiful horse?"

High shook his head. "I need to look at my map."

He found himself suddenly caught in a trap. It took only a moment to see that the trap was of Gino's inadvertent making, but strangely, Gino was caught in it with him.

"Your horse! High! Gino! His *horse?* What about his *wife?* Do you not care if he has any plan where to take his beautiful wife?" Until that moment, High had never seen Savoia Brambilla looking anything but pleasant, even if she could be overly curi-ous. Now he saw her looking far closer to angry than he would ever have wanted to see.

"Well, you know they would go together, dear," corrected Gino, looking helpless. "Of course I didn't need to say it. It isn't as if he would go without his wife."

"No? Well, he should!" Savoia snapped back, her face col-ored with her ire.

Gino, bewildered, looked at High, and High looked his fright back at the man. Gino returned his eyes to his wife, who was un-tying her apron with slow, measured movements. "He should? Why should he, dear?"

"Because! She is not well! And she— She is—"

Once it became obvious that Savoia's speech had hit a dead-end, Gino threw a sideways glance at High, and an almost imper-ceptible nod. He stood slowly, with his fingertips on top of the table. "My dear, would you do me a big favor and step into the other room with me? High, if you would kindly excuse us for a moment."

High only nodded. He didn't dare speak.

After Gino and Savoia walked out of the room, High couldn't make his escape fast enough. He almost bolted down to the bedroom he was sharing with Flo and fled inside.

Flo jerked her eyes open to look up at him as he shut the door behind him. "Are you alright?"

High was staring at her. "Alright? Why?"

"You look like you saw a ghost."

He stared for a moment longer, until a laugh from his own throat surprised him. He had heard that expression often back home from his mother. "Well, maybe I kind of did." He didn't elaborate even though her inquisitive expression begged him to. "How are you feelin' now? Do you think you'll be able to ride?" His seventeen-year-old mind was making plans *fast* to escape this house. Dealing with Flo was enough for him. He was not equipped to fight more than one female at a time.

"I still feel pretty queasy," she replied, and he was astute enough to catch a mild pleading in her eyes. "But ... I'll be ready if you want me to, High. How much time do I have?"

High could feel his innards churning. What kind of a man *was* he? If Flo wasn't feeling good, could he really ask her to get on a horse and ride? He didn't even have any idea how far they were going to have to travel before their next stop, and if he might even be forced to make her sleep out on the ground.

A feeling of helplessness came over him. Taking a deep breath, he walked over and sat on the bed by her. This left him in an awkward position for looking at her, but maybe it was best if she couldn't see his face anyway.

He sat there trying to find the right words to say for so long that she finally decided he wasn't going to speak. "Are you alright, High?"

He held back a laugh. *Alright?* He should be asking *her* that! "I'm fine. But how do *you* feel?" He kept thinking he should say her name to her more often. For some reason uttering it felt too personal, like a big step he simply was not ready to begin taking. And yet she spoke his name all the time.

"I'm okay. I'll get ready—if you want."

"No. No, let's ... Flo, why don't you try to rest some more?" There! He had done it! He looked at her, and she had an almost shocked look on her face, but a happy one.

"Okay," she said. "But it's okay if you want to go sooner. Just tell me when, alright? I can be ready in twenty minutes if you ask me to."

He turned a little more so he could study her eyes. It seemed funny to think about, but he had never spent much time really looking into Florence Starbuck's eyes. In fact, he had spent most of his time around her avoiding them, because they always seemed to harbor anger for him—sometimes even hatred. But he never saw those looks anymore. There was something different in her eyes, but now that he looked in them deeper he wasn't sure a little of whatever this new look was hadn't been there all along.

"Let's stay here today," he said. "It'll be alright. The horses could use the rest too." He knew the horses had been ridden easy. They could travel another easy ten days if every day was the kind of day that had been asked of them so far. But if he blamed his decision to stay on the horses needing rest, then maybe he wouldn't look so much like he was trying to take it easy on Flo. And he didn't want her thinking that, above all else.

"Yeah." Flo nodded. "Yes, I'm sure the horses could use a rest." She was reaching toward his arm when he looked away and stood up abruptly.

"Well, maybe I'll go see if I can split some wood for Gino and Savoia. I'd better do something to earn our keep, huh?"

"Sure," he heard her mumbling as he opened the door. "Sure, they'd like that."

High spent the next three hours doing different chores around the place after Gino went to work at the jewelry store. Savoia acted polite enough toward him, but he had noticed a change in her demeanor. She seemed more distant. Maybe she was only lost deep in thought. He couldn't say for certain, only she didn't seem terribly friendly as she had at first and didn't always have that big smile ready to leap to her face.

Later in the day, when High was almost finished trimming a large pile of dead limbs out of the fruit trees in a small orchard behind the house, he saw Angelina Brambilla driving up in a turquoise-colored Model A Ford. She disappeared at the front of the house, and High put down his saw and looked around frantically. He had been able to handle Savoia alright, and the one time he had gone to check on Flo she had told him Savoia had brought her some chicken soup earlier, which seemed to help settle her stomach. Fortunately, he hadn't had to spend any time today with the two of them together, because he had a gut feeling there was something in the wind, and that getting two females together, with only one of him, was a recipe for disaster.

But now the two sisters-in-law would be together, and High was alone, and helpless as a worm on a hook. Without telling them anything, he went to the pen where the horses were being kept, caught up Wilder, and put a bridle on him, riding him bareback to town. He had gotten to a point where he preferred riding with a saddle, but he wasn't about to take the time to saddle up with two women putting their scheming heads together inside the house—maybe three women, if Flo decided to join the party.

Riding back to the same place he had tied up the horses yesterday, High left Wilder there, trusting Rupert's citizens to follow proper decorum and leave the stallion to himself. He returned to the jewelry store, Rupert Gems. On pushing inside, he was rewarded with Gino Brambilla's huge, friendly smile. "High! I'm so glad you came to see me. I'm surprised you lasted so long as my wife's slave." He laughed to show he was being playful.

"She was very nice," High said, "and I got quite a bit of work done."

"Well, thank you, son. That was very kind of you. Not required, but very kind. So to what do I owe your visit?"

"Oh, I just thought I'd come down an' say hello."

Gino gave him a knowing nod. "It doesn't have anything to do with what I overheard from Angelina earlier, does it? That she thought about going to pay Savoia a visit?"

High couldn't help a sheepish grin. "Well, I thought they might like to talk without any men around," he admitted.

Gino laughed again. "You are very wise, for such a young age. So how would you like to help me here in the shop for a while?"

"I'd like that." And High wasn't only saying that to make Gino happy. He had never spent any time in a jewelry store before, and all this gold, silver and these precious stones were beautiful to him, and intriguing. He didn't care if he ever owned any jewelry, but, like a beautiful sunrise or sunset, he certainly could enjoy looking at them and knowing more about them.

High spent three full hours helping Gino do inventory of his wares, between infrequent visits by citizens of the city, and occasionally someone who lived out on the farms. He heard far more about jewelry and watches, gems, and precious metals than he could ever retain, but it was all fascinating. It gave him a strange yearning to have had the chance to shop in a store like this, seeking out the perfect engagement and wedding ring for his former bride-to-be, Valentina Torreales. Now he would never have that chance. Flo already had her ring, and she didn't seem like the type to wear fancy necklaces or earrings. Anything High learned here today, he guessed he would never have any real use for.

Even as he was trying to write down an inventory of all the things Gino told him as he removed them from their sparkling glass cases—the names of watches, rings, necklaces, pendants and chains—High's mind kept returning to Valentina. What must she think of him today? He had been pushing all thoughts of her from his mind for so long. At nights, being physically so near Flo, he had more terrifying things to think of than what Valentina could be thinking. But now it all came rushing in, all of the terrible, painful things he had tried so hard not to contemplate.

He remembered the pleasant touch of Valentina's hands on his. He remembered the feel of her lips against his lips, and her breath in his ear. He remembered being close to her face when she told him she loved him, and he could almost taste the words as much as he could hear them.

The sound of Gino's voice finally broke through to him. "High! High?"

"Yes, sir? Sorry!"

"Are you still with me, son? Did you write that down?"

"I'm sorry. My mind wandered a little. Can you tell me again?"

Gino smiled, the picture of patience. "Aw, you know what, High? It's alright. You know, I think it's time we took a rest anyway. What do you say? In fact, why don't you run over to the drug store and buy a soda pop and a chocolate bar for us? You would like that, wouldn't you?"

High didn't care about either one at the moment. He was only embarrassed he had been caught letting his mind drift when Gino was relying on his help. But the light in Gino's eyes could not be denied. "Sure. Sure, just tell me what you want, an' I'll buy."

"Oh, no! No, no, no! You are our guest, my son. I will have you tell them at the counter to put these things on my bill. In fact, I'll send a note along with you."

So High thanked Gino and did as he was told, picking up six Milky Way bars, something he had only ever tasted once, and six bottles of chilled grape Nehi, which he took back to the jewelry store with him.

While no one was in the store, Gino and High kicked back in their chairs behind the counter and popped the metal caps off two of the Nehis, sipping at the sparkling drink inside. It was a little taste of heaven. The Milky Way High bit into was the same. The soft chocolate and caramel melted in his mouth, and he wondered how he had survived his whole life without eating one of these every day. They kept the extra candy and bottles of soda pop in a brown paper bag, to be delivered home with them later.

They took a full ten minutes enjoying every last morsel of the chocolate bar, then sipped the last drops out of the soda bottles before Gino smacked his lips and smiled broadly at his young friend. "Good, yes? Ah! This is the life God intended us to follow, I believe."

High grinned back. "Yes, sir."

"So, High, have you given any more thought to my earlier question?"

"Question, sir?"

"About where you'll go next with the horse?" He smiled sheepishly and added, "And your wife, of course."

"No, sir, I still haven't looked at the map. But ... sir? I hoped I might ask you a favor."

"Certainly."

"I told Flo she could rest for another day. I'm sorry I didn't ask you first, but would it be alright if we stay another night? Just one more, and then I promise we'll go."

"Oh, High! High! No, of course! Please don't give it a second thought. I promise you that Savoia will be overjoyed. It will be wonderful to have you for a while longer."

Gino suddenly dropped his eyes and began fidgeting with a beautiful golden cross on a chain of such exquisite twenty-four carat gold it looked like it might melt in his hands. It was obvious he had something on his mind, but High didn't have the social skill to ask him what it might be. Finally, Gino took a deep breath.

"High? I would like to ask you something. Actually, it is about what my wife took me out of the room to talk about this morning."

High felt the grip of nervousness. "Sure."

Gino cleared his throat. "This is going to sound presumptuous, and perhaps more than a little strange, my son, but please— just tell me you will think about it before you make any reply." High waited. "I wonder if you might consider letting Florence stay here with us for a while. With my brother-in-law, Salvatore, actually. I told you about him, didn't I? The shoemaker?"

"Yes, sir, I think so." He didn't say anything about the main subject. He had no idea *what* to say, although as the idea began to sink into his head it seemed like it might be something really good, for both him *and* Flo.

"Well, Salvatore—most of us know him as Sally—he has a nice little farm a mile or so out of town. He pays a father and son team to work it for him. He and his wife have their own residence there, but they also have two small cottages. One of them is where the two men stay, but the other is empty, and ... Well, I think that Sally and his wife would love for Florence to stay with them— you know, while you are away showing off your beautiful horse and making money."

High's guts clenched up. He didn't want to jump to any decision, but ... Wouldn't what Gino was suggesting be perfect? Flo would be away from Oakley, away from gossiping mouths, away from all the shame, and High would *still* be able to travel! He would still be able to experience all the freedom he had been craving, and dreaming of for so long! He knew he couldn't simply agree and go running off on the road without asking Flo about it, but of course she would say yes! It was more than either of them could have dreamed of. It was the ultimate example of High having his cake and eating it too, just as his teacher had always said he couldn't do!

So many times he had feared that a time would come when Flo might want to do something physical with him. Even if it was only to hug him, or to kiss him, the idea was too much. The mere thought made High cringe. They had become friendlier to each other lately, and that was wonderful. It would make their lives so much easier. But any thought of having some kind of husband-wife relationship together ... Well, High wouldn't go so far as to say the thought turned his stomach, but ... On second thought, it did. How could he ever go from knowing Flo Starbuck couldn't stand the sight of him to sleeping with her, and doing things with her that ... He shuddered and pushed the thoughts from his mind.

Flo *had* to agree to a temporary separation. She would be here, with people who truly seemed to care for her and had proven that they would spoil her, and he would have his freedom on the road! It would be the perfect chance for him to live out his dream and slowly get used to the idea of being stuck in a marriage he hadn't asked for, while knowing that the woman he had chosen to keep safe was exactly that—safe with people who cared about her, and, from what Savoia had revealed, would not think to judge her.

For the first time, High was excited about the prospect of seeing Flo later that afternoon. He could hardly wait to tell her the news!

CHAPTER SEVENTEEN

SOMEHOW IT DIDN'T FEEL right, but High let Gino Brambilla talk him into doing a show that evening in the town square
without Flo there. Gino went home with Angelina to let Savoia,
Flo and the children know High would be out until his show was
over, but handsome Luca Brambilla went with High to help him
collect money, and to keep it safe.

Wilder was in high form tonight, and High knew it. The
crowd was going wild. Wilder got up on his hind feet and walked
all of ten steps with High clinging to his back, the farthest High
had ever convinced the stallion to walk. He counted to ten with
both feet, let High "shoot" him with his finger, and flopped over
on the ground to play dead until High knelt down and kissed him
on the nose, making Wilder lunge up, shaking his head as if shaking off having just been deceased.

With a great big yell, he got Wilder to leap first to the left,
then the right, to whirl five or six times each direction in a tight
circle. Every time they would pause between tricks, High would
greet Luca Brambilla's huge grin with one of his own, and watch
people rushing forward to throw their nickels and dimes into his
hat. The hat was half full after thirty minutes, and since the great
crash of Black Tuesday, people simply didn't have that kind of
money anymore. But what they did have it must have seemed that
High's and Wilder's show made it worth parting with some.

High was in his glory.

Throughout the presentation, he had been seeing three men in particular who watched him and Wilder with rapt attention. One of them was tall and rangy looking, with a nearly bald head and baggy, patched trousers. A bulge at his right hip made High guess he was carrying a handgun there.

The second man, black of hair and black of eye, with huge bushy eyebrows, kept laughing and cheering High on louder than anyone. In his exuberance, now and then he would turn and hit one of his companions a hard-looking blow to the shoulder, and that one would glare at him before turning back to watch High and his horse.

The third man was shorter, not much over five-six, and he wore a snap cap and plain blue shirt. In spite of his diminutive size, in comparison to his companions, this man, who held onto a gunny sack out of whose end protruded the neck and head of a guitar, had the most commanding presence, which puzzled High. He finally decided the man had the same kind of aura his father had had, what people called charisma. It surely helped that the man was dashingly handsome, with deep, flashy dimples he liked to show off while grinning at High and his exhibition.

When High and Wilder bowed for the last time, to the crazy cheering of the crowd, and after the usual group of young people ran up to shake High's hand and try to see Wilder closer up, Luca Brambilla came over carrying his hat, which was obviously even heavier than it had been the night before, with both coins and some cash. The three men who had been watching High and the horse so intently also sauntered over, looking at Luca with practiced patience as he stopped near High, but stood back from the stallion because all his family had been made aware that Wilder still didn't particularly like adult males.

"That was even better than last night!" said Luca, grinning and looking up at the big horse.

High started to thank him as the three men stopped close by, the tall, rangy one edging close to Wilder and starting to put out a hand. "Don't get too close," High warned, taking his eyes away from Luca. "He's not too keen on men."

The man slowly lowered his hand, seeming only then to notice the horse's laid-back ears and the warning look in his eyes. "Yeah, so I see. Still needs some manners, huh?"

High instantly started to bridle up, but the short man cut in, "Ha! Listen to you, Heavy! Looks like you're the one who needs some manners!" The man instantly whirled back to High, thrusting out a hand and smiling disarmingly. "The name's Legend, son. Roy Legend."

On the instant, High couldn't help but like Roy Legend. He towered over him by close to a foot, but as he had noticed before, something about Legend made him seem much bigger, and he was nearly as handsome as Luca Brambilla, although not what someone might call pretty. Even at five-six, Legend was all man's man. High took his hand and introduced himself.

"Warning!" Legend repeated. "That's pure capital! What a name. Legend and Warning. With names like that, I think it was destiny for us to meet. High—do you mind if I call you High? I'd like you to meet my traveling companions. This here gentleman with the big mouth is Heavy Beecher, and Mr. Smooth, here, is Damian Prentiss, but we just call him Browsy."

High couldn't help being amused by the name, obviously given to Prentiss because of his over-sized eyebrows.

"You put on quite a show, High," Roy Legend went on, smooth as warm grease. "I declare, I don't think I've ever seen a thing quite like it. I'd sure like to buy you a drink, if you're not doing anything else."

High looked quickly over at Luca Brambilla, who shrugged and smiled at Roy Legend. "The family is actually waiting for us even as we speak," Luca said. He looked at High, raising an eyebrow. "Maybe another time?"

High returned his eyes to Legend, feeling disappointed. But it was only polite for him to return to the company of the people who were so kind as to put him and Flo up for free. "I'll be in town tomorrow sometime," he said with a suggestive shrug of the shoulder.

"Well, we will be too," said Roy. "We sure will. Stayin' in town, actually, over on the northwest corner of Fourth and J Street where some house burned down last year. Come see us, if you get back in town. I'll buy you a drink, and I'd like to talk to you about something."

"Sure," High said. He of course had no idea what Legend would want to talk about. He had simply taken to the man, which he didn't do all that often with strangers, and he was hankering to spend time around some men who seemed to be living the wild and easy life High himself had hoped to be living by this time.

"I'll give you a hint, so you don't forget," Legend added. "It has to do with makin' money. Me and the boys, we do an exhibition too. Not just like yours, of course, but we make a sizable amount of money doin' what we do. Come on into town tomorrow and look us up. We'll talk."

"I will," replied High, with a grin, again shaking Roy Legend's outstretched hand. Somehow, even though physically he towered over this man, High felt small, but fortunate, in his shadow. He seldom remembered liking another man so quickly.

When High returned to the Brambillas and set Wilder loose out in the pen with the other horses, he took a moment to get his crazy grin under control after Luca left him and went to the house. It seemed to High like his life was actually coming together. No, he wasn't marrying the woman he had dreamed of, the woman he had been promised to, then not even had the nerve to tell how and why things had changed. But he was finally going to get to live the free life he had dreamed of, Flo would be well cared for in his absence, relieving him of any obligation he felt toward Seth, at least until his return. And he was meeting people he was sure could help him on his way. Things could not be going better.

Once Wilder had been brushed out to a sleek shine, High gave him grain, mixed in with a little corn, then walked away from his horse after giving him two sugar cubes. His horse was king that night. Soon, there would not be a soul in Idaho who didn't know about the wild pinto stallion and the young man named High Warning.

As High knocked lightly on the front door of the Brambillas', then walked in, he had his first moment of doubt about talking to Flo. He had been so excited when Gino first told him his family's proposition, and he had thought a lot about it since. He could see no downside to the plan, and yet something nagged at the back of his mind. He had to force himself not to think about it. He knew everything would work out, and Flo would be happy.

Everyone greeted High with great fanfare as he came in, congratulating him on the wonderful evening's show Luca had just told them all about, and on the great amount of money he had made, which he hadn't counted yet but he was certain was over thirty dollars.

Savoia left the others and pulled High aside in the hallway. "I'm afraid Flo is still feeling a little bit under the weather. You ... you're certain everything is alright, High—aren't you?"

"Yes, ma'am. Yes, ma'am, I think so," High replied. He wondered if there wasn't more to her question than he read on the surface. She had been with Flo more than he had today, and she had a woman's intuition. If there was something wrong with Flo, wouldn't Flo know as much as he did? But then again, Savoia had no way of knowing how little he knew about Flo. She didn't even have a clue the two of them hadn't bothered to find a preacher yet.

"Alright. Well, you should go check on her. Supper will be ready soon." High had guessed as much. The whole house was filled with an aroma the likes of which he wasn't sure he had ever smelled before.

High knocked on the bedroom door. He didn't enter until he heard Flo's invitation.

Flo was sitting up in bed, and she smiled at him, but she didn't look well. Her face looked abnormally pale, even for her. Somehow, it made her cornflower-blue eyes stand out more in her face, and even while she appeared to be on the verge of being really ill, somehow her eyes seemed even more beautiful than normal. He could never have dreamed he would think Flo's eyes beautiful, but they were. Even a blind hick from the boondocks could see beauty when it was shoved in his face.

"Are you alright?" Again, he stumbled on pronouncing her name, cursing himself inside.

"Hi, High," she said, then let out a weak giggle. "I'm sorry. I guess I never said hi to you before and said your name."

He laughed. "It's okay. I'm used to it. It was a big joke at my house forever. My first name. Our last name. There's a lot of funny things you can say with both of 'em."

"Well. I always loved your name," she said, a little of the color coming back to her face. "I think it's majestic. And it fits you perfectly."

He gave another laugh. "I guess, but I'm not sure if that's such a good thing!" He walked over and sat on the bed, and she startled him by putting her hand on his. He jerked a little, and she quickly removed her hand, apologizing. That made him feel worse than he already did.

"You don't have to apologize. It's okay. Hey—did anyone tell you how much money we made tonight?"

She shook her head, looking back and forth at his eyes. "No. A lot?"

"Well, I'm not exactly sure," he said, feeling sheepish. "It looks like a lot."

"That's good. We will go to a new place tomorrow then?"

He looked at her for a few seconds, trying to decide how to tell her about Gino and Savoia's offer. He didn't feel certain anymore how she would take it, and that was a disconcerting thought. He wanted her to be as excited as he was.

"Hey," he said on a whim. "I was thinking about Seth's ring."

"I know," she said hurriedly. "I'm sorry, High. I'll put it on so nobody asks about it anymore."

"No!" he said. "No, it's okay. But ... Maybe we should try to find a preacher soon. Or at least a judge. You know, before ..." He glanced down at her belly, feeling heat rise into his face.

"Oh! Yes. Yes, I ... I guess we have to, right?"

Have to? Did they have to? He wondered if there wasn't something more behind her words than there seemed to be. They did have to, didn't they? They couldn't just go through life pretending to be married but never actually doing it. Or could they? If they weren't going to actually do anything physical in their marriage, did it matter if they had a piece of paper saying they were married? How much did that kind of thing cost anyway? What if they each held onto their true freedom? Nobody would ever really know. How could they?

He shrugged, finding himself tongue-tied. If Flo was really wondering about getting married, maybe she didn't think it was necessary. Maybe he didn't need to force it. Maybe there could still be some way that it never had to happen at all ...

He stopped himself there. He had promised Flo to look after her and not ever let anyone know what she had done. He had promised Seth, too. There was no way he could go back on his word.

"Well, we don't have to talk about it right now, I guess. But ... Hey. I have some pretty exciting news to tell you." And there it was. He was jumping in with both feet, and there was no turning back now, not when he had landed in the middle of a raging river, and a cliff was behind him, keeping him from turning back.

"What is it, High?" When she said his name again, he gritted his teeth, determining to pronounce her name the first chance he got and when it didn't sound forced.

"Well, Gino asked me something today. Something he and Mrs. Brambilla were talking about. He ... well, he wanted me to ask you ... Flo." He cursed himself. Why did it sound phony when he said her name? It didn't sound at all that way when she said his.

"What?" She searched his eyes, and in her face he thought he saw some anticipation, but also something more. Maybe it was doubt. Was he that readable?

"He and Mrs. Brambilla ..." High started out strong, then stopped. Out of the blue, something struck him that hadn't even occurred to him before. Now he felt like a fool!

"High, what is it?"

"Flo ... did you tell the Brambillas you're ... I mean ... Well, did you tell them you're going to have a baby?"

She shook her head. "No. I didn't want to say anything before we talked about it."

High clamped his mouth shut. Why would the Brambillas suggest that a new young couple be split up if they didn't know she was with child? Why would any wise older couple think newlyweds should not be with each other, especially in the first part of their marriage?

"I think they know," he said.

She blinked, and in her eyes he saw concern growing. Oh, how he wished he could read what a woman thought about!

"How could they know?"

He froze. Everything was clear. Flo wasn't only sick. She hadn't eaten anything bad. She had the morning sickness he had heard about. The Brambillas knew that was why she was sick. They wanted her to stay with them because of the baby!

"Because you're ..." His voice faded out. He wished he were with Murk Bowen, Tommy Hawk or one of his brothers, talking about wild horses. "They guessed because you're sick," he said quietly.

"Oh." By the shocked look on her face, he could tell the thought had never crossed her mind either. "Okay. I guess you're right."

They sat in silence for a while, neither of them seeming to know what to say. Finally, Flo's lips parted, and she reached out and touched his hand again, this time gingerly. "What was it you started to tell me earlier, High?"

"Well ..." He stared at her, starting to feel petrified. How was he going to tell her now? How was he going to tell her he was going to leave her here with people she hardly knew, that he was going to scramble off like a coward, taking life easy on the road, while she, the woman he was supposed to be caring for, stayed with strangers to have her baby?

"I'm getting scared now," Flo said softly. "Please tell me, High. Just spit it out."

"They want you to stay here with one of their relatives and not travel with me anymore. They want me to go on the road and make money and leave you. And I thought ..." Again, his voice trailed off. "I think they want you to stay because of the baby," he finally said.

"Oh." Looking brave, Flo nodded quickly, trying to gaze into his eyes until moisture came into hers and made her look away. "So ... they asked you to leave me here?"

He could only nod.

"And you're going to do it."

"Well ... I thought you'd be happy not to have to travel." Even as he said that, he saw pain wash over her face before she could hide it.

"I think they know something, High."

"That you're gonna have a baby," he affirmed.

"Not only that," she said. "They know there's something else wrong. At least Savoia does."

"Why? How do you know?"

"Because. Of things she was asking me today. And she ... She told me a story. She ..."

"She told me too," he revealed. "You mean how her and Gino had to get married an' come over here from Italy because of their families?"

Flo nodded, swallowing audibly. Finally, she said, "Why would she volunteer to tell us that? Why would she unless she was trying to make us tell her about ... You know."

High felt sick. Now they *had* to get married! They couldn't wait any longer. They couldn't take any more chances. He felt hot all over. He almost wished they had never come here.

"We gotta go find a judge or somebody tomorrow," he said. "I'll take you, Flo."

She quickly shook her head. She couldn't meet his gaze. "I'm not feeling very good. I think I'm going to try and rest."

"Are you ... You sure? Do you want me to bring you some-thin'? To eat?" He was almost frantic. He had no idea what to do with a pregnant girl. And suddenly Flo seemed just like that: a pregnant little girl, scared out of her mind. He didn't know much about the first part, but right now he knew the second part plenty well.

High left Flo alone, lying on her side crying. She pretended she wasn't, but he had seen her tears before she pulled the edge of the bedspread over her face to try to hide them.

CHAPTER EIGHTEEN

IN THE MORNING, HIGH ate breakfast in silence. Gino and Savoia were silent as well, as were their four children. The children were always well behaved, but this morning their normal polite chatter was absent. It seemed as if a pall was over the room, perhaps even the whole house.

In the early morning, hours before sunrise, Flo had taken to throwing up again. This time High took care of it by himself. Savoia, planning ahead, had left him a bucket and some old rags. She had made him promise to come and wake her up if anything happened, but when it did he couldn't bring himself to knock on the Brambillas' door, not when he had everything he needed and they could get the sleep they deserved.

Savoia must have heard something through the thin walls, because that morning before breakfast she asked High if everything had gone alright during the night, and the way she kept pressing him for information, he could tell she knew more than she was letting on. After High valiantly fought the woman's curiosity off, the room settled into a silence broken only by the metallic click of utensils against plates, glasses being set down, or water or milk trickling into an emptied glass, and sometimes nearly boiling coffee into a mug.

Savoia excused herself when everyone was halfway or more through their meal, and she went down the hall to check on Flo. When she came back, she picked her glass up off the table and paused before taking it to the sink. "High? Do you think I could have a word with you in private?"

High's insides tightened up, a feeling he had come to hate. Again, he wished fervently they hadn't stopped here. He wished he and Flo were in a hotel somewhere, away from prying people, whether they meant well or not. "Sure." He got up and followed her out the back door of the kitchen and into the bright new sunlight.

Savoia turned and looked at him and tried to comfort him with a smile. High knew she and Gino liked him, as did their children. But he could sense in Savoia a frustration with him that felt like it was growing stronger and stronger.

"High, I feel like I need to be nosy. And I'm sorry. Please forgive me. Wives sometimes have to stick together—you know?"

He nodded, now dreading with his entire being whatever she was going to say.

"What are your plans for today?" she asked bluntly.

"Uh ... Well, I'm supposed to go into town and meet some fellows who saw me and Wilder last night."

"And?"

He stared at her. *And?* He wasn't sure what she wanted him to say.

"I'm sorry. I just don't know if you should be taking off like this too much. I feel like Florence might be much sicker than you realize."

High's heart leaped. Sicker? Sicker how? One thing was certain—Savoia's comment confirmed what he had suspected, that she had heard Flo being sick in the night.

"What do you mean sicker?" he managed to ask.

"Like it might take her a while to get better. And she might need a lot more constant care than she is getting—except from me."

He swallowed hard, gritting his teeth. Here it came. The big speech about how he needed to be a better husband. He would have expected something like this from his mother, but not from someone who was almost a complete stranger.

"I'm sorry, ma'am. I'm not really sure what to do for her. Maybe we should move on," he blurted out, the first thing he thought of to say that might make good his escape from this pressure.

"Move on? You would try to make your wife leave, right now when she's sick and obviously needs rest, not travel?"

So much for making an escape. The woman's look of disappointment in him was the farthest thing from an escape.

"I'm sorry, ma'am. I'm tryin' to figure things out."

Savoia's face softened, and suddenly she sighed and stepped close, taking hold of him by the back of the neck and pulling him into an embrace. Even though he was a good eight inches taller than she was, right then he felt very much like a child. She stepped back from him again.

"I'm sorry too, High. I know you're struggling. You're so young. High, let me ask you something. Can you remember any time when you were really sick? The sickest you've ever been. Was someone there for you, someone who wouldn't leave your side? And can you imagine if that person wasn't there?"

In asking the question, Savoia was surely thinking it would call to mind his mother. But while he could remember his mother caring for him, the worst times he remembered, when he was truly hurt, it was his sister Ava who remained by his side, nursing him, putting cold cloths on his face, praying for him. But Flo ... she wasn't even truly his wife in the first place! Besides, how did a dumb kid who only knew about horses take care of a sick girl who wouldn't even have been part of his life if bad circumstances hadn't forced her into his care? He had already been asked to do so much, cleaning up after her, even emptying her bed pan, a thought which left him feeling cold inside, and almost sick.

"As soon as I get back from town, I'll stay with her," he said with resignation. "I promise I'll come right back."

The woman stared at him, her wheels of thought churning behind her eyes. Finally, she nodded. "Well, you must do what you feel is right. I am not your mother. I'll stay with her and take care of her while you're gone, but I hope you'll think about what I said. A stranger's care will only go so far, and whether you choose to be with her in her time of struggle, or you decide not to, I think it's a choice that she will forever remember."

High rode into town two hours later, an hour after Gino Brambilla's departure. He was fighting an entire gamut of feelings. He didn't want to be frustrated or angry with Savoia Brambilla, whose family had taken him and Flo in with so much kindness, given them a warm, comfortable place to sleep, and fed them wonderful meals, all for free. But he hated being preached to, and if that woman wasn't preaching to him he didn't know what she was doing.

On the other hand, he had to give her grudging thanks for choosing not to argue any more about his coming into town. After all, hadn't he promised Roy Legend and his friends that he would come? And didn't a man have to keep his promises, at least if he meant to be a man people respected? High really liked Gino and Savoia, but he sure wished Flo hadn't gotten sick right now, because he wasn't sure he liked being around Savoia as much as he had before.

And then came the guilt.

He gritted his teeth and forced that last emotion away even while he knew deep in his heart that it was the entire reason for his not liking Savoia Brambilla's presence as much as before.

Riding directly to Fourth Street, then to the place where it intersected with J, the remains of a burned-out home's foundation were instantly obvious. Right there, between the rock foundation and the trunk of a big elm tree, he saw what amounted to a camp.

Two men were lying there with hats over their faces as he drew close. The third man, tall, rangy Heavy Beecher, was sitting up. He looked almost startled to see High riding their way. Turning, he nudged the knee of the man next to him, then hit him a little harder when he didn't respond right away, and turned to say something to him.

By the time High was within ear shot, Heavy Beecher was unpeeling his frame like a huge banana and standing up, grinning like a fox at High, and nodding. He dipped the brim of his faded, sweat-stained fedora.

"Well, howdy. Nice to see you."

Roy Legend was scrambling to his feet by now, and Browsy Prentiss was starting to stir, his snap cap only now falling away from his eyes to let in the brilliant sunlight.

High climbed off Wilder and looked about for a convenient place to tie him as Roy Legend came striding over, all smiles, with Heavy Beecher coming along a few steps behind him.

"Mornin', High," Legend said. "It's a beautiful one, isn't it?"

"It sure is," High said, feeling some of the morning's stress fade out of him. Legend's nature seemed to do that.

Legend thrust out his hand, and High shook it, feeling the warmth and the strength of it. "Why don't you grab onto one of those limbs yonder and tie your horse up there?" Legend suggested, jerking his thumb toward a pile of logs that had been stacked up beside the remains of the house and obviously had been sawed from the dying elm tree.

High did as suggested, as Legend followed him, keeping a safe distance from Wilder. "I'm sure glad you came back," Legend said as High turned back around. "Man! I still can't believe that show you put on. You should be famous, High. I mean it! You could take that horse around the world!"

Hearing those words, High tried to hold back his excitement. Without knowing it, Roy Legend had struck upon one of High's greatest dreams! He remembered the very day he admitted to his father that taking Wilder around the country wasn't enough, and that he wanted to travel the whole world with him. It was like Roy Legend could read his mind!

"I'd sure like that," High admitted. "It's been one of my biggest dreams."

Grinning bigger, Legend slapped High on the shoulder, turning to give another grin and a wink to Heavy, and to Browsy Prentiss, who had finally made it to his feet and was stretching, his face groggy and his eyes squinted almost shut under his bushy black eyebrows.

"You boys hear that? High dreams as big as I do, huh?"

Heavy grinned. He had one gold eye tooth that winked in the sunlight when he smiled big enough. Browsy yawned, then somehow found the ability to give an exuberant nod. "That's great, High," Browsy said. "Just great!"

"Yeah, great," agreed Legend. "Man, you need to come travel with us, High! How you set for cash and what not, anyhow?" He scanned all around High, then glanced casually toward Wilder. High hadn't brought any traveling bags. He hadn't seen any reason to, since he couldn't leave without Flo—at least not yet.

The thought of Flo gave High a jolt. In all the rush and excitement the night before, he had never told Roy Legend about Flo. That knowledge was going to change everything! But he couldn't keep it from them.

"I, uh ... I have cash. Quite a bit. People have been giving me a lot of money."

"Yeah? That's great! Us too!" Legend said, and to prove it he reached into his pants pocket and lifted a wad of greenbacks partway out, riffling through them with his thumbnail. Winking, he stowed the money back away. "High, you come travel with us, we'll make you a rich man—and famous!"

High thought of Jim Martin, who had told him much the same. Martin seemed like an alright sort, too, but there was something he was truly drawn to in Roy Legend. This was a man who wouldn't look down on him, but a man he believed would treat him as an equal—as a friend.

"I have to tell you somethin', though," High said, feeling queasy. The others must have sensed his trepidation, for they cast suspicious glances at each other.

"Well? What is it, High? You want to travel with us, don't you?" asked Legend.

"Well, sure! More than anything I do! But ... Well, I got somethin' t' take care of."

"To take care of?" repeated Legend, then let out a laugh. "Well, what could there be to take care of? You're a drifter, huh? Just like us, footloose and fancy free. Go get your bags, get your cash—because you'll need it, for the train and such. Let's blow out of this city. Nothing keeping a bunch of traveling men—right?"

"Uh… Yeah. That's right," said High.

Inside, he cursed himself. He had chickened out! What about Flo? What was he going to tell her? She couldn't come along with them. He had to get her settled in. He had to make sure the Brambillas were really going to take care of her.

Then he thought of what Roy Legend had said: the world! They wanted to travel the *world!* It was High's dream, and had been forever, but ... Surely it meant that he would not be able to return to Flo until long after the baby was born!

Trying to hide the sick feeling inside, High said, "So how long you figure it would take to travel the world?" Maybe it would only take months. Maybe he could be back here before the baby was born, and Flo would be fine for that long in the kind care of the Brambilla family.

"Shucks, High, I don't know!" said Legend. "A year? Maybe? Two? Three? Depends on how much territory you want to cover. But I bet if we were gone for three years you could save up maybe ten thousand bucks by then."

High stared at him. *"Ten thousand? For real?"*

"Hell yes! Easy, with that horse and all the tricks he can do. And those Europeans, you know, they aren't in the big fix we got into in this country. I mean you think people here are being generous, just wait till you see how they treat you over there. Shoot! A beautiful stallion like yours? They'll eat that up! It's the Wild West, High. Something like those folks have only dreamed of! And you'd be bringing it right to their front door. Yeah, I'd say two years at least. Maybe four. You'd never have to work again!"

High's heart was pounding—racing! He would never have to work again! Then he could buy a horse ranch of his own, catch some mustangs, breed Wilder, and others. He could have the biggest horse ranch in Idaho. He could tell Roy Legend really believed it, and something about Legend made High believe it too!

But what was he going to do about Flo?

Alright. Alright, he had to tell Legend about Flo. That was all. He couldn't simply avoid it. But Flo would understand, wouldn't she? After all, it wasn't like they were madly in love with each other. They were together only because she had gotten in a bad situation. So if she knew that in somewhere between two and five years' time he would return to her a rich man, and if he could keep sending money back to her, from back east, and from overseas ... She would see the sense in it all. Wouldn't she? She could buy a house fairly fast with the money he would be sending back. In the economy the country was in now, houses must be pretty cheap. This was a sure thing! How could she turn it down? After all, he had already made a huge sacrifice for her, and since they didn't really love each other, the way a normal man and wife would, why would she care if he was here with her, as long as she was taken care of?

"I still have to tell you somethin'," High finally managed to choke out. "But don't worry. I got it all figured out."

"Alright, High. But you keep worrying me, son. What is it that's got you so het up?"

"It's that ... Well, I got somebody I have to take care of."

"Somebody— So like a kid? You mean you have a kid?" Legend's smile vanished. "Tell me that isn't it, High!"

"No," said High, feeling his face get hot. "Well, not exactly. But I ... Well, I'm kind of traveling with somebody else." He instantly felt ashamed of himself, ashamed that he couldn't even tell them that for all intents and purposes, Flo was his wife.

"Oh no!" exclaimed Legend, glancing over at his partners, who suddenly didn't look so chipper anymore. "What do you mean? You already have another partner?"

"Not really a partner, like you'd be," said High. "But ... Well, I got me a wife."

Roy Legend swore. A tentative smile started to come onto his face, and then it vanished, and he swore again. "You're not pulling my leg, are you? You're really hitched, High? A young, footloose fellow like you? *Married?*"

High felt more sick than ever. He was sure none of these three men was foolish enough to have gotten themselves married, not when there was so much of the world left to see. How had he gotten himself into his situation? Right now he almost hated his brother Seth—and Flo, too.

"Yeah," he said, feeling crestfallen at the admission. "I'm married, but I already have a place lined up where she's gonna stay. It's all arranged. Honest! I just have to go back and make sure it's all set."

Legend stared High down. The grin wasn't on his face any-more, and all pretense of smiles was gone from the faces of the other two. Browsy Prentiss had turned around and gone back to sit down on his pile of rumpled blankets.

"You serious, High? You think you can really leave your wife here? No fooling? I mean, you sure as heck can't take her with us. You know that—right?"

"Of course!" said High. "Sure! She wouldn't want to go any-way. I'll tell her I'm going to be making a lot of money, and send-ing it back to her. She'll be alright."

Roy Legend looked doubtful. "I don't know, High. Maybe it's not such a good idea. Married!" he said suddenly, with great feel-ing. "Man! I never thought you'd say that."

"Hey," said Heavy Beecher suddenly. "Come on, Roy. Listen to the kid. He already said it would be fine. He knows his own wife better than we do, huh? Let him make his own choices. Come on, brother! The kid wants to see the world, can't you see? Why don't you let him live his dream too? Who're you to take that away from him?"

Legend listened peacefully to his partner for a while, frown-ing. He finally looked back over at High. "Aw, I don't know. Man. That seems pretty big. I mean ... a *wife?* But no kids—right?" High's mouth was open, but words were lost to him. "Right, High?" Legend repeated. "You told me you don't have any kids—right?"

"Not just yet," said High, his voice quiet.

Legend searched his eyes. "But she's ... Aw, High! Damn it! Well, that's that then."

Browsy Prentiss had lunged back up off his blankets, as if re-joining a brawl. He stomped over to stand shoulder to shoulder with Heavy. "Now come on, Roy! You heard the kid. It's his life! Listen to Heavy. If the kid still wants to come, let's let 'im! I mean what's the harm in it, right? Let 'im come! What would you've done if somebody had tried to get you to stay with Lana?"

"Shut up about her," Legend growled. It was the first time High had seen even the littlest bit of irritation in Roy Legend, to say nothing of anger.

"Let me at least go talk to my wife," said High, feeling suddenly desperate.

Heavy and Browsy stared at Legend, while Legend studied High, biting his lip. "Alright. Alright, go talk to her, High," he said, the smile seeming to be gone permanently from his lips. "But I don't know if I have a good feeling about it anymore. I mean ... I just don't know."

"I'll be back," said High. "Will you be stayin' here?"

"Sure! Sure, kid, we'll be here," Browsy assured him. "Right here waitin' for you. How long you think you'll need?"

"I'm not sure."

"How'll we know you're comin' back?" asked Heavy. "I mean, we can't stay here forever, of course."

"I'll be back," High said, feeling desperate. He had three men standing right in front of him who wanted to travel the world, and who seemed like they would know how to do it. This might be the best chance he would ever have!

"Don't rush it, alright, High?" said Roy Legend. "Don't rush it. And don't believe that woman of yours just because she tells you one thing. Sometimes what they'll tell you, and what the truth is, are two totally different things. You got a kid on the way ... Well, you just go on now and sort it all out. Take your time."

"Three days," Heavy Beecher cut in, glowering at Roy Legend before looking back at High. "Three days, kid. Then we'll have to go. You'll be back before that—right?"

"Yeah. Before three days from right now I'll be back," promised High. And he would. Come hell or high water, he was coming back.

High Warning and Wilder Heart were going to travel the world!

CHAPTER NINETEEN

IN SPITE OF HIS excitement, High about made himself sick by the time he got back to the Brambillas', trying to think of all the ways he might break the news to Flo about what he intended to do. He had stopped off at Rupert Gems, Gino Brambilla's store, and he had something in his pocket that he hoped might make things go down easier with Flo, but the more he thought about it the less sure he was that he wanted to give it to her—or anything else beyond money to live on.

The one thing he knew above everything else was that he had to go. Traveling the world with Wilder had been his dream for far too long to simply toss it aside and forget it now. He was sorry for Flo, but he hadn't put her in the situation she was in. That was her own doing, and that of his fool of a brother. Besides, it wasn't like he was going to abandon her and leave her penniless. The opposite was true—she would be living better than any of the rest of his family, even if she did have to stay with the Brambillas. They were nice people anyway. They would treat her well. Most likely, she would feel like part of their family. So why should he feel guilty?

The more accurate question—why *did* he feel so guilty? Curse Seth! Curse Flo! And curse High Warning, for foolishly telling the girl he would take care of her, when none of what had happened was through any fault of his own! He never stopped to think until later, of course, that he wouldn't even have been out on the road until he turned eighteen if it hadn't been for the situation Flo had put him in. He never would have met Roy Legend.

High brushed Wilder down in the barn and grained him before turning him loose into the pen with Flo's horse, Bragger, and their dark dun packhorse, Honcho. Then he went to the house, hating how his heart was pounding.

Savoia met him inside, and his guts knotted up on the instant. But when their eyes met, he saw a different look in her face from earlier, when she had seemed almost angry with him.

"Hello, High. I'm glad you're back."

"Thank you." What else could he say? At least she didn't seem perturbed now, but still he couldn't erase how she had made him feel earlier.

"Is Flo feeling better?" he asked, hoping to turn the woman's attention away from him.

Savoia frowned. "No. She doesn't seem to be. You should go in to her, High. Be with her. If you want to."

That last part sounded odd. Had she had a change of heart since he left? She didn't want to make demands of him anymore? Only suggestions? Anyway, he jumped at the opportunity to get away from her before she started in on him again about anything.

Going down the hall, he knocked lightly. There was no sound behind the door, so he knocked a little louder. "It's okay," he heard Flo's voice. "You can come in."

High stepped inside, finding the girl propped up in bed with a number of pillows. "Hi," she said. He guessed she had learned her lesson about making herself sound foolish by putting his name with it.

"Hi. How are you feelin'?"

"Not very good."

He had guessed as much, even beyond what Savoia had already told him. Flo looked as wan as a scrap of cotton batting with lips and blue eyes.

"Anything I can do?" he asked. She was going to have to help him. He didn't know how to care for her without her guidance.

"I need to talk to you," she said in reply, surprising him.

"Oh. You do? About what?" He wondered if what she had to talk to him about was going to be anywhere near as much fun as what he had to talk to her about.

"Can you come closer?" Her voice was shaking, and he realized suddenly that she was about to cry again. Were all women this emotional, or was she this way only because she was sick, or pregnant?

He walked close, but when her lower lip started to tremble, he wanted to run. How had he gotten himself into this predicament? He should not have to be here!

"What's wrong, Flo?" he managed to ask, proud of himself for saying her name. "It's alright—talk to me."

"High ... I think I did something bad."

Those words frightened him. Was whatever she was about to tell him going to make him angry? "What? What did you do?"

"I told Mrs. Brambilla everything, High. Everything about us. I'm sorry." Instead of dropping her eyes, she stared at him, bringing both tight fists up to her mouth. Her eyes started to water so he wondered how she could even focus on him, but she forced herself not to drop her gaze away.

He stared back at her, his whirling mind trying to process what she had said. It began slowly to dawn on him, and then the realization that this was why Savoia Brambilla had greeted him differently from the way she had been acting that morning.

"But, Flo ... You told her about *us?* Wait. I'm not sure what you mean. What did you tell her? That we're ..." Flo was openly crying now, but in silence. "I'm so sorry, High. I'm so sorry I dragged you into my messed-up life."

"You didn't drag me in," he said, his mind scrambling through emotions, trying to make sense of everything. "I told you I'd fix everything, that's all. And take care of you. You didn't ask me to."

She shook her head quickly, which he guessed somehow was her agreeing with him. At this point she was crying too hard to say anything else.

Feeling awkward, he stepped closer and put a hand on her shoulder. Of course his intention was to comfort her, but she only cried harder. He was left wondering, until she got control of herself, exactly what she had meant saying she had told Savoia "everything". As he thought about it, left to his own devices while he waited for her to stop crying, it started to seem like it might be a really good thing if she had told Savoia everything. Did that mean ... Had she even told Savoia they weren't married? And that she was with child, by his brother? If Savoia knew literally everything, wouldn't she and her family all look at him in a different light? Wouldn't they think he was a good guy for trying to protect a girl he had no real responsibility for? He couldn't stop his mind from racing. Maybe all this was perfect! Maybe now when he left to travel the world, no one would think poorly of him. Maybe they would realize he deserved to be free!

It was a good five minutes of High standing there with his hand on Flo's shoulder before his arm got tired and he decided to sit down on the bed by her. At that point, it was either put it on her leg, the only convenient part of her, or put it in his lap. Of course he chose his lap.

"High?" Flo's voice broke a long period of complete stillness.

"Yeah?"

"Could you ... I mean, do you think you maybe could ... Oh, I'm sorry. Never mind." She was fighting tears again.

"There's no 'never mind'," he said, trying to sound gentle, because he had always had a soft spot for suffering animals, and people in pain, even if he really didn't know what to do for them. "What is it, Flo?"

"I just need you to hold me. Only for a little while. I need you to tell me it'll be alright. That we're going to be okay."

Feeling almost like he had been kicked in the stomach, High turned to her, scooted closer, and put his arms around her. He thought it would feel awkward, but it didn't. It felt natural, as it had the day she came to the house with her confession. He patted her back, almost unconsciously, as she intermittently cried in silence, then let out a wracking sob. How was she going to take his news? Would she be as happy as he wanted her to be, to think that not only did she not have to do anything physical with him, but that she would have all she needed in the way of money, and shelter? She would still have her fond memories of Seth, and she and their baby would have a safe place to stay, far away from gossip, far away from prying minds. How could any of it be a bad thing?

"I'm okay," Flo finally said, sniffling. "Can you get me a handkerchief from my bag? I'm afraid my nose has run all over your shoulder. I'm so sorry."

He laughed, not feeling exactly comfortable, but not uncomfortable either. He simply felt sort of neutral.

Getting up, he got into her clothing bag, embarrassed when he saw items of clothing in there that he had seen before, but never actually had to touch. He found a handkerchief and stepped back over to hand it to her. Then he stood there awkwardly while she blew her nose, trying unsuccessfully to be dainty. He wondered if he should sit down again, to tell her his plans. He wondered a lot of things, and he kept hating the feelings of tenseness in his guts. Why should he be worried about telling her? What could possibly be bad in his plans?

Finally, he sat down. They remained silent for a time, until she spoke again. "High? You need to tell me something, huh?"

"Maybe you first," he replied quickly.

"Me?"

"Yeah. What did you mean when you said you told Savoia everything? You mean she knows you're going to have a baby? And it's not mine? And we're not even married yet?"

She nodded, as his questions obviously came too fast for her to make any intelligent reply. When he stopped, she said, "Are you mad at me?"

"Why would I be mad at you? No! I think it will make a lot of things make more sense to them now. I think it's good!"

She gave him a weak smile. "You're sure?"

"Sure I'm sure. I think you did a good thing."

"Okay. I'm glad. So ... what about you? You've been wanting to tell me something too."

"Yeah. I mean, sure. Maybe a couple things. First, I was thinking ..."

"Wait." She stopped him abruptly. Was she as scared about his revelation as he had been about hers earlier? "Before you tell me," she said, "I wanted to tell you I've been thinking about something. I think I should go back home. And you should find that man, that Jim Martin. You should travel, High. That's your dream! You should take Wilder and travel around, and don't think about me."

He stared at her, but she couldn't meet his gaze. She looked quickly down, and once more her lip began to tremble, and he knew it had taken everything in her to say what she had.

"Why, Flo? Why would you decide something like that? Why would you want to go back home right now, when you know everything people are going to say?"

"It's just ..." She stopped, pressing the handkerchief against her nose and lips. "I just think it's for the best. You don't—"

"Don't what?" he pressed.

"Nothing," she said softly, looking at the handkerchief she had crumpled in her lap. "I'm so tired, High. I think I might try to sleep some more."

He stared at her, feeling confused. He hadn't even been able to tell her his plans. She had asked him to, but when he started, she cut him right off, with the strangest of revelations. Was it all going to be this easy then? Was she actually going to free him to travel? Or even to return home and marry Valentina Torreales? Could his escape from his own stupidity really happen like this, with hardly any effort on his part?

There was part of him that wanted to leap for joy.

But there was another part that felt strangely dejected. Was it that easy for Flo to walk away from the chance of being cared for, and to look like an honest Christian woman? Did she simply not want to be with him?

Well, if that was the answer, then he guessed this was God's plan. And who was he to deny God's plans?

CHAPTER TWENTY

IN THE NIGHT, FLO woke High up, groaning. He rolled over in the dark, slipping quickly from feeling groggy to feeling faintly frantic. This sound wasn't like anything he had heard from Flo.

"Flo, what's wrong?"

"Oh, High. High, I'm hurting. Really bad."

"How? Where?"

She hesitated, from pain or from embarrassment he couldn't tell. "Down there. High, I'm scared."

Rolling out of bed, he accidentally dragged most of the covers with him, and the tangled mess brought him to his knees beside the bed. He scrambled up, feeling along the wall for the light switch. When it was on, he whirled to look at Flo. She looked ghastly white and was clutching her abdomen.

"What do I do? What do you want me to do?" High wasn't a young man who normally went right into a state of panic. He was calm in situations with horses, bears, cows and other animals and situations that could hurt him bad. But panic seemed to be the order of the day when it came to woman stuff.

"Maybe go get Mrs. Brambilla," she said through clenched teeth.

And High was gone.

He brought the older woman back with him, Gino following them as far as the hall. Savoia took one look at Flo, who had sweat beaded all over her face. "Oh, you poor thing! High—go tell Gino to go to town and bring the doctor."

If High's panic was a jackrabbit sitting frozen under a sage-brush, watching a bobcat lurk past, someone had just sneaked up behind it and poked it in the butt with a sharp stick. He whirled and almost slammed into the edge of the door they had left open. When he made it out into the hall without incident, Gino said, "I heard. Do you want to come with me?"

High stared at the older man, then whipped his head to look back into the room. He surprised himself with his own reply. "Maybe I better stay with Flo."

"Okay. You're right," said Gino. "Good man, High. Keep her safe. I'll be back as soon as I can," Gino called past High into the bedroom. He rushed back down the hall to get dressed.

High took a few deep breaths, trying to remember all the things his father used to tell him would help calm his nerves. More deep breaths. Gritting his teeth. Flexing his hands a few times, hard. He stepped back into the room.

"Can I do anything, ma'am?"

"Yes. Will you go get Mary?" That was the Brambillas' oldest daughter, who was twelve. "Get her and ask her to put a pot of water on to boil and bring some towels."

High did as told. Mary, along with the other children, was already awake, and she went right to work in the kitchen, leaving High to rush back to the room.

"High?" Flo's voice was weak and frightened. Her pale blue eyes stared at him, into his soul, it seemed. "Will you hold my hand?"

Anxious, High looked over at Savoia. This was no time to hesitate, with not just one, but two women in the room, and one of them pleading for him. Reaching down, he took her hand, the hand of the woman who was supposed to have been his wife. It was as cold as snow melt, but also sweaty. Flo tried to smile up at him, but it was a frightened attempt, and it made him feel no better.

"High, perhaps you should look away for a moment," Savoia suggested. He started to question her, realized in his foggy mind that she meant to do something that would horrify him, and whirled away from the scene, looking at the door.

Savoia was talking softly to Flo, moving her around. High tried not to hear anything she was saying, because the little bit he allowed himself to hear was more than enough. High had seen plenty of blood and destruction in his life—more death than most city kids would see in a lifetime. But none of it involved bleeding from the area Savoia seemed to be examining!

"Okay," he heard the woman say. "Okay, you just rest, sweetheart, and try not to worry. The doctor will be here soon. He is a good friend of ours. In fact—"

Gino was suddenly at the door. "I'm leaving now," he said. "Why don't you—"

"Call Dr. Akins," Savoia finished his sentence. "I was just about to. Go!"

With what he obviously intended as a reassuring glance at High, and a pump of his fist, also meant to be reassuring, the man turned and hurried down the hall. Not much later, High heard the car roar to life out in the yard, and a few minutes later zoom away into the night.

"Stay with her, High," ordered Savoia, giving his shoulder a squeeze. "I'll call the doctor to let him know Gino is on his way. If you need me, I'll be right within earshot."

The woman left, and High turned back to Flo, his heart racing. What could be wrong? Was it something to do with the baby? Flo had a death grip on his hand, and she reached the other one up toward him as well. He took it in his other hand, and she pulled him close. "Don't leave me, High. Please don't leave."

"I'm not. I won't. I'm right here, Flo. Just hold on, okay? I know everything will be alright." He heard himself speaking as if he were someone else. Faintly, he thought he remembered his mother saying things like that to him when he was hurt, or sick. His mother or maybe Ava, his most wonderful guardian.

Flo shuddered. She tried to smile again. "High, I'm so cold. So cold ..." She shivered violently. "Please hold me for a minute. Like you did before. Hold me, High."

He didn't even need to steel himself, as he would have at one time. Without hesitation, he lay down on the bed, which was damp with her sweat, and lay his arm across her, pulling himself close and squeezing tight. He soon heard silence from the other room, realizing that Savoia Brambilla had hung up the phone even though it hadn't registered on him until just now that she had been talking. Savoia and Mary came to the door at the same time. High heard them, but he didn't look up. He just kept holding tight to Flo.

Savoia's hand came down to lay softly on High's shoulder, and her voice sounded even softer. "That's perfect, High. You hold onto her good and snug. Dr. Akins will be here soon. He's already getting dressed. You will both love him. He is such a sweet, dear old man. He'll make everything all better. I promise." High turned to look up at her. He wanted to smile, but he forgot. He wanted to jump up and hug her, her voice sounded so kind and reassuring. But he wasn't about to let go of Flo.

"We're warming up some towels," Savoia said. "They'll be ready soon. How do you feel, Florence?"

"I'm okay," Flo said. "Just cold. But I don't hurt anymore."

"Oh, that's good. That's very good, sweetheart. You lie still. Those warm towels will be ready soon. Would you like any tea?"

"No, thank you." Flo's voice was faint. She sounded very tired, like she might fade to sleep. "Thank you, Mrs. Brambilla."

"You're welcome, dear. We'll make you all better."

Savoia took the water Mary had heated up, dipped a wash-cloth in it, and started gently to wipe the sweat off Flo's face and neck. "Does your skin hurt?" she asked.

Flo didn't reply. High started to come up, but Savoia's hand dropped to his shoulder and firmly held him down. When he turned to look up at her, she put her finger to her lips. He looked over at Flo, and her eyes were shut.

"Stay," Savoia whispered. "Stay with her. I'll be back soon, but if you need me before that, you call me. Promise?"

He nodded, holding his tongue because if Flo really had gone to sleep he didn't want to wake her.

"High?" He looked up at the woman again. "She'll be okay. She will. You just stay with her. I have a feeling that's the most important thing in the world to her right now."

Savoia came back a few minutes later and lay warm towels over Flo's chest and abdomen, giving High a smile. "You could be a good nurse," she whispered. "You sure put your baby right to sleep."

His baby ... The words echoed in High's head for long after Savoia left the room, turning the light off as she went. Flo's breathing was soft. She had turned her face a little toward him, and it brushed against his cheek like the wings of a butterfly. It seemed so strange to be lying here with Florence Starbuck. So many times he had thought how if he were choosing a wife, of all the girls he had known, she would have been about the last on his list. And yet right now, in the silence, holding her didn't seem so terrible after all. She didn't seem like such a distasteful person, not the way he had always envisioned her, especially when she used to look at him with such hatred glowing in her eyes. He raised his face to look at her. She seemed so peaceful now, in sleep. Some moments he really had to concentrate even to tell if she was still breathing. Florence Starbuck ... Now that she planned on leaving him, he found himself strangely wondering what kind of life they could really have had together. He wondered if in time he really might have come to love her. And he wondered, too, where she would go now. What she would do.

How she would raise Seth's baby on her own, although surely she would have the help of her mother as well.

He thought of the baby and glanced down, wondering if anything was wrong with it. It was kind of the only thing left of Seth except memories now. He hoped Flo wasn't losing it, the way he had seen some of their cattle and horses lose young. He recalled the feeling he had sensed around mares and cows after they gave stillbirth. The animals always seemed so forlorn, and the heart-wrenching sadness and loss he sensed in them stayed with him sometimes for weeks, even after the animal didn't seem to think anything of it anymore. The thought of Flo going through that was almost more than he could bear, even though this baby was nothing to do with him. He simply didn't want to see Flo suffering.

When the doctor came, they shooed High out of the room. As High was leaving, he heard Flo waking up, and the first thing she did was to start was calling his name. The doctor and Savoia shushed her and calmed her, and the door closed softly. Gino walked over and put a hand on High's shoulder. "It can be pretty frightening, High. I certainly remember. You did well. I'm glad you wanted to stay with her. She sure needed you."

High nodded, trying to smile.

"It isn't my business, son," said Gino, "but I guess Flo must have told you by now that she told Savoia your story."

Again, High nodded. "Yes, sir."

"Well, it is a very brave thing, what you're doing. Most young men your age would never have taken on this responsibility. Especially when ... Well, Flo told us that you also were engaged to be married, to another young lady."

"Yeah." High swallowed hard against a lump that rose in his throat. Flo really had told them everything!

"What is her name? If you don't mind talking about her."

"Valentina Torreales. But usually I called her Val." He gritted his teeth as he felt a lump rise in his throat.

"Valentina. It is a beautiful name. Just lovely. Did you have a chance to talk to her? To tell her what happened?"

High shook his head. He wanted to speak, but he couldn't let Gino Brambilla see him break down.

"That is hard, young man," Gino said. "It makes me respect you very much. What you have done ... That is the kind of sacrifice a person doesn't hear too much about in this world, where most people are really selfish. Truly they are."

"She's going home, though," High revealed.

Gino nodded. "I know. She told us of her decision. How does it make you feel?"

High almost chuckled, trying to meet the man's eyes. "I thought I'd be happy. I thought I'd like to feel free again. Now I don't know. It makes me feel sad—well, for her, I mean." But that wasn't what he meant. He had said exactly what it made him feel—sad. And he didn't even know why. Having Flo release him from his decision to be her life-long guardian should have left him feeling elated.

"Oh, sure," said Gino. "I knew you meant sad for her." But in the man's eyes High read the truth. Gino Brambilla knew High was hurting. Maybe he knew this part of High better than he knew himself.

The doctor finally came back out, after what seemed like an eternity. He studied High, a kindly look in his eyes. "I'm sorry to have kept you waiting so long, young fellow. The young lady ... is your wife?"

A rush of feeling went through High, and he looked over at Savoia. She had kept everything to herself!

"Yes, sir," said High.

"Well, she is going to need some rest. Perhaps for a few weeks, even. I'm sorry, that's probably not what you hoped to hear. But the baby I think is fine. Not to say anything to embarrass you, but just so you understand, Florence was cramping up a little, but that isn't completely abnormal. And there was a little spotting of blood, but don't let it startle you. In my experience, the vast majority of pregnancies that experience a little spotting will go to full term and be fine.

"I am telling you, though, as I told Savoia, that the girl should not be put under any sort of undue stress. That is the main thing, you understand. Keep her calm, and let her rest as much as she wants to. I'll come back to check on her now and then—every few days. I promise. In the meantime, I've given her a mild sedative, to help her rest. Try to keep her warm, but if she starts to experience any high fever, please call me back. A mild fever is alright—nothing over one hundred degrees, or one hundred one at most, for short periods of time. Give her plenty of water, and mild soups or broth. I think she'll feel better in a day or so. Just try to comfort her and mostly be there for her emotionally. This is her first pregnancy, and I know she is very anxious. Do you have any questions?"

High knew everyone was watching him, so he tried to sound as much like a responsible adult as he could. "No, sir, I think you answered them all."

"Fine. Fine, then. You seem like a capable young man, so I'm sure your wife is in good hands. One thing I feel like telling you, though, on a personal note—of course it's only my personal opinion, but son? I think that young lady is madly in love with her husband. In case you ever wonder about it." The doctor winked and shifted his bag to his left hand, offering the other to High, who shook it, feeling a tremble in his own.

When the doctor was gone, Savoia offered High to make tea or coffee, and since he was too keyed up to go back to bed he took her offer of coffee. She made tea for herself, Gino and Mary, who was too anxious to go back to sleep as well. Later, they sat in the living room, on the two sofas, and sipped on their hot drinks. For a while, no one spoke, so the tinkle of china was the only sound. Finally, Gino broke the quiet. "Dr. Akins sounded pretty promising, yes?"

High looked over to find the man looking at him. "Yes, sir. I think so."

"What will you do?" asked Savoia. Since the silence was already broken by her husband, apparently she felt alright to open the conversation up to deeper subjects.

"What will I do?"

"Yes. Florence plans to go home now. Will you let her?"

The question was a bit like a kick in the guts to High. Not only did Savoia seem to be hanging on his reply, but Gino and Mary were right there as well. Why would she put him on the spot like that, in front of everyone? How did he know what he was going to do anyway? And how could he feel like he had any say about what Flo chose to do? She had made it pretty clear that she was going home to Oakley and his input didn't make much difference. Since it would free him to travel with Roy Legend and his companions, it was High's first choice anyway.

And then he thought of what the doctor had said, that Flo was madly in love with her husband. Why did people keep saying things like that? High sure couldn't see it. She seemed to appreciate it when he was there to comfort her, but what else was there? They had never so much as kissed each other, not even a peck on the cheek or forehead. And she had never acted like she wanted to. What had she said or done to make people think she loved him?

"I guess when she's ready to travel I will," he replied.

Savoia and Gino sat nodding thoughtfully, not meeting High's glance. That was alright, because he was too uncomfortable to look at them anyway.

"Will you go with her at least, to make sure she arrives home safely?"

High froze. How could he admit to the Brambillas that he had made plans to go with Roy Legend and his friends, and that he had to go with them in the next three days? It would have to wait, that was all. Maybe he would tell Gino when they were alone. He couldn't bring himself to say it right now, with all three pairs of ears listening.

"Sure," he replied. "Of course."

Later, although with the coffee in him sleep was probably far away, he made his escape back to the bedroom. Even as kind as the Brambillas had been to him, Savoia had begun making him feel uncomfortable, always seeming like she was delving into his private thoughts too much, needing to know too much about his plans. He went in the room to find Flo asleep, so he quietly shut the door and turned the light back off. Going to the chair across from the bed, he took his boots and socks off, then his belt. As usual, he left the rest of his clothing on, although he longed to be back in a bed of his own, and sleeping again in only his underwear. Wearing a shirt and trousers to sleep in out on the trail was one thing, but in a nice, clean bed it was completely something else. It didn't matter, though. He wasn't about to take a chance on Flo seeing him in his underwear. And now that the Brambillas knew everything, especially that he and Flo weren't even married, he was certainly not going to be caught in her bed in only his underwear. He was a little surprised that Savoia was even going to continue letting him sleep in the same room with Flo. His own mother certainly wouldn't have.

Long into the last of the dark morning hours, High lay listening to the soft sound of Flo breathing, sometimes coming close to snoring. One of the last things he remembered before fading to sleep was the touch of Flo's hand, as she felt around under the covers, and her hand at last closed over his. He didn't jerk away. In fact, he didn't even mind. And sometime soon after, with Flo's hand holding his, sleep claimed him. It never even hit him until morning that he had finally succumbed and crawled back into the bed with Flo.

The next day, Flo went back to being nauseous, throwing up almost anything she took in except some water. She went through bouts of mild fever and chills, but never a fever over one hundred, so Savoia decided not to bother Doctor Akins. High left the room that day only five times, three of them to eat, and the other two to feed and brush Wilder and to use the privy. The horse seemed to be growing restless of late, but when High was there he would settle back down, enjoying his sessions of being curried all over, and loved on.

One of the little tricks High had taught the stallion was to hug him, by bringing his head around, and pulling High in close to his neck. But the hugs weren't only done for exhibitions. Somehow, the big horse seemed to know when High was feeling needy and emotional, and the horse would pull him into one of his powerful embraces, then hold onto him sometimes for thirty seconds or more. Wilder, outside of perhaps Ava, was the best hugger High had ever known.

The rest of the day, when High wasn't with Wilder, he lay on the bed beside Flo, or sat up reading. If the girl was fast asleep, he might get out of bed to let her rest better, but even then he was in his chair close by. He began and read clear to the ending a book called *All Quiet On the Western Front,* a book that by its end left him feeling breathless, and aching in his heart. He prayed while reading that book that he would never be called upon to take part in any war. He guessed he would enlist, if it was to help preserve his country's freedom, but that book certainly took away any idea that war was a glorious adventure.

The third day after meeting with Roy Legend and the others wasn't much better for Flo, but one of the times when she was awake she begged High at least to go out and take Wilder for a ride. She seemed to know High was dying inside being cooped up in the house all day, and in the one stuffy room.

"Are you sure you'll be alright?" he asked her as he pulled his second boot on and stood up, threading his belt into the loops in his jeans. "I don't know if I should go very far."

Flo gave him a weak smile. "It's okay, High. I promise. But thank you. Savoia will be here. You go. Go have fun. I'm sure Wilder needs it too. I don't suppose you could take Bragger out too."

"Of course. I'll take them both. You—" He stopped. He was only going to ask her again if she would be alright anyway.

He grinned as she waved him on. "Go! Don't come back for at least two hours."

The ride through the Magic Valley countryside was magnificent. Flo had certainly been right about that. High took Wilder out for a while by himself, so he could let him run out some energy at a good speed, then returned and fetched Bragger, and the packhorse, Honcho, and rode for a few miles at a more leisurely pace. It wasn't that he didn't think the other two horses could stand to get some real exercise, but the few times he had ridden Bragger very fast, he found that Bragger had nothing to brag about—his gallop, like his trot, would make a strong man's spine into cornmeal mush in a matter of minutes. And Honcho was too old to run him much. High had seen a horse have a heart attack and die once, and he had no desire to be searching for a new packhorse.

It wasn't until High was back to the house that he decided he had to go see Roy Legend and the others. This was already day three, and that was the day he had promised to be there. He had enjoyed his ride in the valley, trying to relax as much as he could and simply relish in being in the open air with the horses. But the thought of Roy Legend and his friends was always in the back of his mind. He couldn't go with them right now, so he was already breaking one promise. But they would have to understand—wouldn't they? He couldn't simply ride away right now when Flo was so sick. He couldn't ride away, but he couldn't let them sit there in town wondering. If they still wanted him to go with them, they would wait for him a while longer, but either way he owed them an explanation.

He found Legend, Heavy Beecher and Browsy Prentiss at the burned-out house. Beecher and Legend were both standing up smoking cigarettes when he first saw them, and Prentiss lay on the ground resting on his bedroll. This time his bedroll was rolled up, apparently ready for travel.

Beecher turned his head and must have said something to Prentiss, as the latter jumped up and grabbed his bedroll, walking to his partners. For some reason, there was no happy smile from Legend to greet High this time. Instead, he dragged deeper on his cigarette, apparently trying to get the smoke all the way down into his toenails.

"Where's all your gear?" Heavy Beecher asked as he stalked close, his eyebrows lowering suspiciously. "You ain't plannin' to travel with just that, are you?"

"Aw, don't get on him," Legend cut in, his face sour as he drew on the smoke again and blew a cloud out the side of his mouth. "I didn't know if you were comin', High," said Legend. From the look on his face, it almost didn't seem like Legend *wanted* him here.

"My wife got sick," he said. "Real sick. Doctor's been over there a couple times already, and she's havin' a hard time."

Legend swore. "Well, you should be there with her, right? Not here in town with a gang of ne'er-do-wells like us."

"Now who's on 'im?" Heavy growled. "Leave 'im alone. He's the only one c'n know how bad things are. So ... where's your stuff, kid?"

High stared at Heavy, bumped his glance only for a second over to Browsy Prentiss, then to Legend, and back to Heavy, since he was the one addressing him and since Heavy Beecher, with his sheer look of animal toughness, commanded attention when he spoke.

"I'm not gonna be able to go yet," he said, trying to sound firm.

"Wait—kid, you're gonna miss the chance of a lifetime?" pressed Heavy. His eyes looked somehow flat and cold. He licked his fingertips and pinched the end of his cigarette, dropping it on the ground at his feet. It was like he tried to make the movement seem casual, but at the same time it seemed like he got rid of that cigarette with more force than was necessary.

"His wife's pregnant," growled Legend. "And sick. Let 'im be, Heavy. Just let 'im be."

Feeling much more encouraged now by Legend's words than he had at first by his lack of a friendly greeting, High looked his silent thanks at the charismatic shorter man, then returned his eyes to Heavy. "I'm real sorry. I sure do mean to go with you still, if you'll let me. I just ... I'll need at least a day or two more."

"Well, I apologize, kid, but we really need to get down the road," Legend said. "I mean, we've stayed longer than we intended to anyway, and most everybody around here who ever meant to see us do our show already has. I hope your wife gets better and you get a chance to travel around the world with your horse, but maybe you need to wait for another chance. You never know—we might even travel back by this way sometime."

"Don't listen to him, kid," Beecher said, trying to put on a friendly look, then turning to look at Browsy Prentiss. "Come on,

Browsy, help me out here. You think the kid should go with us, don't you?"

Browsy had been bringing a cigarette to his lips, but he stopped, surprised. He shot a glance between Heavy and Legend. "Well, uh ... I mean, sure. I wouldn't want 'im to miss out, that's for sure. Chance of a lifetime, right?" He put on a grin.

"I'll be back," High promised earnestly. "I will. Just ... If you could only give me a few more days."

"Well, why not?" said Heavy with an elaborate shrug. "Hell, I don't know why Roy's so all-fired in a hurry t' go anyway. It ain't like we got any place t' be. Is it, Roy?"

Roy shrugged, looking sullen. "His wife isn't going to be all better in a day or two if she's that sick. Come on!" He looked back at High, thrusting out a hand. "It's alright, friend. It's a good dream, and you c'n still do it. I don't think you should be takin' off on your little woman like that right now, that's all."

"But ... I wanna go with you," High said. "Honestly, I do. Hey—I think my wife's goin' home anyhow."

Legend's mouth dropped open. "She's— Wait, she's *what?* You say she's going home? Like as in leaving you? What happened, kid?"

High didn't usually care to be called names like kid or son, but somehow with Roy Legend it didn't bother him. "Nothin'. She just told me she might go home. And she kinda told me her own self to go travel. So ..."

A big ugly grin washing over his face, Heavy turned partway and stiff-armed Legend in the shoulder with the palm of his hand, pushing him back. "You see? You oughtta mind yer own business. It'll all be fine!"

Legend frowned and sighed, looking at High. "I want you to know I can't promise we'll still be here by the time your wife gets better. At least I need to say that."

"Oh, don't mind him!" Browsy Prentiss interjected. "We'll be here. At least me 'n' Heavy will be. We'll be right here—long as you don't take long."

Heavy gave a big, succinct nod. "Exactly, kid. We got you covered. Just make sure you bring all your truck next time—'specially all your cash money. It ain't cheap out on the road, you know—trains 'n' such," he added.

"I'll bring everything next time," promised High. "As soon as my wife gets feelin' good."

Feeling at least a little relieved that he had been able to buy some time with Legend and the others, although he wasn't sure he was liking Heavy Beecher all that much, High returned sometime later and brushed down all three horses, then went into the house after seeing Savoia out hanging up clothes on a line between two metal poles. The children were all in school, so High and Flo had the house to themselves at least until school was out or Savoia came back in from her laundry.

Entering the room quietly, the way he had learned to do as a young man trying to sneak back in without his parents knowing he had been gone, he found Flo asleep. She was in a partially seated position, with a pad of paper and a pencil in front of her, where they had collapsed at the same time she did.

Gently, he took the paper and pencil from her, glancing down at Flo's words as he was setting them on the nightstand. He froze. Flo had been writing a letter, and the first words leaped off the page at him like a rattlesnake: *Dear Mama*

The letter was written in a fine hand, and it filled most of two pages. Something like trepidation clutched High's insides, and he didn't even know why. There was nothing Flo could write to her mother that wouldn't paint him in a better light, not a worse one, than whatever her mother had been thinking before—at least assuming she would write her only the truth, and that was one thing

High didn't doubt. He didn't even know why, he just knew he could fully trust Flo not to tell anyone something about him that made him look bad.

High looked over at Flo. She seemed fully at peace in sleep. He glanced back at her letter. A gallant boy would have turned it over, so no one could accidentally see it. But he wasn't accidentally seeing it.

Picking up the note pad, he sat down on the chair, glanced over at Flo one more time, then looked down and began to read.

CHAPTER TWENTY-ONE

DEAR MAMA,

I am not really sure how I should start this letter, so I know I have to just start. I hope I will say something to make you not hate me, as I fear by now you must.

High's heart leaped at the sound of Flo's voice. His body leaped as well, coming up out of the chair and whipping the letter down to his side as he started turning to and fro, pretending to be looking for something.

It wasn't until Flo moaned again in apparent pain or discomfort that he realized she was still asleep. He practically jumped to the girl, doing his best to arrange her note pad and pencil the same way he had found it. As he was taking a step back, her eyes fluttered open. She looked up at him, and it seemed that either her eyes wouldn't quite focus or, worse, she didn't recognize him.

"Flo?"

Her eyes flying open wider, she struggled to sit up straight, her hand clumsily slapping around on the rumpled covers until it closed over the letter. She looked down at it, then back up at him. Pushing away his guilt, he said, "Are you alright? It's me. It's High."

She slowly sank back into her pillows. "I'm alright. Sorry, High. You just startled me."

I startled you! That was what he wanted to say, but of course he didn't. He only apologized, as she had.

"How was your ride?" Her voice sounded so weak it was like her writing pencil was being shoved slowly into his heart.

"Alright. It's a nice day."

"Yes," she agreed, her eyes fluttering closed again for a moment, then opening on him once more. "I saw that, out the window. A beautiful day for a ride."

"Yep."

She cringed, but made no noise. He watched her, and waited. Finally, she looked at him again. "High?"

"Yeah?"

"Do you ever think about what it would be like to die? Before you really even get started living?"

The question shocked him into a thoughtful ten seconds. He guessed that he, of all the people he knew, should be thinking about that all the time. He had had more brushes with death by his seventeenth year than anyone should have the right to survive, he guessed.

"You're gonna be alright," he assured her. "The doctor came last night. Do you remember? He said everything was going to be fine."

She gave him a wan smile. "Yeah. He did say that, huh?"

He forced himself to gaze her down. It wasn't hard to see that right now she wasn't believing the doctor's words so much.

"Is somethin' changing? You feelin' worse? The doc said to call him back right away if somethin' changed."

"I don't know if I want the doctor, High. I'm not sure if I want anything but just to be left alone."

"What're you talkin' about, Flo?" He felt like he knew what she meant—that she wanted to let go and die, and the thought made him panic. Was she worse off than anyone guessed? "I'm gonna go get Savoia, alright? Just wait here."

She gave out with a little, weak laugh as he was turning away, and it made him turn back, staring at her. "What?"

"You. You tellin' me to wait here. Where am I gonna go?"

He gave her a sheepish grin, turning back to her. If she was able to laugh, even a little bit, could it be she was alright? Could it be she was only still a little bit under the weather, and feeling down?

"You feelin' hot or anything?" he asked.

"Sometimes. Then real cold. Then I just hurt. All over, but ... especially ... down there."

He felt his face grow warm. He wanted to ask her about blood, but he couldn't get the words out. He had to go get Savoia. She would know what to ask. She would know how to help.

"I'll be right back," he said, trying to make himself sound brave. He stepped out of the room as if nothing were wrong, but the moment he was out of sight he practically ran through the house, searching for Savoia Brambilla. He finally found her hanging up the last of her laundry on the line.

Savoia turned when she saw him out the corner of her eye. Instantly, she was on alert when she saw his face. "High? Is everything alright?"

He stared at her for a second, hoping he wasn't just panicking, like a dumb little kid. "I'm not sure, ma'am. Flo just ... Well, she doesn't seem right."

"What do you mean 'right'?"

"Well, she doesn't seem like she's doing any better. And ... I don't know, exactly. Somethin' doesn't feel right. Sorry. I can't put it in words. She was askin' me if I ever thought about what it would be like to die, when I was still so young I hadn't even started livin'."

Savoia stepped closer, touching his arm. "High, you really care for that girl, don't you?"

The words shocked him. What did she mean by "care for" her? Of course he cared for her, but probably not in the way the woman meant. "Uh, yeah. Of course, I care for her. I hate to see her hurtin'."

With a little frown, Savoia said, "High, we will go in together and make sure she is alright. Hopefully it is nothing. But I hope when this is all over you will do the right thing. You need to decide whether you want to keep taking care of her, or you want to be free and ride your horse around the country. You simply cannot do both. And if you want to keep taking care of her, you need to find a priest and make everything right."

He stared at the woman, not knowing what to say. Should he be angry that she couldn't mind her own business? Should he be thankful to know she actually cared? Either way, he wasn't ready to make choices like that.

"High Warning," said Savoia in a firm voice. "I do not know if you know it, but that girl is in love with you. If you do not think you can feel the same, then it truly is time to tell her goodbye."

High didn't go back to the bedroom with Savoia. He didn't feel comfortable in there while the woman was in there too. He wasn't angry with Savoia, he decided. But he didn't like anyone trying to force him to make big decisions that only he and God could rightly make. He had told Flo he would take care of her, and he was trying. He had found a way that he could have his freedom for a while, and she could still be taken care of. This country was in a hard time. People were struggling, some of them starving. A lot of good men were out of work, and more were losing their occupations every day. People couldn't live the way they used to be accustomed to in the Twenties, back in a decade when most people were feeling pretty flush. He was *lucky* to have found a way to make money in the harsh environment the country was in the middle of. Who was Savoia Brambilla or anyone else to try and take that away from him? Or to take that financial security away from Flo either, for that matter?

He stayed in the sitting room and waited for Savoia to come out of the bedroom, when he would much rather have been out with Wilder. "I'm going to call the doctor back," Savoia said when she finally came out, avoiding his eyes.

"Why?" He tried to make himself sound calm. "Is she gettin' worse?"

"I'm not sure. But as you said, it feels like something isn't right. Let's let the doctor check her. I will not take a chance with her health. If you cannot pay for it, High, then we will."

"I'll pay," he said proudly. "I got money. I've got a lot of money right now."

She gave him a preoccupied nod, and without another word, she stalked down the hall to the phone, ringing the operator and asking for the doctor.

This time when the doctor came out of Flo's room, his face looked drawn and gray. High stared at him, too frozen to say anything. Doctor Akins stopped in front of him. "Well, I'm not sure, young man. She's very weak. She has all the symptoms of the flu, but—" He stopped when Savoia walked in from the kitchen, now dividing his attention between them. "I was telling the young man that she seems as if she might have the flu. All of those symptoms are there. But ... there's more spotting, I'm afraid, and it's a concerning amount. And ... well, frankly, I'm beginning to worry that she may be turning septic."

"What does that mean?" High blurted, immediately embarrassed at his outburst.

"It would mean she has an infection from something. An infection through her body. In her blood. Please understand what I'm saying—I'm simply not sure. We have to watch her closely. I've given her another sedative that should help her rest, but she's very weak. We need to try to get some fluids into her, through salty broth if possible, but I think if she can't keep anything down—and a significant amount—I may have to come back and give her some saline by hypodermic needle to rehydrate her. Young man, I'm sorry to have to say the frightening part out loud, but your little lady is really not well."

"Is there anything we can give her when she starts hurting again?" asked Savoia. High was glad she asked, because he wanted to but was finding himself tongue-tied.

Doctor Akins bunched his lips, scrubbing a hand across them. "I am contemplating the use of morphine," he said. "I think she is in that much pain, but hiding it. But with the baby ..."

"Yes," said Savoia, nodding quickly. "Yes, the baby. No, I think morphine should be the last thing we think of."

"I agree, Savoia. I certainly do. But the kind of pain I think she's been experiencing ... Well, we're just going to have to see what she is able to endure. I'm sorry," he told High. "I sure wish I had something more promising to tell you. You watch her fever now, do you hear? That is the most important thing I need you to keep track of right now—and blood loss. And make her drink broth, whenever she's awake—even if she balks at it. Tepid broth in small amounts—with a little more salt in it than normal. I wouldn't worry too much about straight water. Right now, in her present condition, salty broth is more important."

"Doc?" High managed to stammer out. When the older man only cocked an ear and looked at him, waiting, he said, "Could she die?"

The doctor flexed his jaw muscles, looking over at Savoia, then back to lock his gaze on High. "Your wife is strong, and young. She has those two things going for her. I think until this she has been a very healthy young lady. But yes, young man. I would be lying if I told you that sepsis, or even influenza, cannot kill her."

All the rest of that day, High sat in the chair by Flo's bedside. If he did try to get up, other than to use the outhouse, it was to try to go to the kitchen to get some broth. But Savoia, Mary or even Gino, once he got home from the store, was always there to meet him. High couldn't fix anything; broth was ready on demand.

Gino walked with High to the doorway of the bedroom when it was close to his family's bedtime. Savoia had already been standing at the partly open door, looking in at Flo, and she turned to greet them.

"High, I'm proud of you," said Gino. "But I have to caution you that if you get sick from Flo, you won't be able to help her anymore. And being in that room so much, with no fresh air ..."

High nodded. "I know. I'm sorry. I don't want anyone to have to take care of me, too. But ..."

Gino smiled when High couldn't go on. "It's alright. I under-stand."

High fought the lump in his throat. "I just can't leave her," he said, and gritted his teeth.

Savoia had tears in her eyes, High noticed when he managed to look at her. "You would be a wonderful husband, High," she said.

In the night, Flo woke up with a terrible case of the chills and threw up all over the bed clothes. High didn't bother the Brambillas. They had to be getting as weary as he was, and he couldn't stand the thought of getting them sick too. He simply pulled off the bedspread, which had been the main target of Flo's vomitus, and folded it up in a corner for the night, and then he got as many clothes as he could out of his and Flo's traveling bags and laid them over her with the remaining sheets and blankets because she was shivering violently. Finally, in desperation, he got on the bed with her, and with her back to him he snuggled as close as he could to her and pulled her in tight.

The bouts of savage chilling, intermingled with high fever, went through the night, and Flo moaned in delirium, saying crazy, senseless things, some of which ended in mid-sentence, some which seemed to go on and on, as if she were recounting some crazy scene in her mind.

High couldn't stop thinking about the blood. He knew a good husband might be able to bring himself to check for blood loss, but it was one thing High simply could not do. He didn't know if he was more ashamed of himself for his cowardice, or if he felt like he would be more ashamed if he gave in and looked for blood. But some things even the bravest of wild horse hunters simply cannot do.

Through the last hours of darkness, High brought Flo new broth three times, and she managed to keep it down. Her highest fever seemed to subside, and that was the first time in the night that he felt any relief over her condition.

The morning light exploded brutally through curtains that seemed suddenly thin. High tried to open his eyes, but the blazing light seemed to stab like fire into them.

"High." The voice was soft at first, the second time more insistent.

"You have to get up and eat something." His groggy, almost fevered mind recognized the voice of Savoia Brambilla. A warm hand squeezed his shoulder. "Come on. Come get some rest. Come. I promise I'll stay with her."

Managing to roll over and get his feet on the floor, High let Savoia help him stand, then stumbled down the hall with her to a pallet of blankets she had made on her own bedroom floor. "You rest here, High. I will be with your sweetheart. Mary stayed home from school to help as well. Go ahead." She motioned toward the blankets. "I'll come for you if anything changes."

Exhaustion and bitter emotion made tears well up in High, and before he could step forward and embrace Savoia, like he suddenly wanted to, she was hugging him to her, patting his back. "Sleep, young man," she said, in a voice full of love and kindness. "I'll clean everything up for you and change the bedding. You've earned a rest."

High slept only an hour or two before waking with a start. He lay on the floor staring at the ceiling, wondering where he was, and what had brought him there. After a while, conscious thought returned, and he struggled up off the blankets. He had to get to Flo! He had to bring her some broth and check her fever!

Stumbling out of the room, leaving the door open, he hurried down the hall to the closed door of the bedroom Flo was in. A light knock brought back no reply, but ten seconds or so later the door cracked open, revealing Savoia's face.

"High!" she exclaimed. "Why are you up? You've hardly had time to rest!"

"I can't," he said. "I have to be here. Did she drink any broth?"

"She did. She couldn't take in very much, but she kept it all down. And the doctor will be here in an hour or two to check her signs. High, please go back to bed."

"I have to see her," he insisted. "Just let me see her."

With a little smile, and a nod, Savoia opened the door and stepped aside. High went in and walked to the other side of the bed, because Flo's face was turned that way. At the moment, it seemed a dark pink color, but was it simply the shade that was cast on her now that the sun had risen farther and was no longer smashing through the window? He reached down, feeling her head, and looked over at Savoia.

"Yes," the woman said. "Yes, she is still hot. But it's better. I promise, it's better."

"Did she ... Is there any more blood?"

Savoia quickly shook her head. "She had a ..." She stopped. Apparently High didn't need to hear everything. "No, there hasn't been any more blood."

High had a strange urge suddenly to lean down and put his cheek to Flo's. What was wrong with him? But he couldn't do it. Not with Savoia right there watching. Reaching a tentative hand down, he squeezed Flo's fingers, then set her hand gently back down and darted out of the room, shutting the door behind.

He went down the hall and stood for a while, feeling dazed and more than a little confused as adrenalin subsided and sleepiness began to reclaim him. Finally, he returned to his and Flo's room and knocked again, then pushed it open. "I have to go feed the horses," he said.

"High. It's okay," Savoia stopped him. "I had the boys take care of everything, because Gino couldn't get near your horse. They're already fed, okay? Gino watched to make sure they did everything right. Go sleep, please? Before you make yourself ill."

And this time High did. He felt like he slept for twelve hours straight.

CHAPTER TWENTY-TWO

THERE WAS A WHOLE shipload of pirates—apparently really tiny pirates, but with undeniably sharp boot heels and peg legs—walking on High's eyelids when he tried to open them later.

He lay still, wanting his eyes open, but not wanting to fight pirates—even tiny ones. Let them have his eyes!

Light stabbed in under the slits of his eyelids when he got energetic enough to try opening them again. It wasn't even sunlight, merely daylight. But it hurt, and he lay still for what seemed like another ten minutes.

Finally, at least half the pirates seemed to march off his eyelids and down into his bowels, forcing him to struggle to his knees. Now he looked around, remembering that he was on Gino and Savoia's bedroom floor. He managed to get the rest of the way up and stumbled out to the outhouse. It was a strange time for a memory to crop up, but he recalled Gino mentioning a plan of having a real, indoor bathroom, with running water and an indoor toilet built on to the house. The idea of doing certain things inside the walls of a home people resided in seemed odd, but right now he almost wished they had already done it. As bright as the light in the bedroom had been, the sunlight on the way to the privy was like hot pokers burning through his eyes and down into his soul.

High went back in the house and washed his hands at the kitchen sink, using water poured over them from an old-fashioned ewer. At least the Brambillas were civilized enough to have a sink whose drain you could pour water down and have it go outside.

Knowing he had slept too long, he crept down the hall, feeling bad about making Savoia care for Flo all these many hours. He tapped on the door.

"Yes?" came Savoia's quiet reply.

"Ma'am? Is it alright if I come in?"

"High?" Her voice came through the closed door again, and then the door cracked open a few inches, and he could see part of her face. "What are you doing up? Two hours is not enough sleep!"

"Two hours?" he repeated dully.

Savoia opened the door wider, frowning at him. "You've been asleep barely over two. Go back and sleep some more, High."

He shook his head. "I can't. I feel like I've been asleep for half a day."

"You should be trying to!" she scolded.

"I just ... I can't leave her that long."

Savoia drew a big breath of resignation and sighed it out. "Alright, young man. Alright, I can't blame you. I'm sure I would do the same—but women are supposed to be that way."

He grinned at her. It seemed like whatever had been such a rub between them for a while—he guessed because she didn't think he cared enough about Flo—was completely gone now, and they were back to being friendly again.

Savoia started to let him in, then stopped at the same time he saw a thought enter her head. She gently pushed him back out into the hall, stepping out with him.

"She's been asleep this whole time. When she wakes up, she might have to go to the outhouse. Will you want to help her, or should I?"

"I will," he said, feeling courageous. "If she'll let me."

"Okay. If you change your mind, come and find me. And, High? She doesn't seem to be any better. I just wanted to prepare you."

"Her fever …" High stopped. His question seemed too obvious to need speaking.

"It still comes and goes. She is between spells now, but her clothes are damp from the last one. I have warm towels on her, but she'll wake up with chills soon, and I can come help you change her clothes if you would like."

Help change her clothes? Inside, High was panicky. Helping Flo out to the privy was one thing, but helping to change her clothes? Maybe right down to her bare skin? Some places a seventeen-year-old boy had to draw a hard line!

"Uh … ma'am, I uh …" He felt his face begin to burn. He was helpless to go on.

Savoia smiled her understanding. "Come find me. I forget you and Flo ... Never mind. Just come and find me."

High closed the bedroom door behind him after Savoia went away. He leaned against it with his palms flat on the door behind him and stared at Flo. She looked so bad—not much better than the last time he had seen her fiancé, in fact. And Seth was pale in death at the time.

Why did this illness have to strike Flo? And right when she had been starting to seem so happy, and they had started to have fun-loving moments between them. Right when he had started to think maybe he could look past all his lifelong dreams and see his way clear to coming home, after touring the world for a while, and marrying her. Of course she would never have been his first choice. They would always have too much rough history between them. But it would be alright. She was a good person, and not so hard to look at as he had once believed. Heck, he wasn't any prize himself. Maybe they would make an alright couple—or at least they might have.

Looking at her right now, he had to face the fact that if she didn't start to improve soon, he was probably never going to have to honor his promise to care for her. He had a terrible feeling that Florence Starbuck was never going to get up out of this bed.

High never thought much about things like getting sick from other people. He had spent time around Seth when he was sick, and Ava, Eve and Clementine had all had their terrible bouts with the flu. But somehow, his parents and Grant and Owen never seemed to get anything worse than a common cold, and High didn't seem even to get those. Fate seemed to think having him try to commit suicide by horse, goat, rooster, cow or weak tree limb was enough of a challenge and didn't want to bother saddling him with the simpler ailments of life.

He thought nothing of crawling onto the bed with Flo, and he draped his arm over her body. He told himself that was so if she started to wake up or move around, and he was asleep, it would alert him.

He lay there for a while, staring at the side of her face. He was still plenty young enough to focus on very close objects, and he focused on her straight, fine nose, her full, almost pouty lips that used to be a dark wine color but now were a sickly pink. He focused on the damp strands of her dark corn silk-colored hair that twisted around beside her face, clinging to her cheeks and forehead. He suddenly wondered how soft it would feel.

Raising a shaking hand, he touched the edge of her hair, feeling the damp coolness of her cheek. "Flo ..." He didn't know he was going to speak until he heard his own whisper. "Flo, you gotta get better soon. I gotta go travel Europe. I can't leave with you bein' sick. Get better. I was gonna send you a lot o' money. I was gonna make you an' the baby feel rich."

His voice went still, with his fingers still up along the side of her face. He stroked her cheek. Flo wasn't supposed to be sick like this. She was supposed to be standing at her new residence, smiling at him and waving goodbye as he rode off on Wilder to make them a fortune. That was the dream he had been having, at least.

Perhaps it was only a silly dream. Perhaps this was God's way of answering all his prayers to spend the rest of his life with Valentina Torreales, riding horses, and eating tamales until he burst.

High woke later to Flo stirring around under his arm. He had no way of knowing how long he had been here with her this time, but the first thing he noticed was that she was burning with fever again.

He raised up on his elbow, staring at her deep red face, where sweat beads dotted her forehead, upper lip, cheeks and chin. Her eyes were still closed, but she started moving her face back and forth, moaning. "Mama ... Mama, please. It's burning. Mama ... make it stop. Mama, that's enough. Enough hot water now."

High sat up, staring at the girl, frightened. She was caught in some wicked dream. He had seen Clementine like this before, and Seth too. She was far from any state of consciousness, and she wouldn't likely even remember what these nightmares were about when she finally woke.

Should he shake her awake? Should he let her fight on in her dreams? He watched her until she finally grew still again, so still that he reached out in a panic to feel the pulse at her throat. Her heart was still beating, but it felt so weak, and fast.

High had never been one to go straight to praying, not like his mother, Ava and Eve talked a lot about, and demonstrated to others by their actions. Right now, however, he was desperate. He couldn't stand to see Flo like this.

He didn't close his eyes at first. He couldn't take them off Flo. Staring at her tortured face, he said, "God, please make her well again. Let her go home and see her mom, and Lilia. Don't take her now. Please. She's too young." He kept staring. He didn't know if he expected to see some miraculous change. But he sort of expected at least to *feel* something different, and there was nothing. He thought of his mother, of Eve, but especially of Ava, who was so sweet and seemed so angelic and sincere. When he saw them pray, they always closed their eyes and bowed their heads, so he mimicked them.

He prayed again, once more out loud. "God, please don't take her away. She's got a lot of things to do. A lot of life to live." He held still for a long time, his brow furrowed so hard he started to notice it almost hurt. "God?" A panicked feeling clutched his guts. He didn't want to say what he knew he was going to. But desperation was setting in. "If you'll make her better, I won't leave her. I'll stay with her and take her wherever she wants to go to feel safe. I'll even ... I'll even marry her if you want me to, and if you just make her better. Please, God. I never asked for anything before now." That wasn't entirely true, for he had said prayers over different circumstances involving Wilder. But he had sure never tried to pray since Washington Starbuck killed his father and Seth.

"God," he said once more, closing his eyes tighter. "You heard me, right? I'll marry her and stay with her if you only make her better."

The thing that scared him near to death was knowing he meant it. All of a sudden, not having Flo die meant more to him than his own freedom. Whatever was suddenly wrong with him he had no way in hell of knowing.

He only knew that in his head he must be sicker than any illness Florence Starbuck might have.

CHAPTER TWENTY-THREE

LATE THAT EVENING, HIGH wasn't certain Flo wasn't dying. He sat up on the bed with her, listening to her breathe too fast, and moan like a horrible wind moans around the eaves of a house. Had God listened to his prayer, or was he too much of a sinner to draw God's attention? Was Flo just going to waste away and die, right when he was getting used to the idea of living with her?

He looked over at her, able to see her fever by the flush of her skin and by the sweat matting her hair to her temples. Anymore, the fever never seemed to go away, and it never seemed to lessen. The doctor had come and checked her, giving her a sedative, and whatever medicines he could. He had put some saline into her intravenously since she wasn't holding in enough fluid. But never in all the time he had spent there had he had so much as a promising look, or even a kindly one, on his face. He acted like he couldn't even bear to look at High, and he only said what he absolutely had to, then left.

Out of the blue, High thought of the letter Flo had been writing to her mother. He wondered if he would have to send it on with a letter of his own, trying to explain to Mrs. Starbuck how her daughter had died, and possibly because he had taken her out on the road with him. If Flo died, he wondered if he would ever be able to shake that very thought. What if they had stayed in Oakley? What if he had convinced Flo simply to stay there and face the shame of what she had done, and she had never contracted whatever was ailing her now? If Flo died, High would indeed be "free", but it wasn't a kind of freedom he wanted. He would rather die with the girl than live knowing her death might have been his fault.

On a whim, he got up and looked around in Flo's things. He found the letter, now folded up in an envelope, apparently ready to be sent when Flo chose to. Again, he looked down at her, his heart pounding. The girl was not going to wake up any time soon. That much he knew. And somehow he simply had to know what she had written home, and what he might be forced to add to it.

With trembling fingers, he pulled the two folded pieces of paper out of the envelope and laid them open on his lap. Again, he began to read.

DEAR MAMA,

I am not really sure how I should start this letter, so I know I have to just start. I hope I will say something to make you not hate me, as I fear by now you must. I know you also must know that I am with High Warning, and so I have to say some things to you to be sure that you don't hate him, and in fact, that perhaps you will come to love him, as I have.

Mama, I have sinned before God. I have brought so much shame on myself, and on you. I was with Seth Warning, and I became pregnant with his baby. I couldn't bear to tell you what happened, but Seth and me thought if we could hurry and get married then no one would ever know, and I wouldn't bring any shame upon you and our home.

When Seth died, I felt desperate and lost. Again I wanted to come to you, but instead I turned to High. I am not sure if you know, but High was to marry a Mexican girl in town, the little girl whose father and mother make the tamales to sell. Instead, he chose to take me away and pretend this baby was his. He told me we would marry, and when the baby was close we would return home and everything would be fine. Nobody would ever know the truth, except that we had eloped. So please never be angry with High. He is a good man, and he only wanted to protect us, and Seth.

Mama, I got sick. I am scared I am going to lose this baby. I suppose it would be for the best, but the thought breaks my heart. This baby would be the only thing I have left of Seth, and I know High would have been a wonderful father to it. But I am so sick. I have not admitted to High just how sick I am, or to the nice Italian people who took us into their home. They are really good people, Gino and Savoia Brambilla, and, Mama, he is the mayor here!

Mama, this next part is hardest. I am partly writing because I want to see if I can come home. I know that may be startling. Maybe it will be that you do not want me to bring this shame home. Please consider what I am asking, however, and I will do as you say.

High does not love me, Mama. I wanted him to, because I have come to truly love him. He is so strong and kind and good. And I know in my heart he would be such a wonderful provider for me and our children. But he does not love me, and I know he never will. High wishes to travel the world with his horse. He has been doing it, and he is making a large amount of money from donations. I cannot keep him from his dream, especially since he is only marrying me to protect me and not because he loves me.

Without telling High, I contacted a man we met who is a businessman from Boise. He wanted to be a sponsor for High. Or I think you might call it a manager. Anyway, he wanted to travel together with High around the country, arranging exhibitions for High and his horse, Wilder. I think it would have been grand to travel with High, if he loved me as I do him. I honestly would have done anything for him. But he believes this man, Mr. Martin, will not allow me to go with them, especially when he learns I am pregnant, and so High turned him down because he didn't want me to have to go back home by myself to the shame he knows I will face in Oakley. See, Mama? High is sweet, and so very protective of me and my honor, and Seth's.

When I spoke with Mr. Martin on the telephone and he found out I am going to have a baby, he told me he did not feel good about taking High away from me, and that he would regret breaking us up, so he turned me down, which I was very sad about, as I had made up my mind.

Mama, I am going to contact Mr. Martin again and tell him I am coming home, that is if you will let me. I won't be any burden to you, or at least any more than I have to. I can do all the house chores or whatever you need, if you want to try and find work in town. I just don't know what else to do. I simply cannot tie High down when his heart isn't in this marriage. So perhaps it will work out that High will go with Mr. Martin still, if I am out of his way.

I hope I don't lose my baby, Mama. I hoped he would be like Seth, and I so wanted you to be able to hold him. But I don't have a good feeling about it, and I believe God is preparing me for a great, sad loss.

I thought I would keep it a secret from you where I am at the moment, but I guess I was being silly, as you would not know where to write me back if I don't tell you. By the time this letter reaches you, though, I suppose High will be on his way to some place across the world with his horses, and I will probably come home on the train. I know High will make sure I have enough money. I honestly think he might even send us some from what he makes while traveling, if he can. So please, I beg of you not to be angry with him for taking me away. We both agreed this was the best way to keep your reputation safe, as well as mine.

I love you, Mama, and I look forward greatly to hearing back from you. I will understand, however you should choose.

With all my love,

Flo

High sat there stunned. What was he to think of this letter? There were so many emotions assaulting him right now. Part of him felt almost angry that Flo had gone behind his back and contacted Jim Martin about being his manager. He thought they had pretty much decided together that they wouldn't do that, because Martin would probably not allow Flo to travel with them. Then she would be forced to go home after all, which was the whole reason they were traveling in the first place, so no one would know she was having the baby.

Another emotion that pulled at him was Flo's outright statement that he didn't love her. Was Flo right about that? He didn't even know. He didn't feel the same excited feelings he did around Valentina, that was true. Or even pretty little Lilia. But he had gotten used to being with Flo, and he had decided they would be alright together. Maybe that wasn't enough. Maybe Flo was right. Maybe he didn't really love her, at least not the same way Seth had. He guessed perhaps he never would. But what right did she have to decide that? He had promised he would take care of her. What right did she have to take that choice away from him? After all, it would affect his family too, as everyone in Oakley would know what Seth had done.

He sat there staring at the girl, once he finally got his thoughts sorted enough that he was able to. He didn't know what his real emotions were right now. The ugly truth was no one knew how bad off Flo was, not really. The doctor could examine her, and he could make all his guesses. But how could anyone else know how bad she was? Maybe Flo really would lose her baby. And just as possibly, judging from the way Doctor Akins was acting, she could lose her own life.

If that happened, when all was said and done, nothing in Flo's letter was going to mean a thing. She would be gone, and High and Wilder would be traveling the world. Whether it was with Roy Legend or not, High would be traveling the world.

It suddenly hit him like a kick to the guts that he would probably be traveling alone with Wilder anyway, if not with Legend. It didn't sound like Flo planned on giving him any choice.

If that was the case, then one thing was sure: Never again would he put himself in a situation where he had to feel responsible for another human being. This one time was enough to last the rest of his life.

CHAPTER TWENTY-FOUR

IN SPITE OF EVERYTHING he had read in Flo's letter—and he didn't believe anyone would lie in such a letter—High found that he was unable to leave Flo's side. He sat there watching her toss and turn, her flushed face dotted with the same sweat that was gluing strands of her hair to the sides of her face. He sat listening to her moan, and mumble strange words that often didn't even sound like words, and when they did, they made no sense to-gether.

He kept going to get cool water, put washcloths in it and dab the sweat from her face. He wondered if she was losing blood "down there", where he would never dare try to check. Was she losing Seth's baby, the thing he guessed she must want and need the most in the world?

Savoia came in now and then and sat with him, or did little things for Flo, hovering around her like a mother blackbird, watching out for its young. But no one else came. High sensed that those who might have, Gino and Mary, were simply too afraid. He was pretty sure that everyone in this house had at last come to wonder if Flo had much chance to survive this illness.

When Savoia came, there was little conversation. There were precious few times when she could even meet his eyes. But one time she pulled a chair in and sat beside him, and without saying anything she reached over and took his hand, squeezing it and holding on for a good ten minutes. Finally, she got up, putting her hand on his cheek and looked deep into his eyes.

"Pray for her, High, and be strong. She would have wanted that."

Then she left the room.

It wasn't until Savoia had been gone for five or ten minutes that the woman's words hit him full force. *She would have wanted that?* The way she had formed the words made it sound as if Flo were already dead!

Whipping his eyes over to Flo, he stared at her. She had gone quiet for a long time now. He didn't even know how long. He stared at her face. There was no sweat. He stared at the blankets that covered her torso. The labored breathing had ceased. In fact, he could see no movement of her chest at all!

Leaping out of his chair, with chills covering his skin, he dug at his eyes, clearing them of the sudden tears of his fear. He stood over Flo, staring at her face, watching her slightly parted lips.

"Flo!" He couldn't stop himself from leaning over and grabbing her shoulders, shaking her motionless body. "Flo!"

Suddenly, to his shock, her eyes fluttered open, and she looked right up at him. A little smile came to her lips. "Hi ... High."

He stared at her, trying to process everything he could see. He felt tears wanting to come, and he hated himself for it. So many times he had heard that a man doesn't cry, and he believed it. He couldn't let her see him be any less than a man, and yet the emotion of the moment was tearing his heart to shreds.

"Flo ... You weren't breathing! And ..." He scanned her face. It was dry, and the color was pink, the way she used to look. "How do you feel?"

"Tired," she replied, with another smile parting her lips. "So tired. And I'm dying of thirst."

He grinned. "You are? You're thirsty?"

"I could drink water out of a hoof print."

After staring at her for a moment, High remembered it wasn't that long ago when he had said that to her, one day when they were traveling, and she had laughed at him. Now she was using his own humor—actually an old saying from his dad—on him! He laughed and put his hand on her cheek without even thinking about it, feeling an urge to touch her, to feel closer to her.

"Flo! You aren't hot!"

She shook her head and shrugged a shoulder. "Uh-uh. High? How long have I been here?"

He dug into his memory. Was it three days? Or four? "Half a week," he said. That was a safe enough reply.

"I feel like I haven't had a drink for that long."

"Oh! Sorry!" He actually heard himself giggle. "Wait here! I'll get you some water."

As he whirled away, he heard her say his name, and he turned back. "Yeah?"

"I'm pretty sure I don't have any choice but to wait here."

He laughed, and feeling elated, he ran from the room.

In the kitchen, Savoia was stirring something in a bowl, and she turned to see his face. Her eyes widened. "High?"

"She's awake!" he said. "She wants water!"

"Are you—" She stopped herself. "Run back to her. I'll bring water. Go!"

High went back to Flo's side. She had somehow found strength enough to struggle up to a position on the bed that was half sitting, half lying. She smiled at his concerned face. "I feel like I've been dragged by a goat."

After staring at her for several seconds, High started laughing, and he had to fight hard to stop. Soon, the whole Brambilla family was gathering in the room, all staring down at Flo with big smiles. Gino and Savoia were busy firing questions at her at the same time, at such a speed there was no way she could answer them.

At last, Savoia let out a laugh, reaching over to squeeze her husband's forearm and effectively shut off his voice from whatever question he was asking at the moment. "I'm sorry, *cara*. We are stampeding over you with questions. But ... we are so happy to see you like this!"

Flo smiled weakly, scanning the whole family. "Thank you, but I bet I must look a fright."

"You are the most beautiful thing I have seen in weeks. *Bella!*" said Savoia. *"Bella donna."*

"What's that?" asked Flo.

"Beautiful lady," Gino interpreted for his wife. "And you sure are, to our eyes."

Blushing, Flo looked over at High. "I am very doubtful of that, but thank you." She sipped the cool water Savoia had brought her, closing her eyes for a moment as if experiencing the most exquisite wine. "It tastes like heaven, Mrs. Brambilla. Thank you."

"No, cara. No, thank *you*. Your waking is a gift to us all."

High's heart was racing. Savoia was right—Flo's waking was a gift, especially if, as it appeared, she was recovering. Yet so much had changed since she fell sick, and much of it was in Flo's letter, which now he could never erase from his mind.

High slept beside Flo all night, except that to say he actually slept would have been an exaggeration. For most of the night, he lay there awake, wondering if he should talk to her about the things in her letter, or if he should simply let them go and allow things to play out as they would. It sure did seem, however, that if he didn't say anything to her she was going to have to say something to him. That is, unless she had changed her mind about everything she had written to her mother.

High chose to wait, at least until she had had a full night's rest.

When morning came, much to High's surprise, he found he had finally fallen asleep. He was only waking now because he could feel someone gently brushing the hair away from his forehead. When he stirred, that someone stopped and settled back down onto the bed beside him.

For a few more minutes, he lay there, then finally opened his eyes. He turned his head to look at Flo, who was already watching him.

High didn't know where his words came from. Perhaps it was because he had heard them running through his mind for so much of the night, while he tried to decide if he should say them. But now, suddenly, they were spilling out, out loud, and once he started there was no way to take any of them back.

"I guess you made a lot of decisions about us, huh?"

Flo blinked, and she stared at him, looking confused. Finally, she leaned a little away from him. "What?"

"I guess you made a lot of decisions, I said."

"What do you mean?"

He raised himself up and rested his head on the palm of his hand, hating how his pounding heart made him feel. But he had kicked over the beehive, and he had to go on.

"You decided on your own that I should let Jim Martin decide what's best for my life. And you decided to go home—and leave me."

For five or ten seconds, Flo stared at him. When the realization finally hit her, she came up off the bed almost as if her torso was on springs that had popped loose. Her face was on the verge of anger, perhaps as close as he had seen in her in years. "Did you read my letter?"

Feeling a little guilty, but doing his best not to let her see it, he said, "It was sitting out right in plain sight."

"So? You don't read other people's letters. I would never have read something private of yours."

"Well ..." Now he was finding himself on the defensive, but if he hadn't given in and read it, how would he even have known what was going through her mind? Besides, he didn't believe for a single second that if the tables had been turned she wouldn't have read a letter he wrote home.

"Well what? High, you didn't have any right to read that." She pushed herself up, then got to her feet, having to steady herself for a few seconds with her hand on the wall.

"You shouldn't get up," High said, getting off the bed and facing her. "Lie back down, okay?"

"I'll do whatever I damn well please!" she said, her nostrils flaring. "This isn't over, High. What have you done?"

"What have I *done?* What have *I* done?" It was time. High didn't rile easy, but he was not going to go down easy for reading a letter that had been left out in the open, for anyone to read, and which in fact had ended up having a huge bearing on his relationship with this girl—or woman, whatever someone wanted to call her. He wasn't going to be vilified for doing exactly as she—or anyone else—would have done in his place. "Don't start in on *me.* Okay, I read your letter. You would have done the same, and you know it. Besides, the point is I sure didn't go try to get some guy to be your partner without any by-your-leave from you. I didn't make a decision about what you were going to do with your life, either. I didn't decide what I was going to do without even asking you, no matter if it affected you too."

Flo's chin and lower lip were trembling now, and tears were running down her cheeks. They stared each other down, probably looking for all the world like they hated each other. Flo finally found her voice. "I was trying to help you! I'm so sorry for trying to do something I thought would make you happy."

"How do you know what would make me happy? You didn't even ask! I told you what would happen if I told that man I'd travel with him."

"Well, good! That's what *should* happen!" she snapped.

"Why?" He knew his own voice came out as a growl, but he was getting so angry he didn't care.

"Because! You don't love me, High. You never did, and you never will, and you can't tell me any different. I don't need any more of your pity. I'm going home."

Incredulous, High stared at her, knowing his mouth was hanging open—catching flies, as his dad used to say. How had this gone from his innocently reading a letter to this horrible fight between them, the first real, angry fight they had ever had, or at least in adulthood? He thought these things, but none of his thoughts helped him escape the anger, shame and embarrassment he felt right now, in part because he felt stupid for ever offering to help her in the first place, if she was going to attack him like this for such a stupid reason. *He* was the one who should be attacking *her,* not the other way around. She was the one trying to make life-altering decisions for him without even asking how he felt!

"Well, go ahead!" he said angrily. "Go home. I don't give a—" He stopped shy of using the kind of language she had. One thing he wasn't going to do was swear in front of a woman, no matter how angry she made him.

It was Flo's turn to stand and stare again, her lips clamped tight together, and the tears on her cheeks that she couldn't stop. Before he finally turned away to stomp to his travel bag and start packing it, he saw her slap the tears away, her eyes blazing at him. "What are you doing?"

"I'm leaving," he said. "Just like you tried to make me do without even askin' me."

"I was trying to help you!"

"Ha! Like I need your help. I was doing just fine without Jim Martin. Besides, I got three guys in town I'm gonna go travel around the world with an' make some *real* money. I was gonna start sendin' a bunch of it home to you that you could share with your family, and a bunch to my family too."

"Home to *me*? Home *where?*"

"Here! Here with the Brambillas—just till I could get back from Europe."

"I don't want any of your money!" she said, hardly even waiting to recover from his barrage of revelations. "You can keep it all—every last penny!"

"Good! Then I will!"

He spun away again and began packing, shoving clothing and anything else he needed into his bag, the last item being his holstered pistol and cartridge belt. He already had four good-sized bags of coins and several hundred dollars in cash stowed down deep under his clothes.

When everything was packed, he turned back to Flo, who stood there with her arms folded tightly. It was almost as if she didn't dare let go of herself for fear her clothes would go flying off.

"Do you want to sell me Bragger? Or just figure out a way to get him home?"

"Mom wouldn't like me getting rid of him," she said, her voice much quieter, but sounding sullen.

"Okay." He took a deep breath, then dug into his pants pocket and stepped toward her, holding his hand out. "Take this, I guess. I bought it at Gino's store. He helped me pick it out. I won't need it, and maybe he'll give you the money back so you can get a train ticket home."

She just glared at him, her chin starting to quiver again. She only glanced down at his hand, not moving to take whatever was in it.

"Go on," he insisted. "Take it."

When she finally put her hand out, a small black box rolled into it, and she snatched it back to her without opening it. The tears were running down her face freely again. He had to look away from her because she was a mess, and he was starting to feel bad.

"Wait a second," he said, and he unbuckled his travel bag and dug down into it. He came up with cash and counted off several bills, equaling a hundred and twenty dollars. He held it out to her. "Just in case you need more to get home, and some for food for you and your family."

"Take your money!" she said. "Take it and just go. That's what you've been wanting all along anyway."

He could only hold her eyes for so long this time. Keeping the cash in one hand, he buckled the bag again, shaking, walked to the door, and went out. Savoia was standing there not far away, and it was obvious she had heard way too much of the exchange in the bedroom.

"I have to leave," he said. "Can you give this to her when she's not so mad?"

"High ..." Savoia obviously wanted to plead with him, but when she saw the determination in his face, she stopped and simply took the cash he offered. "Okay. I will. Travel safe, High Warning. You're a good young man, and it has been a blessing to have you in our home."

"Thank you. You sure made me feel like part of your family."

High could see when Savoia's decision not to interfere vanished from her face. A certain set came to her jaw and mouth and eyes that he had seen before, and he steeled himself for what was about to come. "Are you sure you won't stay a while and see if Flo will feel differently? What you have both done seems to be a very rash decision, and I think you'll both change your minds if you only give yourselves a chance."

"I won't change my mind," he said firmly. "And neither will she. This wasn't right from the start."

"High, that girl loves you. She loves you with all of her heart. Do you not see that?"

He stared at her, starting to tremble and not knowing why. He stared until he felt his resolve begin to crumble. "I have to go. Thanks again for everything your family did."

Savoia frowned sadly. "Okay. I see you have your mind set. Should I tell Gino and the children anything for you?"

He ground his teeth together to steady his emotions, then tried to smile, although he knew it was an ugly attempt. "Yeah, can you tell them I've enjoyed them all? And I'll miss them? And if I make it back this way, I'll stop and say hello."

"I'll tell them," she said, and she stepped forward and hugged him, almost crushing the breath from him.

Without another word, High went down the hall, trying to walk with poise but fearing that to Savoia he must look like an angry little kid bolting for the first way out of the house.

He went out and threw his saddle on Wilder, tied his blankets and his traveling bag on behind the saddle, then loaded up Honcho the packhorse, climbed onto Wilder, and headed for town.

He prayed he would not be too late to catch Roy Legend, Browsy Prentiss and Heavy Beecher. If he had missed them, it was going to be a long time before he ever again had a chance to travel the world. Especially with someone who was willing to take him along and who seemed familiar with the ways of the world.

He wished Honcho wasn't behind him, because right now he wanted to use his spurs on Wilder and put him into a gallop fast enough to leave behind all the pain he had just ridden away from.

CHAPTER TWENTY-FIVE

HIGH'S THOUGHTS WERE TORN in the ugliest of ways. He knew he had to get to town as fast as possible, in hopes of catching Roy Legend still there, and he was angry at Honcho for being behind him and holding him back. He even found himself wishing he had left Honcho and his packs behind. Maybe he wouldn't need all those things anyway, since according to Roy Legend he would be making enough money to buy anything he needed. All those things fought for a place in his head, but then every few minutes Flo clawed her way back in, and he got angry at her again.

How did that girl think she had any right to be angry with him? Sure, he had read her private letter—the exact same way she would have with the tables turned and she thought he was dying! But what if he hadn't? He would never have known she was making plans behind his back, trying to force him to work with Jim Martin. He had already told her he didn't want to, and it was because Martin wouldn't let her go. Didn't she understand that? Didn't she see he didn't want her to be forced to leave and go back to Oakley to face the horrible gossip? And then, for her to reveal in that letter that she had decided to go home, when he had promised to take care of her! When had she planned on telling him?

The truth was, *he* was the one who had all the right to be angry. And here he had bought her that ring from Gino Brambilla, planning on marrying her so no one would think badly of her! He had decided they should marry, and she hadn't even let him say it! Then she didn't even bother to look in the box! She obviously didn't care! Didn't care what gift he might have given her. Savoia and the others said Flo loved him—even people who had barely spoken to her! How could anyone possibly think that? Flo loved Seth, not him! She had never had any interest in him past knowing he was trying to keep her honor safe. She had never cared, other than to know that he meant to feed and clothe her and provide her a place to live.

Flo sat on the bed and wept for five or ten minutes. She lost all track of time. No one came to the door, mercifully. She had been certain for a while that Savoia would, because Savoia always seemed intent on making everyone else's business her own. She no sooner thought that than she felt bad. Savoia had been nothing but kind to her, and caring. She had done so much for her, even risking getting the flu, or whatever Flo might have had. That woman could have distanced herself completely when she learned Flo was ill. She had every reason to, not the least of which was the safety of her own family. She could even have forced Flo to go to the hospital and not let her stay in their home anymore at all. Savoia Brambilla was a dear, kind woman, and Flo was a horrible person to think badly of her even for only a moment.

Sniffling, she looked through tear-dimmed eyes at the little black box in her hands. She didn't realize she was shaking until she went to open it. The lid came up very slowly, and Flo gasped. It wasn't a necklace of fake jewels, or a chain with a cross on it. It wasn't earrings, or any of the nice little things High could have wanted to give her as a gift—the kind of things she had envisioned it might be. What glittered up at her out of the velvet bed inside the box was a ring. A diamond wedding ring.

What did I do? she thought. *What have I done to my High?*

Clambering up off the bed, she had to stand still for a moment to regain her equilibrium. Her head whirled mercilessly. She thought she would have to lie back down. She even thought for a moment from the sudden nauseous feeling in her stomach that she was going to throw up again. But she couldn't! She couldn't afford to be sick! Not now! Not when High Warning was riding away from her! Not when she had so much she needed to tell him, especially how bad she felt for trying to make his decisions for him. High was right to be mad! It had not been her place to do that, even to make the decision to go home without discussing it with him.

Turning, using her hands along the edge of the bed to steady herself, she went to her clothing bag and pulled out a skirt, and a blouse. Trembling, crying and hardly able to see what she was doing, she managed to pull off the nightgown she had been wearing and struggle into the fresh clothes. She pulled on her shoes and clumsily laced them, pausing every little bit to rub angrily at her eyes, which with their tears kept betraying her.

She struggled up again, her body covered in chills. She had to get to High! She had to reach him before he was gone!

She threw open the door, surprising Savoia standing there. For only a few seconds, they stared at each other, until Savoia found her voice. "I'm sorry to startle you, cara. Are you alright?"

"I have to go after High," Flo blurted out. "I have to tell him I love him and I don't want him to go!"

"But he's gone, Flo. He has a long headstart on you, and you surely can't travel right now. You're far too weak."

"I have to," Flo cried. "I have to!"

"Let me at least call Gino," Savoia said. "He could bring the car."

"No. I'm sorry! I have to go now, on my horse."

"Child, please!" It was the closest Flo could imagine to Savoia Brambilla pleading with her. "You're not ready to ride a horse."

"I'm not ready to lose High," Flo said firmly, and then she was gone down the hall, and out the front door.

High made Wilder walk so fast that Honcho, with his shorter legs, almost had to trot to keep up. They rode into Rupert, and even though he thought of stopping and tying Honcho up somewhere, to come back for him later, he didn't. He kept pushing on, feeling like he needed to have everything with him when he saw Roy Legend and his partners, so they wouldn't have any excuse not to let him come along with them.

The lot with the burned-out house stood empty. Empty but for the signs of where men had walked, and where they had slept. Empty but for the remains of the foundation, and the dust, and the dying elm tree. High felt like someone had kicked him in the stomach. With his heart thudding dully, as if it was up in his throat, he rode slowly through the yard. There was a pile of ashes where a campfire had been, and disturbed places in the earth where the three men's beds had been. After half a day of wind, there would be little sign that Legend, Beecher and Prentiss had ever been here.

High looked about, his vision dull. What had he done? Why had he waited so long? He should have come sooner! He should have been packed up and ready on that third day, when he had promised them he would. Savoia would have looked after Flo. He knew she would have!

Thinking of Flo made him grit his teeth. He had to stop thinking about her. He had to get away. Just ride. Ride as far and as fast as he could, until all memory of her was ground out of his mind. He couldn't say goodbye to Gino, or to Luca or Angelina. He didn't have the heart for it, nor the mind. With Roy Legend gone, effectively deserting him, forcing him to go back to traveling the road, only this time alone, he could have stayed long enough at least to thank Gino, his brother, and Angelina. But he had already used up all the grace that was in him. All the good manners.

One day perhaps he would come back, but even as he thought that he knew it wasn't true. His father had told him once, a year or so before his death, that he should get used to one thing in life: losing all touch with friends and family. You might think when you parted ways with people that you would come back one day to see them again, but ninety-nine times out of a hundred you wouldn't. Life was too busy, time was too precious and miles of separation were simply too great. When you walked away from people, or they walked away from you, most of them became only memories. High would never see the Brambillas again.

Aimlessly, High started to ride back toward the center of town. He would stop to eat, somewhere other than the Brambillas' restaurant. He might go to a grocery store and buy a few more supplies for the road, perhaps another box of ammunition for the pistol, for any time he might spot a rabbit, a partridge or a pheasant. He had even shot ducks and geese before, one of them as it was trying to lift off the river.

As he was passing the train depot, he saw a sight that set him back in the saddle. He jerked Wilder to a stop, making the horse grunt in displeasure. There at the station was a group of people, and among them were three men easily recognizable, especially with rangy Heavy Beecher's ragged head and fedora sticking up above the average traveler in the crowd.

It looked like Roy Legend, who was up at the ticket window, was about to purchase a ticket for the train. High took a chance and yelled out to him. It was Heavy Beecher who heard him and whipped around first, searching the street only for a second before his eyes registered on Wilder, and a huge grin split his face.

"Hey, kid!" He turned and said something to Legend, nudging him in the side, and both Legend and Browsy Prentiss pivoted about as well, looking toward High. High was taken aback to see that Prentiss also got a big smile, but Legend's face, the one High was most happy to see, wasn't even what he would call sober, so much as it was almost disgusted.

Legend turned back and leaned down, apparently to say something through the open window where High could see glimpses of a clerk. Then Legend and the other two came trooping toward him, still all smiles except for Legend, who lagged behind the others, looking almost sour of face.

"Kid, you made it!" said Heavy. "Damn, we almost give up on you!"

High gave them a tentative smile, as he reined Wilder around, controlling him against the horse's obvious urge to continue down the street. He tried to avoid looking at Legend, but that man was all he could think about. Was he only having a bad day, for him not to have any welcoming greeting for High?

"Sorry I'm so late. I just now got away."

"What happened with your wife, High?" asked Legend, the first time he openly acknowledged High and met his eyes.

"Well ... She's alright. She got all better." He said that even while he knew Flo wasn't exactly "all better", but she was certainly not on the brink of death, as she had seemed to be before.

"And she didn't have any problem with you coming with us?" Legend pressed further, looking troubled.

"No. Well, we had kind of a falling out. Hey—should I buy a train ticket? What about my horses?"

Heavy Beecher replied before Legend could say anything. "Naw, since you're here, we was thinkin' maybe we all could go a-horseback. I mean why not, right? Horses are sellin' perty cheap right now, what I hear."

High's own disappointment surprised him, since normally he was more than happy to be riding. This time, he had actually been looking forward to putting Wilder and Honcho in a box car, then taking a much more leisurely means of getting far away from Rupert—and Flo—as fast as he could.

"Alright," High agreed. After all, what else could he do?

"Let's go along and find a stable," Beecher said. "See what kind of deal we could get on some horses."

Roy Legend wasn't finished with High, however. "So kid, what do you mean you and your missus had a falling out? You didn't split the sheets!"

"No, I ..."

"Come on, let 'im be," interjected Heavy. "That ain't none of our business what he does. He wants to travel the world—lay off 'im and let 'im do what makes 'im happy."

Legend's face soured even more as he looked at his partner. "Shut up for a bit, would you? I'm talking to the kid."

"Don't you tell me to shut up. You don't run me."

Legend stared at Heavy, finally turning to spit his anger out at the road. "Why don't you crawl down off that horse, High?" he asked after a few more seconds, turning his attention away from Heavy like a palpable slap in the face. "Hey, listen, I just don't know how comfortable I feel about your wife."

High suddenly knew he had to come clean. For one thing, if these men were going to be his traveling companions, they should know they could trust each other. It wasn't good to start out on a pack of lies.

"Mr. Legend, I have to tell you somethin'."

"Come on, High—it's Roy. Alright? Now what do you have to tell me that's so important?"

The stream of life in Rupert was flowing around High and his three companions now, with people stopping now and then to stare in awe at the stallion. Some of them smiled at High, and he knew they must have seen one of his performances.

High took a deep breath and held Legend's gaze. "What I told you the other day wasn't exactly the truth. Flo an' me were never actually married, like I told you. An' the baby ain't even mine. It's my brother's, an' he got killed in a car accident."

Legend stared at High. "You aren't married? I don't get it. What were you doing with the girl then?"

"I told her I'd take her with me. You know, so she wouldn't have to face up to all the folks around that'd look down their noses at her."

"There you go!" Heavy cut in, crowing in his triumph. "Now it don't matter one bit, Roy. Jeez, let's go get some horses. What are we standin' around here jawin' for?"

Grimacing, Roy Legend looked around. He glanced at his companions, then at High. "Kid ..."

"Damn! Leave 'im the hell alone, Roy!" Browsy Prentiss spoke for the first time. "Let's go, already! If he wants to go travel the world and show off his horse, what's it to you anyway? What's gettin' into you?"

"I don't like it," Legend said. "The kid said he'd take care of the girl, so ..." He turned suddenly on High again, who was standing on the street with them and holding Wilder's reins, with Honcho standing dutifully behind. "I don't think you should go with us, kid. No offense, but I think we'll travel better alone."

The statement was like a kick in the guts to High. He looked helplessly over at Heavy, wanting to plead with him because suddenly the bigger man seemed to be the one on his side.

"You go on and get on the train then," Heavy growled at Legend. "Hell, you can see the kid wants to come with us. Maybe it's time we go our separate ways."

Legend stared Heavy down. He switched his gaze to Browsy Prentiss. At last, his eyes returned to High, whom he studied at length. Finally, he looked again at Heavy. "Is that the way you want it then? After all we've been through?"

"I guess it's the way *you* want it. It's the way it's gotta be, if you won't quit ridin' the poor kid."

Legend at last heaved out a big breath. "Fine then. Go on. Go on and to hell with the both of you." He looked at High. "I think you're making a bad choice, kid, that's all I can tell you. I think there's something you aren't telling us, something about that girl. I think you're going to regret riding off, but you do what you want. I'm done with the bunch of you."

Having said that, Legend turned and stalked back toward the train station platform and the ticket office.

Shocked, High finally stopped watching Roy Legend walk away only when he heard Browsy Prentiss's voice. "Come on, kid. Forget about him. We don't need 'im. Come on with us. We'll be the Three Musketeers."

"Yeah, kid, come on to the stable," said Heavy. "Come show us how to go about pickin' a good horse."

CHAPTER TWENTY-SIX

DOWN THE SAME STREET, there was a livery stable. Over the tall, wide door, where deep shadow lay behind, it said simply CONYERS STABLE. "Let's try this one," Beecher said. "Good as any place, right?"

High agreed, tying Wilder and Honcho off one corner of the building by huge iron rings set in the wall. He always felt nervous tying the stallion anywhere, but whenever he did, he tied him up very short, in hopes that if any adult male who didn't know the signs of an unhappy horse tried to touch him around the face, Wilder wouldn't have enough rope to move fast and far enough to take the man's hand off.

High was starting to feel an uncomfortable sensation creep up from his innards into his chest as they went inside the dark stable, and a tall but slightly stooped man with a stocky upper body but toothpicks for legs, a man whose appearance spoke of shoulders once broad, now narrow and thin, with a small, bristly mustache and weary, wrinkle-shrouded eyes that had seen too much in his life, limped to them. "Kay Conyers," he said. "How can I help you gentlemen?" He directed most of his attention to Heavy Beecher, which most people probably would now that the more charismatic Roy Legend was no longer around. That was a thought that for some reason wrenched at High's heart. He really liked Legend, and it was only beginning to hit home that he wasn't going to get to travel with him now, and try to learn all the things Legend must know about staying alive and well on the road.

"Me and my partner here wanna buy a couple horses. Horses that'd be good for long spells ridin' on the road," Heavy said.

"I have a few," Conyers replied. "Wanna follow me out back?"

Heavy, Browsy and High followed the older man, walking slowly because any fast walk would have put them past him and his uncertain, shuffling pace in seconds. In a corral out back, Conyers waved his hand over a smattering of horses, mostly browns and reds, with one piebald and a strawberry roan thrown in.

"What's your preference?"

"They have to be geldings," said High. "I'm traveling with a stallion."

"Gutsy of you, son," said Conyers. "Too bad, though. Nicest horse on the place is my black mare. But alright. These are mostly geldings. 'Cept those two sorrels right there, and the dark bay. And if you want to make your life easier and sell that stud, I'll look him over, maybe even give you two geldings, if he's stout and well-bred."

High instantly shook his head. "He'd be worth at least a thousand, but I wouldn't sell him."

The liveryman got a sly little smile under his mustache. "Thousand, huh?" He had obviously heard such things before. Then he paused, looking at High closer. "Say! Are you the kid who puts on that show with the big pinto stud?"

High grinned. "Yes, sir. That's me."

"Then my doubts are quieted. Your horse might be worth a thousand at that—and be a darn fine match for my black mare, too."

High could only keep on grinning and thank him. Every time he heard anything like this praise, it was a promise that his future traveling the world, whether with Roy Legend, Heavy and Browsy, or with a man like Jim Martin, was going to be a rich and fulfilling one.

Conyers cleared his throat. "Well, alright. So you just needed the two, right? A pretty good-size one for you," he said, looking Heavy up and down, then appraising Browsy Prentiss. "For you prob'ly too." His heavy-lidded eyes told a different story, but High guessed a man wouldn't sell many horses by making potential customers feel bad about their stature.

"I like the looks of that bay. The one with the crooked blaze," High said, pointing. "His feet good?"

"Oh, sure. Hard as nails. Same with that sorrel. He's got just the one white sock, but even that foot's pretty hard. Don't take much shooin', not even if you're out on the road a lot, I'd expect."

"Good enough," said Heavy. "Need a couple saddles too, I guess. And you mind if we ride 'em around a while? Get the feel for 'em?"

"Don't mind, not if you have somethin' for security. Like the kid's stallion or the like."

"Sure," Heavy replied without even looking at High. "Sure, he don't mind."

High did mind, but what was he going to say? He didn't expect any man to buy a horse he didn't even know would suit him. High left Honcho tied outside and brought Wilder in, putting him in a high-boarded stall. While he was doing that, Heavy and Browsy picked out two saddles from a dingy tack room where sunlight filtered through cracks in the wall and dust danced on its beams. They came back out and saddled the horses Conyers had pointed out. They started them out riding in the corral for a while, pushing through the other horses, who curiously looked on and only reluctantly stepped out of the way when the riders wanted past.

Next, they rode up and down the aisle between stalls, and then took them outside. High followed them out into the sunlight, watching them and finding himself unimpressed by the stiff, uneasy way Heavy bounced around on his saddle. Browsy, meanwhile, had evidently spent more time around horses, for he rode with some poise.

The two riders were coming back up the street, with High waiting in the stable doorway, when a sorrel horse appeared down the street, jogging their way. High stared at it for a moment, at first feeling confused as he tried to focus in on the rider, quite obviously a female. In a flash, his confusion vanished. His heart leaped. This couldn't be, but it was! It was Flo, riding Bragger!

High was hardly conscious of Heavy's and Browsy's horses getting too close until he felt as much as heard Heavy's horse snort, and mucus sprinkled his face. He lurched backward out of the doorway, almost running right into the open barn door, which was hooked by a chain to the outer wall, to keep it open.

"High!" Flo's weak-sounding voice sounded along the street.

High stared her down, stepping toward her, still confused. What had she done? Why had she left her room when there was no way she could even be close to a full recovery? She appeared ready to drop dead over the side of Bragger, whom he saw was streaming with foamy sweat around his chest and neck. That horse had been ridden way too hard, especially by a girl as sick as Flo. She had no business even being in the saddle at all!

"Flo! What in the name of— What are you doing?"

"I'm sorry." She looked about ready to burst into tears. "I had to come after you! I had to find you."

He hurried over to the side of her horse, almost expecting her to fall out of the saddle into his arms. "You shouldn't have come! Look at you!"

Flo stared down at him, then without warning tried to slip over the horse's side. As High had expected, and prepared for, she nearly collapsed into his arms. She turned almost drunkenly toward him, her face terribly flushed and hair plastered to her forehead and cheeks with sweat. He grabbed her arm, trying to steady her. "Flo," he repeated. "Why are you here? What on God's green earth are you thinkin'? You're gonna kill yourself!"

Flo looked dazed, startled, and most of all ill—very ill. "High, please don't leave me. I can't bear the thought of letting you go."

High felt his face redden, hoping Heavy and Browsy were nowhere close enough to hear this. Then, from the shifting of Flo's eyes, he knew they were. They were coming up behind his left shoulder, and now he heard their footsteps.

"Who're you?" High heard Heavy's voice.

"This is Flo," High said. He didn't think to introduce Heavy and Browsy, even when he turned and saw them glaring at her.

"Your wife?" asked Heavy. "Or whatever."

The heat around High's collar grew warmer. "Yeah. My wife. Flo! Come into the shade with me," High encouraged her. "Come on. Don't stay out in this hot sun."

"What the hell you doin' here, girl?" Heavy cut in. "You're wastin' your time—and ours. The kid's comin' with us. He already decided he wants to travel the world an' get rich."

High ignored Heavy's harsh-sounding voice, so Flo was forced to as well when he turned, steadying her and walking with her toward the barn doors. High didn't even bother with Bragger. He could leave and wander off down the street as far as High was concerned, although most likely he would simply go over by Honcho. The important thing was Flo; she was about to collapse in a pile on the ground, and anyone could see it.

He took her into the shade of the stable, and Conyers came limping up from the back. "Hey! Everything alright?" High could sense the genuine concern in the older man's voice, and see it in his face.

"My ... friend is sick," he said, instantly hating himself for choosing that word, although the hurt in Flo's face didn't even register on him for a second or two more.

"She sure is! This girl needs a doctor."

"She can get her own doctor!" Heavy growled. "Kid! Don't do this! Don't let her ruin all your dreams right when you're almost on your way! You told us what she is!"

High looked sharply over at Heavy as the man's words registered on him. *"What?"*

The change that came over Heavy's face didn't really mean he was sorry for what he had said. It only meant he was scrambling to salve it over because he didn't want to push High away. "I mean ... Well ... Oh, sorry. But ... you said you wanted to travel the world, right? Said you wanted to make some money?"

"I did. I do!" High said. "But she's sick. I can't just leave her like this."

Heavy tried to strengthen the phony look of concern on his face. "We should get her to a doctor then, huh? They'll be able to take care of her. You and me, kid—and Browsy—we gotta go, right? The three of us, remember? The Three Musketeers?"

High nodded, feeling suddenly unsure of so much, so many things he had thought he wanted more than anything. "Yeah, sure. As soon as we get her to the doctor."

Flo lunged off the chair they had settled her onto. At least it was as much of a lunge as she could perform in her present condition, having worn herself to nothing riding Bragger to town as fast as she must have to catch High.

"High, please!" The expression on her face was one of desperation. "I'm sorry for everything I said. And did. I'm sorry! I'll beg you if I have to. Please don't leave me."

"I won't," High said. "I won't leave you." He reached out gently, taking both her upper arms. "Come on, sit back down. Sit and somebody will go get the doctor."

"I'll go," old Conyers said. "Won't take me five minutes to be back. Just get her some water from the pump out back, and I'll be back right quick." With that, Conyers started down the street. As High watched him go, he wondered how smart it was letting him be the one to go for help, since the old man himself also seemed to be on his last legs.

Heavy and Browsy had crowded up shoulder to shoulder now. High could hear the bigger man whispering something to his partner.

High rested his hand on Flo's shoulder. "I'll get you some water. Just rest, alright? Stay right there."

"I'll get the water, kid," said Browsy. High noticed a strange alteration to the tone of his voice. It was almost strained, as if something was pinching off his air. With one last, almost frightened look at Heavy Beecher, Browsy started down the aisle for the back of the stable. High didn't notice when he stopped partway along. He didn't notice even when he heard Wilder starting to fuss in his stall.

A couple minutes later, however, wondering where Browsy was with the water, High looked up in time to notice Wilder's stall coming open. The horse was walking out of it, apparently almost willingly, with Browsy leading him. Behind the cantle of the saddle were his saddlebags and traveling bag, which contained both his revolver and all his money except for five or ten dollars he carried in his pants.

Standing up straighter, it took High a moment to recognize that there was a twitch cinched tight around Wilder's ear, a small length of chain that Browsy was using in a very cruel way to control the stallion and make him meekly come along. That explained how Browsy had Wilder on his way, when he never could have otherwise! Just when everything began to register on High, he heard a click. He looked over at Heavy Beecher. The rangy big man had a sneer on his face. He was looking over a snub-nose revolver at High.

"You hold right still, kid. So still I can shoot a fly off your nose. You ain't gonna ruin this for us. We're all goin' to Europe together, remember? An' we're leavin' *now*."

High felt his guts grow tighter. He glanced down at Flo, then back at Heavy. He heard Browsy coming up with Wilder, who was breathing heavier than normal, and obviously in significant pain. He clenched his teeth.

"I changed my mind. I ain't goin' to Europe. Not anymore. I'm stayin' here. With Flo."

Heavy bunched his jaw muscles. He spat hard to one side, wiping his free hand across his sneer. "Fine. Stay then. But every dime you got is goin' with us. We need a stake."

"How do you think you'll get away with that?" asked High. "There's people all over outside."

"Easy. We're takin' you with us. An' the girl, too. When we're a long ways from this town, we'll let you go, an' then we'll keep your horse."

"No! You can't have the horse!"

"You'll get 'im back. And he'll be alive, even—that is, if you play your cards right. But you send anybody after us, I'll put a bullet in his head just as sure as your name is Ugly Bug."

High's heart was racing. Heavy's pistol, to judge by its bore, couldn't have been much more than a .32, but at this range, if the bullet was placed right, that was plenty to kill him … or Flo … or even Wilder, if a shot went astray.

"Drop that damn gun!"

High heard the voice behind him. Involuntarily he whirled to see Roy Legend standing there! The man's hands were empty, which made his words sound ludicrous, but the threatening look on his face said he didn't care. "Heavy, you son of a bitch. I told you we're not doing this. Look at this girl! She's sick as anybody could be! Don't you have a heart anywhere in that chest?"

"Sure I do. A heart beggin' to quit bein' poor. To quit starvin' on the road, an' beggin' scraps. An' a heart to stop listenin' to your mouth. *We're* not doin' anything, by the way. You ain't with me and Browsy anymore. Get in here, or I'll shoot you in the face right where you stand."

High was staring at Roy Legend, still trying to comprehend how everything had changed, and so fast. Legend's glance flitted over to High, then away. "You can't do this, Heavy. That shot'd be heard all up and down the street. Put the gun away. Don't make it all worse. You don't want to go to jail."

"What do I have to lose?" Heavy said. High could almost hear his sneer right through his voice, even with his back to him. "I go to jail, at least I get three squares a day."

High heard a sudden scraping noise behind him, and then an explosion, which was magnified in the close quarters of the barn. He saw Legend rush forward, even as he himself whirled toward the sound of the shot. As he turned, he saw Heavy Beecher viciously strike Flo across the side of the face with the side of his gun. The blow drove her toward the earth. High could only think Flo must have jumped up and tried to grab Heavy's gun!

Before High could react, Heavy's gun came up again. He leveled it and fired as Legend blurred past.

Legend clutched at his arm. Heavy's gun exploded again. This time Legend dropped to one knee, crying out in pain. High started forward, but the gun barrel erupted upward, driven by Heavy's fist. It struck High under the chin with all the furious force the man must possess.

The gun must have hit just right. High's world flashed to a brilliant white, and then to black. He felt a tremendous impact against his back. He heard a commotion down the aisle, then a scream from Wilder. He heard the stallion's hooves pounding against the hard-packed soil of the barn. He heard Browsy Prentiss growling frantically, still trying to control the horse with the cruel chain twitch.

High peeled his eyes open. He found himself on his back, staring at the ceiling of the barn. Everything was turning in a slow circle. Browsy's frightened voice registered on him. "I can't hold this thing, Heavy. Shoot it! *Shoot it!* For the love of—"

The gun cracked again. Wilder let out a ferocious cry. Browsy groaned in pain. High thought he could hear the man running, but every sound now whirled in a cloud of confusion. High struggled to find his equilibrium. He tried to push to his feet. He heard a roaring voice. It took him a few seconds to realize it was his! He was reaching for Heavy Beecher's arm when the man turned again. High saw a flash. He heard another sharp crack. Something kicked him hard in the side.

A sickening pain swept over him. He dropped to his knees. He looked down for a moment, trying to fathom the cause of his pain. A dark red spot was swiftly forming on his side. Confused, he looked up. He saw Flo getting up off the ground as he grimaced and clutched his side, trying somehow to contain the pain.

Heavy Beecher pointed his gun at High's face and pulled the trigger. His gun clicked on an empty chamber! Throwing it down with a snarl, he reached to the side, clutching a broken tool handle that leaned up against an empty stall. Turning, he rushed High. He raised his club above his head, towering over him. He obviously meant to brain him!

Flo let out a scream. From the corner of his eye High saw Wilder make a rush for Heavy Beecher, teeth flashing. Beecher instinctively whirled. He struck out at the horse. He managed to give him a crippling blow on the bridge of the nose, but the effort broke his tool handle club into two pieces.

Wilder shook his head, trying to chase away his pain. He reared again and pawed the air. He belted out a wild cry the likes of which had probably sent many a rival stallion fleeing during Wilder's feral life on the range. The ferocious horse came at Heavy with hateful vengeance in his eyes. He stretched out with his clashing teeth. Heavy, his eyes filled with terror, thrust forward with what was left of his wooden club, which now had formed itself into a spear. At the same time, Wilder brought his face down, aiming his teeth for Heavy's chest and neck. The end of the now sharpened stick drove in hard. Far back in High's consciousness, as he knelt there knowing he was dying. He heard a ripping noise and saw the stick tear deep into Wilder's skull. It must have sunk clear to his ears!

The wound didn't stop the horse. His ferocity was too great. His momentum alone carried him forward, his head tilted over to one side. His teeth closed over Heavy's face with a snapping noise, and he bore down and ripped to the side. When the horse jerked back, with a grisly trophy between his teeth, High didn't want to see Heavy Beecher's face, or what was left of it. But he couldn't look away. He kept staring until a surge of energy temporarily made him forget the bullet Heavy Beecher had sunk deep in his side.

High, helpless on his knees, with a searing pain marching throughout his body as he felt his lifeblood trickling out of him, watched Flo. Her face now ashen, she staggered toward Wilder, soothing him, reaching for his trailing lead rope. The stallion screamed and made three half-hearted attempts to rear up. Blood was rushing down his face almost in waves, dripping down over his nostrils and lips, then to the ground. It also trailed down from a hole in his neck. The horse began to stagger as Flo's soothing words seemed finally to reach his ears. Those big, attentive ears came forward, now having to take the place of his vision, which was flooded with an unreal amount of bright red blood.

Flo reached upward as High watched, unable to move or speak. He saw her hand rest on the huge, round flat of the stallion's cheek just as the horse went down to one knee.

High stared mesmerized at Flo and the horse until his vision began to go black. He struggled to speak. There came no resulting sound. As everything faded, he could see the girl turning toward him, the stallion's lead rope tight in her hand. The great, beautiful horse had sunk to both knees now, his life's blood flowing down his face and neck.

Wilder was going. High's beautiful, wonderful stallion, the stallion who loved but one man. And that man he loved was going too. Poetically, they would go home together.

And High's whole world faded into black.

CHAPTER TWENTY-SEVEN

THE FEVER CAME AND went. Perhaps for days. It felt like weeks. But in reality, for how aware High Warning was, it might have been hours.

He had no concept of time. No grasp on reality. Sometimes the fever burned in his head and in his side so hot it felt as if he would burst into flames. More than once, he dreamed he was no longer High Warning. He was Flo Starbuck! His bizarre, twisted dreams even went so far that he thought once he saw his own self, High Warning, leaning over him, stretching his hands down to touch his face. But that High seemed to be getting pulled farther and farther up and away, toward the ceiling. His arms, no matter how long they stretched away from his body, never seemed to reach quite far enough for his fingertips to make contact. *Reach me!* he thought. *Try a little harder! Pull me up, High Warning, or I'll never make it back from this dark, hot place!*

In time his sensation of being Flo would vanish—simply fizzle away—but he still would not be High Warning. He would be nothing but fire. Or he might be sizzling beds of coals. It never seemed like he was a man. Perhaps it was because he had observed her in a fevered state for so long that he so often dreamed he was Flo, being consumed by fire, or he was some form of fire itself.

He was moving, marching up and down barren, rounded hills, hills that seemed without any vegetation except that sometimes one of them would have a tree growing out its top. It was always a heavy, straight-trunked black tree with a million intertwined branches reaching out in the shape of an umbrella. Not a leaf upon it.

The fires in him grew hotter. He began to see armies of capsule-shaped soldiers, some of them white, some black, but all of them shaped like stubby cucumbers. There were thousands of them. Tens of thousands. The white ones marched together, and the black ones in groups of their own. They met on the high-humped, camel-back hills and clashed in mighty but deathly silent battles, battles he could never witness the endings of, for he would fade into oblivion before the end.

Rain fell. On his face. His cheeks. His neck, his chest. Cooling rain, gentle rain. Days, or maybe weeks, wandering into the hot, fire-blackened hills, he began to smell strange, fleeting hints of aromas he remembered. Cinnamon … cloves … peppermint. Strange perfumes, scents that called back faded, but somehow comforting memories. Horses. Cattle. The tailpipe fumes out of his father's automobile.

The fire came, and his subconscious began to understand that when it did, the rain came sometime after, washing over him. Once, he thought he heard the odd singing of a bird. Not a songbird. More the sound of a dove. It cooed softly: *High! High! High … High … High. High.* Long later, the dove—it seemed always to be the same one—began to make other noises, noises he could never comprehend, no matter how hard he strove to.

He rolled one way, then the other. Cool rushes of wind swept around him. Then soon there would be something that pressed

him down. Down, down, into utter softness that even in its softness felt like it was going to drive all the way through his back.

Finally, wandering the blackened, empty hills, he saw three
armies coming together. One of them was the darker kind, which
looked like black beans. The other two armies were more numer-
ous. There were the white ones, and then a vast army of stubby
gray ones marched in to join them. They came down the valley
on either side of the black bean army.

The three groups met in a mighty battle, an engagement that
made all the others seem small. High tossed and rolled around
and could hear the dove crying frantically. Yet it wouldn't try to
fly away. The heat around him grew unbearable. The gentle rains
came down and splashed his face, although the coolness evapo-
rated instantly in the torrid heat. The dove left off crying its dove
sounds and began to coo in muddled gibberish.

All of a sudden, like a flash of light, the white, navy bean-
looking armies and the stubby gray army rose and stood still.
High saw that not only had the black army been all vanquished
and were strewn everywhere, but now they were melting away--
vanishing. They seemed to be turning into fog, then burning off.

The terrible heat slowly lifted. Even though the sun came out
over the barren hills, the soft rains came again. Green grass and
yellow and white and blue flowers began to spring up all over the
rolling hills. Soft, velvet green leaves began to burst forth on the
trees.

The dove cooed again, now with the sound of a real dove.
Songbirds joined in, and a cool breeze came over his face, along
with the welcome rains.

The gibberish he had been thinking came from the dove began
again. But it wasn't the dove. It was closer. It was almost upon
him. And then he heard a voice say, "High? High, are you waking
up? Come back to me."

He knew he had to look. He had to see who spoke with this voice, a voice he strangely longed for. He tried so hard to open his eyes, but they wouldn't obey him. He struggled, trying to reach upward with one hand.

Then blackness folded over him, and there were no more dreams of strange soldiers or barren hills, or even soft doves crying with forlorn voices.

The world now was silent. But it was bathed by a gentle light, and everything felt softly warm. A fragrance swirled about him, something he was intimately familiar with and yet couldn't place.

He tried his eyes. They merely fluttered. The strain was too much, so he rested.

What seemed like long minutes later, he tried to open his eyes again. Slowly his eyelids struggled upward, and whiteness like a freshly laundered sheet met his weak and weary gaze. He let his eyes drift closed, like two autumn leaves floating together to earth, partners on a tree, and partners to the end.

He let breaths of cool air seep on their own into his nostrils. The odor, a sweet, compelling odor, flooded through him. Hay! Freshly cut hay … He sighed out a long breath. An involuntary smile bent his lips. He opened his eyes, this time to a face. He stared at it. It wore a smile like his.

Savoia …

"High? Are you really awake?"

Her voice was soft. For a moment, he thought it could be the sound of the dove he had been listening to, but it wasn't quite the same.

He nodded when he realized he was far too exhausted to speak.

Savoia Brambilla's smile widened. "We all thought we had lost you," she cooed. "Like I have seen others slip away before. You are quite a fighter, High Warning. I must say."

He smiled. He wasn't sure what he meant to do with it, but he raised a hand toward her. She reached down and took his fingers.

High tried to open his lips to speak, but no sound came. His throat felt caked with dust.

"Oh! You wait, High. Do you want water? Rest. I'll be right back."

Then she was gone from the room, silently, and he stared at the white ceiling.

The first dark wave came over him as he lay there alone—a wave of heart-broken emotion. Wilder Heart! Wilder, his dearest, most loyal friend, was gone. He had seen him going, and in his heart he had known there was no way to stop it.

But what about Flo? What about that helpless girl who had ridden herself near to death to stop him from leaving? The girl he knew had tried to stop Heavy Beecher's attack and who in turn had taken a blow from his gun to the side of her face? Where was Flo? Had she lived through that day? Had she at last decided he wasn't worth her trouble? Had she left and returned to her family? He had never spent much time or money on betting games, but if he were betting now, he would bet she was gone. He could hardly blame her. He had treated her like dirt, when he knew now how deeply she had loved him.

Savoia came back with a glass of water. She helped him struggle to sit up against the head of the bed. She held the glass to his lips, letting the water find its way into his mouth. It felt like the most miraculous thing in the universe.

The woman turned and sat on the bed beside him, then smiled. "Do you mind?"

He shook his head, feeling himself go dizzy, but feeling so much better than he had in ... he was afraid to guess how long. "Of course not," he said, and when Savoia heard his voice, tears came to swim in her eyes. Shaking her head, in embarrassment, it seemed, she got up and hurried from the room.

High was left once more sitting there alone. In spite of the cool air, and the salving feel of the water in his throat, and the beautiful scent of the fresh-cut hay, he tasted bitterness.

He had had a lot of blessings in his life. Even since coming out on the road, he had met so many kind and generous people, the Brambilla family being of course the best of them.

But he had lost his horse. His pal. His amigo.

And he had lost Flo, the girl he had thought meant nothing to him, and who to his astonishment suddenly meant everything.

He had to go home. He had to run after her, the way she had run after him. He had to see if she had lost the baby. He had to tell her it was alright—they still had each other! He had to beg her ...

He froze. What was he thinking? All he had ever dreamed of was to be free, to travel the world, to see the elephant that his dad had talked so much of in his childhood.

Now he wanted only one thing, and his stubborn, stupid self-ishness had driven her away.

Savoia came back in, her eyes pink and puffy. "I'm so sorry, High. I think a lot of emotion just came over me, too much to handle. We all ... Well." She paused and clasped her hands to-gether down in front of her, giving a huge shrug. "I can't lie. We all prayed so hard that you would live, but after a while I'm ashamed to say all our faith started to fade. Except for hers."

High stared at the woman, not knowing what to say, but she must have read the question in his eyes.

"Florence. Oh, High. She was so sick, and so hurt by that man, and by that foolish ride she made to stop you from leaving."

Chills began at the back of High's skull. In seconds they cov-ered his entire body. He stared up at Savoia until his throat began to feel as if it were closing over with emotion. Flo ... *Flo!* Savoia was going to tell him Flo Starbuck had died!

It wasn't enough to lose Wilder, but Flo too?

"Savoia ..." He started to speak, but emotion clutched his throat harder and closed it over. All he could do was stare at her. He managed finally to choke out, "Flo ... Oh no."

Savoia smiled gently. "You should have seen her, High. She was in so much pain, but she was the strongest out of us all. She prayed harder than anyone. She wouldn't leave your side. She stayed in bed with you for so long, until the doctor finally convinced her she had to leave you alone to toss and turn, or her exhaustion would kill her too."

High knitted his brow. He could feel his heart pounding so hard, and his stomach felt so sick he wondered if he would throw up.

"But she ... Savoia ... Did she ..." He couldn't even voice the question.

"She hasn't left you, cara. She has been here all along." Saying that, Savoia walked around the bed, stepping carefully around something on the floor on the other side of the bed from High. The woman reached a hand across the bed, and High took it.

Savoia helped High scoot to the left, and as he did so it was the first time he was conscious of an aching pain sort of like a digging sensation in his left side, where Heavy Beecher's bullet had gone in. Then, on the instant that he leaned far over and saw her lying on the floor beside the bed, the pain fled from his consciousness!

Her face was pink skinned. Angelic. Her ruffled golden hair was a wonderful, tangled, beautiful mess. He couldn't swear to it, but it seemed like there was a little smile on her lips. The only thing that might have marred her appearance was the remains of a large, fading bruise that marked the place on the side of her face where Heavy Beecher had hit her with his gun. But that was a blow she had received trying to defend the man she loved. For that reason, this bruise had its own type of beauty.

High struggled to fight tears that dimmed his vision. He feared he might cry, exactly what his dad and every other man of his life had told him a grown man would never do. A sense of mercy seemed to come over Savoia. "I'll leave you alone, High. But I am so happy you are back."

She fled the room to leave him whatever tiny bit of pride he could salvage. He lay on his fire-rimmed, wounded side and stared down at the girl he was stunned to realize he loved more than anything in the world. Her left hand was out of the blankets that covered her, and on her third finger glittered the ring that Gino Brambilla had helped him pick out special for her.

High rolled over gingerly and struggled off the far side of the bed from Flo. Holding himself up by hanging onto the brass rail of the bed's foot, he worked his way around, and beside Flo he fell to his knees. He reached out with trembling hands, taking her left hand and starting to work the ring off it.

Like two moths, fluttering with the last of their energy to settle into a resting place at the break of day, the girl's blue eyes opened, but she didn't gasp or even act surprised. She simply looked up at him. Her eyes came to focus. A rueful smile came to her lips. She glanced down where his hands had frozen in motion, then back up to his face.

"Hi, High." Her voice was soft. They both giggled at the sound of her words, which had become somewhat of a joke between them. She looked down at the ring again. His hands still held it, along with her hand. "I was being silly, huh? I just didn't want to let go of it yet. You can take it off though."

He swiped quickly at his eyes, wishing her first glimpse of him upon waking could have been the sight of a man, not a blubbering baby.

He cleared his throat. "I wasn't meanin' to keep it. But ..."

Their eyes held for a long time. He finally realized she was waiting for him to finish, and it hit him that neither of them was breathing.

"Flo, I want to put it on your finger myself," he finally managed to say. "Not for you to do it yourself."

Her lip began to tremble. She managed to speak. "High?"

"Yeah?"

He could see she was struggling.

"Are you ... Are you really sure that's what you want?"

He nodded. "I'm sorry how I've treated you. But I ..."

"What, High? What?"

"I didn't mean to do it, and I hope I don't seem like I'm disrespecting Seth. But I think I might've fell in love with you."

Emotion flooded her face, and she started weeping openly. She came up out of her blankets to throw her arms around his neck, trying to squeeze the life right out of him.

"I think Seth would be happy, High," she said in a throaty whisper, past her tears. "I think he would feel honored. And he would be happy to know I fell in love with you too. But I have to confess something to you. Something I've kept to myself way too long. I've always, always loved you, High Warning. I always loved you even after you tied me to that stinky goat. Only ... I never dared to dream a boy like you could ever love someone like me."

CHAPTER TWENTY-EIGHT

HIGH AND FLO COULD not leave yet. Both were smart enough this time to know it. Even to travel on the train, both of them were still too weak, and if they had tried to leave, the Brambillas would have stopped them anyway.

But one thing they *were* strong enough for was a celebratory feast, a gathering of the entire Brambilla clan, along with a friend or two the Brambillas had taken the liberty of inviting.

That evening, a few hours before dark, the beautiful, newly washed and polished cars of the area's local Italian population began to arrive. There was the elegant maroon Buick of the Salvatore Gucci family, the black Ford Phaeton of the Antonio Brambillas, and the blood red 1929 Chrysler Imperial Roadster Luca and Angelina Brambilla had managed to pay cash for only three months prior to the big crash.

All the families' children milled around, excited to be together, while Luca and Angelina came to greet High and Flo, embracing them with huge smiles.

There was one man High never would have expected, a man High would spend much of the evening visiting with. That was Roy Legend, who, like High, was struggling to recover from bullet wounds, one between his left shoulder and his chest, the other in his lower left leg. It was Gino Brambilla who drove into town to bring Legend out to see High. Legend had been asking about him ever since his own regaining of consciousness, which happened two days faster than High's.

"I'd still love to show you the world, if I could," Legend told High when they had a moment of peace alone while Angelina was over doting on Flo and complimenting her on how she looked in the beautiful dress she had brought for her to wear. "Problem is, all I could ever think of was how me and my wife split the sheets before we gave ourselves a chance to make things work, and I just couldn't live with myself if I did the same to you."

"Thanks, Roy. That means a lot. And I'm glad I get a chance to say thanks for comin' that day. I don't know how things would've ended if you didn't."

"You're a good man, High. This damn crash has ruined a lot of us—a lot of good men. I couldn't let it be the ruin of you too. I knew from the start what Heavy wanted to do and got Browsy to go along with. I'm just sorry I didn't stop it before it went so far."

"You risked your life for me," High said. "I won't ever forget it."

It was later in the evening, almost at dark, and High was sitting across a little table from Flo, a table the family had carried out on the front lawn. He was watching his fiancée—his *fiancée,* a thought that still stunned him, yet filled him with happiness— as she sat gaily conversing with Angelina Brambilla. High couldn't help thinking that Angelina Brambilla was still a world class beauty, but Florence Starbuck had somehow become even *more* beautiful … and she was his.

Flo, seeming to feel High's gaze on her, turned her lively, sparkling eyes on him. Then so did Angelina. High couldn't take his eyes off Flo. He couldn't believe how full of light her wonderful, expressive blue eyes had become. How her skin seemed to glow. There was a dark, sad thought deep inside him, but it was a thought he had to keep there until he felt both of them were ready to speak of it. He didn't know yet if Flo still carried Seth's baby, and not knowing that made him ache. But he would have to live with not knowing until the time was right. Perhaps, if she had lost it, there would never be a right time to speak of it. Perhaps it would be one of those things they each took to the grave.

Suddenly, seemingly on a whim, Flo leaned across the table toward him, stretching out both her arms. He took her hands, shocked at himself that it didn't embarrass him to know Angelina was watching. It wasn't long ago that having anyone see him hold Flo's hands would have mortified him.

"High," Flo said, "how do you feel?"

He smiled. "I feel good. Are you alright?"

"I feel wonderful. And I can hardly wait to ride again."

High couldn't help laughing. "After your last ride, I think you should wait a while. That one should last until ..." He froze. He had almost slipped.

"Until the baby comes?" she said, her eyes holding his.

He couldn't speak. He could only stare at her. His emotions tried to take hold of him. At last, he nodded. He didn't look around, but suddenly it felt like many eyes were on him.

"The baby's fine, High," she said softly. "Dr. Akins came and checked me, and he said he thinks everything is still fine."

A big part of High wished Flo would have waited to tell him that until they were alone. The horrible thoughts of her losing that baby had been digging into his soul all day. Now his emotions wanted to let go, but this was one place he never could.

Again, he tried to speak, but an invisible hand had hold of his throat. He nodded, fighting a smile. To be doing some-thing—*anything*—he sipped at the glass of wine Savoia had brought to him, trying to feign a casual look.

Without any warning, a group of people High didn't know started to gather behind Flo, at the direction of Mayor Gino Bram-billa. All of them held some type of musical instrument. On Gino's signal, the group began playing their instruments, and Angelina and Salvatore's wife jumped up and began to sing. It must have been in Italian, for High didn't understand a word of it. Although it was beautiful, their voices, and the musical instruments, seemed unnecessarily loud.

Then the music began to grow quieter, along with the voices of Angelina and Mrs. Gucci. It took a few more seconds for High to realize everyone seemed to be staring at him.

Flo had never let go of High's hands. Now she squeezed them harder. "I think there is someone who would like to give you a hug."

With that, she let go of his hands and stood away from the table. Puzzled, he watched her walk around to him, and right there, in front of everyone, she gave him the warmest embrace he had felt in so long he couldn't remember the last one.

"There's more where that came from," she whispered in his ear as everyone around them began to clap and cheer.

Blushing, but unable to stop grinning from ear to ear, High let out a laugh. "Well, that will be good."

Flo reached down to take his hand. "And there's something else that's good too." She stepped around, gently turning him to face the opposite way.

High stared at the sight in the yard before him. When the realization finally hit him, his knees nearly buckled.

With a huge bandage bound up between his ears, there before High stood a beautiful sight he had never imagined he would see again, and a beautiful spirit he hadn't even dared ask about, because he was so certain he didn't want to hear the answer he was sure he already knew.

There, with the hand of tired old Kay Conyers on his neck, resting gently in a way High had never seen him allow any grown man before, stood the sleek, beautiful paint stallion, Wilder Heart.

"I brought a friend out to see you," Conyers said with a little smile, his warm eyes shining at High. "He kept tellin' me he missed you."

Trembling all over, feeling like he was going to melt into the ground, High stared at his horse. He couldn't even move forward. It felt like his feet were spiked to the ground. "How did he— His head!" High exclaimed. "I saw the blood! I saw that stick go clear through his brain."

Conyers chuckled. "Well, just along the skull, actually. And he took a bullet in the neck. But you know, you pack enough sugar in an ugly wound like that, and clean it up every day ... Well, son, maybe God still does work miracles, huh?"

Tears invaded High's vision, but not so he couldn't see his horse. On shaky legs, he stepped forward. Wilder's big hooves clopped in the grass as he came to meet him.

There, in front of the entire Brambilla clan, and in front of the beautiful angel who was going to be his wife, High threw his arms around the huge neck of his amigo.

Wilder Heart nickered in happiness at his friend, and with his great big, muscular neck, and his wonderful, intelligent head, the wild mustang stallion that no man could tame hugged him back.

THE END

Look next for *High Warning, Book 3*

About the Author

Kirby Frank Jonas was born in 1965 in Bozeman, Montana. His earliest memories are of living seven miles outside of town in a wide crack in the mountains known as Bear Canyon. At that time it was a remote and lonely place, but a place where a boy with an imagination could grow and nurture his mind, body and soul.

From Montana, the Jonas family moved almost as far across the country as they could go, to Broad Run, Virginia, to a place that, although not as deep in the timbered mountains as Bear Canyon was every bit as remote—Roland Farm. Once again, young Jonas spent his time mostly alone, or with his older brother, if he was not in school. Jonas learned to hike with his mother, fish with his father, and to dodge an unruly horse.

Jonas moved to Shelley, Idaho, in 1971, and from that time forth, with the exception of a few sojourns elsewhere, he became an Idahoan. Jonas attended all twelve years of school in Shelley, graduating in 1983. In the sixth grade, he penned his first novel, *The Tumbleweed,* and in high school he wrote his second, *The Vigilante.* It was also during this time that he first became acquainted with Salmon, Idaho, staying toward the end of the road at the Golden Boulder Orchard and taking his first steps to manhood.

Jonas has lived in six cities in France, in Mesa, Arizona, and explored the United States extensively. He has fought fires for the Bureau of Land Management in five western states and carried a gun on his hip in three different jobs.

In 1987, Jonas met his wife-to-be, Debbie Chatterton, and in 1989 took her to the altar. Over some rough and rocky roads they have traveled, and across some raging rivers that have at times threatened to draw them under, but they survived, and with four beautiful children to show for it: Cheyenne, Jacob, Clay and Matthew.

Jonas has been employed as a Wells Fargo armored guard, a wildland firefighter, a security guard and police officer. He is now retired after almost twenty-four years as a municipal firefighter for the city of Pocatello, Idaho, and works full-time as an armed security officer.

One of Jonas's greatest joys in life is watching his second son, Clay, become a recognized writer in his own chosen field, fantasy and science fiction, with his *Descendants of Light* series, *The Truth About Stars* and *Grim Reaper, Inc.* There is no greater compliment a son could give to his father than to follow in his footsteps.

Books by Kirby Jonas

Season of the Vigilante, Book One: The Bloody Season
Season of the Vigilante, Book Two: Season's End
The Dansing Star
Legend of the Tumbleweed
Lady Winchester
The Devil's Blood
The Devil's Blood, the trilogy (Expanded from the original)
    Season of Doom
    The Bloody Season
    Season's End
The Secret of Two Hawks
Knight of the Ribbons
Drygulch to Destiny
Samuel's Angel
The Night of My Hanging (And Other Short Stories)
Russet
Rusted Fence and Broken Cowboys (poetry)
Lying in Wait to Lie in Rhyme (poetry)
Windfall
Tenn Rhoades to Hell
Jinx: A Novel of the Great Depression
High Warning 1: A Wilder Heart
High Warning 2: The Wilder Legend

***Savage Law* series**
    1. *Law of the Lemhi, part 1*
        Law of the Lemhi, part 2
    2. *River of Death*
    3. *Lockdown for Lockwood*
    4. *Like a Man Without a Country*
    5. *Thunderbird*
    6. *Savage Alliance*
    7. *Dark Badger*
    8. *Morgan Rose*
    9. *Bar None*
    10. *The Old Broken Heart (summer-fall 2025)*

pocatellocowboy@gmail.com

The Badlands series
1. *Yaqui Gold* (co-author Clint Walker)
2. *Canyon of the Haunted Shadows*

Legends West series
1. *Disciples of the Wind* (co-author Jamie Jonas)
2. *Reapers of the Wind* (co-author Jamie Jonas)

Lehi's Dream series
1. *Nephi Was My Friend*
2. *The Faith of a Man*
3. *A Land Called Bountiful*

Gray Eagle series
1. *The Fledgling*
2. *Flight of the Fledgling*
3. *Wings on the Wind*
Death of an Eagle—Final novel in the series

Books on audio

The Dansing Star, narrated by James Drury, *"The Virginian"*
Death of an Eagle, narrated by James Drury
Legend of the Tumbleweed, narrated by James Drury
Lady Winchester, narrated by James Drury
Yaqui Gold, narrated by Gene Engene
The Secret of Two Hawks, narrated by Kevin Foley
Knight of the Ribbons, narrated by Rusty Nelson
Drygulch to Destiny, narrated by Kirby Jonas

Available through the author at www.kirbyfjonas.com

Email the author at: pocatellocowboy@gmail.com or write to:

Howling Wolf Publishing
1611 City Creek Road
Pocatello ID 83204

www.ingramcontent.com/pod-product-compliance
Lightning Source LLC
Chambersburg PA
CBHW030405020726
47493CB00003B/957